FRACTIOUS FAIRY TALES

Jessica Palmer

PARALLEL UNIVERSE PUBLICATIONS

ISBN: 978-0-9957173-7-4
Parallel Universe Publications, 130 Union Road,
Oswaldtwistle, Lancashire, BB5 3DR, UK

Contents

The Yellow Brick Road

Glinda the Good trod next to a stream. She jumped into each mud puddle she could find and kicked about a bit. It did no good.

Nothing stuck.

Of course, she was dressed in pink. It came with the job, just like the heavy glittering crown that was fused to the top of her head.

Glinda normally didn't walk anywhere; she wafted in a claustrophobic pink bubble. She hated pink. Anything but pink, black, baby-shit yellow, vomit green, but not pink. However, her attire came with rank, and a name. She was raised above all the nameless people of fairy, those who did the mundane chores and rated only a job title, like the Sandman.

So she put up with pink. Glinda raised her skirts, bounced forward to get a running start at the mire that filled the path ahead of her. She screeched, belly flopped and glided through the mud on her stomach. She luxuriated as muck dribbled between her breasts.

Just as quickly, it dried and crumbled into dust. Glinda stood. She didn't even have to brush herself off. She was pristine.

"Nope, not a thing, not a damn thing," she muttered.

It was a pretty good gig, pink notwithstanding. She saved a lot on laundry. But just try and sleep with a hoop skirt flapping in your face all night, wearing stiletto heels and having a ruddy great crown glued to your scalp.

Glinda never needed to bathe. Probably a good thing. She didn't swim either no matter how hot it got, for the hoop skirt floated to the surface and the weight of the crown ensured she quickly turned upside down.

Today, Glinda was in a particularly bad mood. Her wand was on the fritz, so she had to walk to Emerald City to get it fixed. The bubble was claustrophobic, but it got her where she wanted to go forthwith.

As always, she had places to go, people to see. The Wizard was holding a party to honor Dorothy. The old sot simply doted on the child. From the same hometown, he said. He could not see she was a brat.

It was time to get rid of Dorothy.

It did not pay to be late to one of his dos.

Glinda avoided the Yellow Brick Road. Too many people would recognize her. That path ensured she'd never reach the city. She'd be stopped every yard or so by someone asking for a wish, and she could not refuse them. She was Glinda the Good, after all.

If she were to absent herself from court too long, she would be deemed AWOD, absent while on duty, and demoted to one of the nameless ones.

Glinda shuddered and quickened her pace.

"Oh woe. Oh woe; woe is me." The voice emanated from the marsh.

Compelled, Glinda swung toward the sound. Her gaze dropped to a yellow splotch on a large green lily pad.

"Yes? You are sad, Sir Frog. What ails you that you should cry in this lovely swamp?"

"Can't you tell? Can't you see? Are you blind?"

Glinda pursed her lips. Some invisible hand smoothed her countenance as she said: "Two fine, strong legs, and yes, two big feet. Two scrawny little arms, but you don't use those much. Everything seems to be there that should be there."

"Look at me. I'm yellow. All the other frogs are an emerald green. They blend into the background, and I stick out like a sore thumb. Even a blind woman can see that, or should," he grumbled. "As a result, every hungry stork, hawk or falcon desires me for lunch, and if I leap into the water, the fish can see me too. Who knew they had color vision? I'm treading water under the lily pad trying to hide from the danger above, and I get attacked from below."

The frog lowered his voice conspiratorially. "And it's not very good for the ladies, on the evolutionary scale, to beget yellow offspring with the life expectancy of zero."

At that moment, the frog hopped into the water as a predator approached. His head popped to the surface under a nearby leaf. "I mean I might as well have a sign on my back that says: 'Eat me! Eat me!'"

He glared at her. "You are Glinda the Good. What are you going to do about it?"

Glinda sighed.

He forged on. "If I am to have any luck with the ladies, they can't see me coming. If I am going to mate, if I am going to breed, I must be green." He gave the witch his most endearing smile, which was a bit of a wobbly affair. "Please?"

"My wand's not working. I couldn't even get off the ground in my pink bubble this morning."

"Please?"

Glinda glanced from the frog to the limp wand in her hand. It glared back at her.

"P-l-e-a-s-e!"

"It could turn you into a prince, you know."

"Would I be yellow?"

"Probably not, but there are no guarantees."

"Go for it then."

Glinda glowered at the wand, trying to bend it to her will. "Now behave yourself," she said before she touched the frog with it.

"Ouch," shouted the frog. "It bit me."

The animal would have continued to complain but he was struck by the emerald green legs and feet that appeared between his teeny, tiny, emerald green arms. The frog twisted and turned trying to check his entire body.

Glinda caught a glint of yellow, gasped and stuffed her hand in her mouth.

He heard. "What? What? What did I miss?"

The frog erupted from the water to climb back on the lily pad and gave himself a minute inspection, between toes and under what passed for arms. Then he did what Glinda would have thought impossible. The frog rocked back to his rump, the place where his tail used to be when he was a sprog, and looked between his leg.

"Oh, no. Oh, no, no, no, no, no, no. This will never do. Now I look like I have a social disease."

Glinda clenched the irritated wand to her breast. "I told you. I told you so. I could try to fix it, but you could end up worse than you are now. You could be plaid or paisley. Worse, you could end up human. If you are lucky, you'll be yellow again."

She took a step back. "Yellow is not such a bad color. Sunflowers seem to like it."

"I'm no blooming sunflower. Now, what am I supposed to do?" The frog wailed, but it came out "ribbit."

"If you want it fixed, you'll have to go the Emerald City to see the Wizard. Only he has the power to undo my magic."

"Where's that?"

"You can follow the stream, or you could take the Yellow Brick Road. It's faster," she said helpfully.

"Not bloody likely. With my luck, I'd end up a green smear on the pavement. No thank you very much."

"At least you're not yellow anymore."

"Except for the important bits." The frog hunkered down. "The road is out."

"Okay, suit yourself." Her words, though, were drowned under a splash of water, and the frog began to swim upstream.

"Go fuck yourself," she said, or tried, but it came out fiddle sticks.

She concentrated on the path before her. She could not afford any further distractions if she was going to retain her own shape. When the wand was in a mood like this, she could suddenly find herself a fuzzy pink sheep.

Glinda tucked her head down between her shoulders and strode forward, determined to beat the frog to the city.

It would be bad enough if she appeared late, but to have the gala interrupted by an irate amphibian.

She hadn't got very far when she heard, "Oh, woe, oh, woe is me. Oh, whatever am I going to do? Oh, woe..."

Glinda began to swear. The words froze on her lips. Instead, she found herself saying. "Yes, pray tell, what ails you so?"

Inside her head, her mind was screaming in silent protest. *Damn! Damn! Damn! Not fair. Not fair. This is just not fair.*

"Can you not see?" said the elephant.

She interrupted him abruptly. "Yes, I can see, and no, I'm not blind. You are an elephant. What's your complaint?" She paused. "And don't you dare tell me to look at you. I *am* looking at you."

"My trunk, it's yellow. It was grey a few minutes ago and went well with the great grey ears, handsome grey forehead, fine strong grey legs, but suddenly my trunk turns yellow. It looks like a banana hanging from my face. I've already had a couple of the ladies come over and try to bite it off. They think it's food. Pa-lease."

Glinda deflated. She had most likely caused his problem as some of the yellow from the frog splashed off on this fine fellow.

Normally, she could not refuse, but now she was even more beholden to the word good. She had a moral obligation to correct the matter.

She unwrapped the wand from her cloak, where she hoped it would do the least amount of mischief. Glinda shivered as the star at the top glinted smugly.

The words *over worked and underpaid, but now free-e-e-e* echoed inside her head.

"I told the frog that my wand is not working – it's in a mood – but he didn't listen. He came to regret it Now I'm going to warn you. My wand is broken. Do you think I'd be traipsing along in this jungle," she shuddered, "if I could fly?"

"Well, *I* can't have this banana hanging off my face."

"It's not a banana. It's a perfectly serviceable trunk."

"It won't be if any one of the herd get a hold of it."

The elephants closed in around them, staring at him hungrily.

She conceded. She waved the wand around over her head. Maybe if she got it dizzy.

"Let it be grey," Glinda commanded. "Nice practical grey. Not yellow."

When she felt her arm was going to drop off, she thrust it at the elephant, ramming it into his side, hoping she would knock the wand into submission.

Under her breath, she muttered, "And not pink."

The star burst open and a flag with the word pop appeared.

"Ow!" yelled the elephant. "You trying to kill me?"

Glinda's jaw unhinged as the trunk transformed into the more acceptable grey. She was about to congratulate herself, but the transformation continued. Spots of pink began to appear on his trunk. The pink splotches on his trunk extended, obliterating the grey, until his fine brow ridge became a dusky fuchsia, stretching across the skull and the ears.

Pink.

Over his shoulders, across his belly and down his legs.

Pink.

Gawd, she hated pink. The transformation took only an instant, but she followed it step by step. The elephant matched her dress perfectly.

"Da-ma-ma-ma," she snarled, spitting the incomplete expletive from her lips.

9

The gathering herd shuffled, then trumpeted and roared. Some of them reared, great feet slashing at the air in their startlement. Then all turned tail and ran.

The elephant gawped and caught his reflection in the waters of the stream. He too trumpeted and reared.

"This cannot be. This is so much worse. I look like a hallucination. I look like a *delirium tremen!*" The elephant crumpled in a heap.

"I told you like I told him. There's no telling what can happen when the wand gets in a mood." Glinda rolled the wand into her cloak. "You could have ended up as a mouse and got trampled by the rest of the herd."

"What am I to do?'

"I'll tell you what I told the frog. Maybe this time you'll listen. Go see the wizard."

"Who the hell is he and how am I to find him?"

"He lives in the Emerald City."

"How am I supposed to find the Emerald City?"

Glinda threw up her arms in disgust. She pointed up the stream.

"Follow the yellow-dicked toad."

It's Not Nice to Fool Mother Nature

When the people of Qeplurwonatesxef woke up, it seemed a normal sort of day, bright, disturbingly bright. Only some, the eldest, knew what this portended: a flare.

The rare solar flares were times of rejoicing on the narrow strip in the habitable zone of the planet. The perpetual clouds would part, and the normally black leaves of the planet's produce turned green. The denizens had adapted to this dark world, but they maintained the tales of a time and a place where sky was blue and the sun yellow instead of a bilious ochre-brown.

The process of physical transformation for these people had begun even before the colonists left the mother world. The scientists knew the harsh conditions the immigrants would face to survive in the habitable band under the red dwarf. In their rush to get off the dying world, each immigrant had signed a release allowing the then space administration to modify them to be compatible with their habitat. It absolved the government from responsibility should things go awry.

The willing had been given gills to breathe the water-laden atmosphere and nicotating membranes to protect their eyes. The DNA for this trait had been spliced directly into the human genome to be carried onto the next generation. The first to arrive had both gills and lungs, an attribute they maintained to this day.

Later generations evolved the protective scales of a fish. Their eyes opened and closed with disconcerting effect, especially for the personnel of the cargo ships that brought the supplies to build their domes.

The people of Qeplurwonatesxef also relied on the Jacobson's organ more than visual sighting on a world where light was limited, and the ever-present clouds were dirty brown.

The successful families displayed the releases they signed with pride, a badge of their humanity, their courage, their ties to the mother world and their legitimacy. There were throwbacks, of course, usually hidden away in institutions.

Their behavior adapted accordingly, and they would often open their mouths to taste the world. Their eyes would close in stages and they jumped about like frogs. Overall the Qeplurwonatesxefian presented a decidedly reptilian, almost amphibian, appearance to outsiders that repelled the crew ships, and they were soon abandoned to their fates by the parent planet or, perhaps as predicted, Mother Earth had died.

Buffeted by an eternal gale, the Qeplurwonatesxefian were short and stout. Depending on wind conditions when they left their domes, the people crept on all fours, their sticky pads clung to the rocky soil preventing them from getting carried away by a sudden gust. They had not lost the two-legged stance of their ancestors. It remained the posture of authority and the only proper one for the parties, government facilities, law courts, and in commerce and war.

The brave, who had heard the ancient lore of a benevolent sun, hopped from their beds and threw open their doors to gawp at the aquamarine sky. One lid after another shut with a snap until they could tolerate the orange glow of the sun.

No one in this generation had lived during the last flare, but their thick, scaled skin could deflect much of the heat, and early-on in the human habitation of the planet, the population learned to hop into the nearest body of water to cool themselves. Those who had not perished.

This day a million voices rose in prayer at this miracle of the sun.

The idea of one god previously held had devolved to many – the preferred god usually unique to a region or a country and representing whatever that group held dear. Man also discarded the concept of demons or any sense of a sun-god, since both were unreliable. The words for them had nearly vanished from the vocabulary, except in children's tales.

The planet was not uninhabited. The first ones lived beyond the veil, dimly seen and never met. The elder beings became the gods, for the citizenry had long-since decided that multiple gods were disagreeable enough without adding demons to the mix.

Across the narrow strip of land in countries where holy wars started over the predominate god, the conflict remained a constant, and once begun, no one won.

Until the faint illumination of the unseen sun indicated dawn, combatants hurled epithets across enemy lines as they waited for the battle to commence.

"Unbeliever."

"Heretic."

"Heathen!"

"Infantile."

An argument ensued in one of the ditches.

"That's infidel, you cretin. Infidel not infantile. Don't you know what it means?"

"Infantile? No. What's it mean?"

"Like a baby."

"Well then, they are infantile, worshiping a false god. Infantile!"

There was a splash and a thud. Mud splattered over the side of the ditch. Both adversaries and allies stuck their heads over the lip of their respective trenches to get a better view of the tussle. They were disappointed.

Another voice, the voice of education and command, shouted above the din. "Unshriven!"

The soldiers ducked down, preparing to meet their respective makers.

When it rained, which was all the time, the soldiers and mercenaries huddled in their trenches, emptying their boots into puddles, grown to the size of lakes, and waited until a slight surcease from the storm would initiate the next battle.

Until then, the war was a war of words and the vilification continued.

"Blasphemer... Idolater..."

Occasionally someone would get nasty. "Asshole!"

Then people would die.

Meanwhile the citizens of the battered lands hastened to complete their chores before the bloodshed would begin anew and they would be forced to flee from the barrage of projectiles.

When the heavens darkened, the combatants retreated to their pits and trenches to squat next to insipid fires and rest before the start of the next day's conflagration – some too tired to hurl insults any more. The soldiers would awaken unrefreshed from a dream-riddled sleep for the war to begin anew.

Somewhere in the dark night, a defiant voice shrieked: "Infantile!"

*

The old woman stared at her reflection in the still pond. It was an evil visage. Once Koy had been young and beautiful, and she had been loved, nay, worshiped. Now she was as old as the hills. Older even.

She exhaled sharply. Her gaze dropped from her perch in the dizzying heights to the surrounding mountain range.

Her love had died sometime in dim memory, and the old woman was left alone to fend for herself. She was shunned. People crossed the street to avoid her. She did not look like anyone else. She bore the wrinkled sack-like appearance of skin worn too long. Koy wore veils to hide her eyes from the public, for, through a trick of birth, her eyes did not bear the nicotating membrane that others' sported. Her pupils dilated and contracted, and sometimes the black pupil covered her over-large eyes.

Her damnable eyes also permitted her to see things, secret things. Koy could peer into the human souls and record their sins. Men, women and children would scuttle away from her approach and her flapping veils. They recoiled, too, from the torn dresses and matted hair, as if decrepitude and poverty might be catching.

Yet these same people sought her advice quickly enough when they were ill, and she would treat them with potions and salves made from the harvest of the black forest, hill and vale.

They came in numbers to consult her about their futures, their dreams, or about love, marriage, politics, wealth and its acquisition.

The old woman leaned over the pool and scrubbed at her face where the lines were etched deep so deep they were encrusted with dirt, and it seemed as if her face would never get clean.

Suddenly the clouds parted and a weakly sun appeared. She blinked furiously. Her pupils contracted to pinpricks. Her eyes watered. She covered herself with her shroud.

The sound of distant gunfire issued from the north and the south. Sometimes, it was difficult to distinguish the location where the staccato shots reverberated off rocky outcrops. Day – or what passed for it – had come somewhere in the world.

Koy sighed. Then she pulled herself upright using her walking stick, which the superstitious called her wand. The surrounding air echoed with the clatter of ancient bones and the pop of battered joints.

Someone was going to pay for this – someday – and Koy shuffled off.

*

Xdqtjljlhtkdlffft, god of bureaucrats, sat upon his throne of red tape. He observed the proceedings with no desire to participate. The gods were unruly, not gods at all. The elves resented the invasion of the frog people from earth to their retreat in *Tír na nÓg*. They had flown here in the space boats. They had no need to countenance a dark sky. The masters of illusion, they created theirs.

With the arrival of humanity, their influence was felt as it had in days of yore. The people thought of the fey as godlike, so they became gods, and their physical attributes transformed to fit Man's image of them.

Meetings of the gods were few and far between, beyond the veil, and always contentious. With the wisdom of the ages, Xdqtjljlhtkdlffft had argued against the conclave, but the bonehead god of jurisprudence, *Inlimine*, insisted on it, for there had been an influx of the dead into the land of the gods, thanks to the eternal Holy Wars.

Inlimine, jurisprudence, appeared as one might expect – consisting of an oversized head held aloft by multitudinous arms, reflecting the many arms of the law. He affected a robe that made him look like he was wearing a black rug and a silly wig that did not fit his head.

Xdqtjljlhtkdlffft refused to chair the meeting. The first of the living gods, he could demand certain rights, privileges and responsibilities. This was not one he wanted.

Few in the mortal realm remembered his name, although he had been worshipped once. He was first invoked by the priests of Zoomaria after writing, a knowledge lost in time with the death of computers, was re-invented.

Since then writing had become an arcane art known only to the priestly caste, and the followers of Xdqtjljlhtkdlffft had a chokehold upon the world. They wrote in strange symbols, a language without vowels. Soon kings, nobility and even the common man began to resent their power.

Consequently, Xdqtjljlhtkdlffft's temples had been razed and his name profaned among the common man. The influence of man meant gods appeared as the general populace perceived them. Thus, Xdqtjljlhtkdlffft's robes were rumpled and his hands stained with ink, and the god sported the body of a boar with a weight problem, the wings of the extinct foofu bird, and the spindly legs of a chicken. His elongated torso had several arms and huge hands. His head was an abacus, and his smile, frightening to behold.

But wily humans studied the act of writing and compared it to the spoken word. The cunning saw a pattern and created a vernacular form, using the same symbols incorrectly. One clever fellow had even invented vowels.

Still only papers generated by the priests were trusted in the courts of law. So the clerics of Xdqtjljlhtkdlffft scurried about in their crumpled robes, the blackened hands of their craft, and became fixtures in the temples of the other gods and in the royal courts.

So Xdqtjljlhtkdlffft still had his worshippers, but not among the rank and file. The bureaucrats paid homage to him. Each maintained an individual shrine and wrapped it in copious quantities of the sacred red tape. The cleric who forgot to make obeisance or sinned another way – misfiled a document or misspelled a word – suffered the ultimate punishment, death by a thousand paper cuts.

Because he was oldest, the choice of vantage point was his. Xdqtjljlhtkdlffft sat on the podium, not to lead, but to watch the mêlée he was sure would follow. Around him, the many goddesses, gods and godlings jockeyed for, or argued about, position.

The gods of commerce, Aequitas, Eksjequer and P'lfr, set up their booths close to the throng. Eksjequer had a long nose, good for sniffing out a good deal, a projecting chin which was accentuated by his protruding bottom lips. The tail of a scorpion swished under the merchant surcoat. His cousin Aequitas, the god of fair dealing, sat on a chair with his thumb on the scales of commerce. P'lfr, the symbol wealth, appeared to his followers as a chicken scratching in the sand. He kept on eyeing the animal contingent and sidled closer to them, until Aequitas plucked him from the ground and threw him behind the tables.

"Bird brain," Aequitas snarled. "You stay with us."

Worse, albeit smarter than P'lfr, were the Aladugyamum, the vague spirits of good fortune. They appeared as cloudy, amorphous shapes that would dissipate before a prayer. They had no responsibilities. Instead, they haunted gambling establishments and race tracks. The Aladugyamum never committed to anything, and the faithful took a number at the doors of their temples and soon realized they were playing against the odds.

Aladugyamum stationed their games between the booths and the crowd slightly off the beaten path. Here they could extend their hands to pick the pocket of any passerby.

*

The flaring sun crested the peaks of the mountains and a single shriek rose from a multitude of throats at its arrival. The combatants climbed from their foxholes as one. The opposing sides mowed down their respective enemies. Arms were severed to lie on the ground, twitching, with hands still clenching swords, guns or the weapon of choice. Many soldiers dropped as soon as their faces emerged from the trenches. Their heads exploded while those who made it over the top were hit with a barrage of a thousand projectiles...

*

...and the immortal realm immediately became overcrowded with the spirits of the dead. With a nod from Xdqtjljlhtkdlffft, the god of the dead, whom all agreed had a perverse sense of humor, sent them packing, to reside in the still intact bodies of living mortals. Often souls and sides got switched so that a soldier would stand in the narrow strip of no man's land having fisticuffs with himself. Usually his longevity was measured in seconds.

Necrosis would then find a new abode for these recently deceased souls and the cycle repeated itself.

Xdqtjljlhtkdlffft sighed. The god of death, he thought, enjoyed his job a bit too well.

*

Koy had foreseen the Holy Wars; it was inevitable when man demanded that others follow only one path. Mankind had not evolved much after all, despite the changes to their physical form. The many gods provided only more reasons to fight.

The old woman had settled in the Hepatik Empire, where the gods were allied. Battle raged around the perimeter. Her home was in the interior, straddling the borders of the four Hepatik kingdoms.

And the sounds of war echoed inside her head. She could not escape them.

*

Bonar, one of the minor divinities of the war clan, shoved his way through the crowd to the podium. Bonar was a lesser god, a godling, and a hot head. His father, god of storms and destruction, had disinherited his son, or tried. The youth was stuck in an all-too human form and was not even allowed to throw the lightning bolts that were the symbol of his clan.

The families of war had once been huge, since man loved them so much. Their names ranged from Lively Debate and Mildly Belligerent to Decimation, Holocaust, Apocalypse and Total Annihilation. Years of internal wrangling had done much to thin their ranks. The denizens of war found themselves isolated in a ghetto of their own making, that resembled the aftermath of hostilities because no other god wanted to live near them.

Even the less-favored gods were malicious. The precursor to war and its consequence, Strife wore flayed human skin and a necklace of teeth. He carried both a whip and a club. Two blue hummingbirds perched on his feet and kept drilling at them with their sharp proboscises.

The ill-tempered Strife was reputed to have slaughtered all of his siblings, one sister and four-hundred brothers. Rumor suggested he started an argument between them, and when the dust settled Strife was the only one left standing. He then walked calmly over to his sister and bludgeoned her lifeless corpse until she was putty. Many of the young Lotharios in the immortal realm wept at the young goddess's demise, perhaps because she wore a metal brassiere.

If, Xdqtjljlhtkdlffft thought, you like that sort of thing.

Bonar pushed Contention from the ranks and attempted to mount the podium.

Eh? the Elder had taken a post close to Xdqtjljlhtkdlffft. It seemed the safest place. The listening god was also one of the old-ones, the first gods. He was depicted with enormous ears, but in truth he was stone deaf.

Eh? was much beloved of women, especially those who equated the size of one's ears to other attributes. The elder god had lost popularity when his followers found he didn't actually listen He then bequeathed his primary skill, the art of not listening, to his son Uh-Huh.

On such an important occasion Eh? carried a listening horn to hear the conversation around him. Bonar tipped the wheelchair over that held the elder Eh? and the huge horn was driven into his ear.

Xdqtjljlhtkdlffft shook his head. Humanity thought the gods never aged, but they needed the adoration of the masses to thrive. Thus, the old, forgotten gods showed all the signs of decay and decrepitude as the mortal, only at a much slower rate. Some gave up entirely and faded away. The most stubborn would remain, shrinking so small they could barely be seen except as a gnat reclining before a crumpled temple upon which several other tabernacles – each dedicated to a succession of gods – had been built.

Eh? grappled with the horn, swearing, and screamed his outrage.

*

In the regions where Eh? the Elder still held sway, men fell off their bar stools or toppled along with their chairs. Others grabbed their ears as if in pain while others pulled at their pinnae or tapped them and made snorting noises. In homes, those who were not screeching in distress soon had reason to do so as angry wives invaded the public houses. Driven to distraction by their unheeding spouses, the women walloped them about their collective ears.

*

Eh? shouted, "I am an elder god, you bastard upstart...."

"Shove it, old man," Bonar growled.

Eh? the Elder extracted the listening horn from his ear and inserted it up Bonar's backside and then, with surprising agility, kicked the minor god in the groin from his position on the ground.

The youth grabbed his testicles and began to cry. Then, embarrassed by his own display, he began to expand until he achieved massive height that few others could attain.

His father glowered. "I hate it when he blows up like that," the Big TA exclaimed. "All blow and no show."

Xdqtjljlhtkdlffft stirred himself to pick up the old man, chair and all, before a riot ensued.

The Big TA stood at full height, far taller than his son Bonar, and seized the godling's elbow with one tentacled appendage. "Serves you right."

The irritated youth began to storm around the court. He stepped on many of his fellow gods with his enormous feet, but having no substance, he had little effect. It was like being thonked on the top of the head with a feather duster.

Generations of war and battle clamored to be heard. From the shrunken and shriveled ancestors, more supported by their weapons than their bearers, to their descendants who yammered and yowled, saying the Holy War was not exclusively their responsibility but belonged to all immortals. Cousins so far removed from war they could not even be considered a tepid lament squawked their objections. Tentacles, hooks and claws waved over the heads of the accumulated gods. The feathered sharpened their claws, and the furred stood hackles raised.

Nervously Xdqtjljlhtkdlffft scanned the scene, catching bits and pieces of the surrounding conversation.

Somewhere someone said: "Get off my foot..."

Another retorted, "Well, I never!"

Still another asserted: "I was here first..."

The second answered with a snappy repartee. "Was not."

The return was equally witty. "Was too."

"You stepped on me again and this time it was deliberate..."

"Them's fightin' words, pipsqueak. You willing to put your powers where your, ah, ah?" the god paused seeking the appropriate orifice, "mouth is?"

*

In the mortal realm, warfare descended into bickering farce upon the field of contention, weapons forgotten, until those still in the trenches ascended to bayonet anyone foolish enough to stand still too long.

War was serious, albeit voluble, business.

*

The newly dead floated above the fracas in the immortal world until Death, wearing a pink tutu, touched them with his skeletal wand, and then the souls vanished with a puff.

Xdqtjljlhtkdlffft's shoulders shook as he fought to contain his laughter.

In legends of yore, the gods were the saviors of humanity, fighting against the agents of chaos. Silly mortals didn't realize that the gods were chaos. There was no greater anarchy in the universe than the immortals.

The gods, goddesses and godlings could never act in concert.

For the immortal realm was overcrowded, making the divines a bit petulant at the best of times. Those gods and goddesses who stayed in mortal favor grew bloated and fat with human offerings. Their immortal temples were built on top of the older gods, crushing those who had fallen into disrepute under their weight. Meanwhile their offspring, denied real power, chafed.

The gods and goddesses were always caught up in disputes, usually about real estate and precedence. Their complaints were sent to the heavenly court. Thus, *Inlimine* gained in importance even though he was no longer acknowledge by man, who knew there was no justice.

"Order! Order!" *Inlimine* roared.

The god of jurisprudence loved his gavel and he used it to great effect within the courtroom, and without, when any other god got in his way.

He was pounding it now, hitting the head of an onlooker.

"Order. This meeting will come to order," he bawled. "Or I will put you all in jail."

That had the desired effect. The court fell silent; the gods ceased squabbling and started to giggle. The twitter grew in crescendo to a full-fledged chortle and then into a loud, cumulative guffaw.

Inlimine flushed crimson.

The volume then descended to a few gasping whimpers as the gods and goddesses wiped their eyes.

"Jail. Ha! That's a good one."

"I haven't laughed so hard since I don't know when."

Having angered another god often had amusing results when *Inlimine* transformed into something else. So he might appear as a vulva when he ran afoul of Fanny, one of the many goddesses of fertility, or as a barrel when he outraged one of the Hepatik clan. *Inlimine* had soon learned it was better to thwack an opponent upside the head with his gavel and run like hell before the god regained consciousness. If he was lucky, the offended party would not remember the incident.

"Order," *Inlimine* roared. "Order."

"Give it up."

The gods of the Hepatik Empire finally caught up with the proceedings and began to heckle jurisprudence.

"Order," they parroted. "Order."

"Sure, I'll order. I'll take a wine..." said the goddess of vine and grape.

"... a tequila," said Mezcal, who resembled an overgrown worm.

"... gin..."

"... vodka!"

Whiskey and all the little whiskeys burbled their orders through their stills. "Scotch... *glub, glub, glub*... Bourbon... Single malt... No, double."

The poor man's bevy, beer, was represented by frogs, although no one could remember why. All the god of lager could do was croak his defiance.

"Pissers the lot of them," mumbled Xdqtjljlhtkdlffft to no one in particular.

Next to him the elder god of listening sat up and said: "Eh?"

*

Everywhere on Qeplurwonatesxef, the mortal patrons of public houses stood, raised their glasses, cups and broken pottery to the

Hepatik gods, and toasted them, naming them or the beverage they represented. "Tequila, mezcal, gin, vodka, whiskey, Scotch, bourbon, single malt, double malt, beer..."

"...Tequila, mezcal, gin, vodka, whiskey, Scotch, bourbon, single malt, double malt, beer."

"...Tequila, mezcal, gin, vodka, whiskey, Scotch, bourbon, single malt, double malt, beer."

The words were spoken like a liturgy, mantra or prayer, until a ruddy great cheer erupted from the throats of the happily drunk, breaking the spell.

The gods were venerated in the Hepatik Empire, but they were one of the few that were nearly universal. In one form or another, they were worshipped all across the planet – in dark backrooms of diners and in bright restaurants where the posh ate their evening meal. Even those who did not regularly make offerings to the toilets of the gods knew of them.

In their homes, women who never touched a drop felt an urge to take a little nip. Servants, who kept the keys to the wine cellar, slipped downstairs unseen. Husbands drank deeply from their hip flasks. In the temples across Qeplurwonatesxef, the priests broke into sacramental beverages – wine, tvass or mead, whatever the god demanded – and got legless.

*

These gods of the Hepatik Empire had their hangers-on, Jeuse and Ahcancun, the friend of boozers and sunburn. Of all the gods, goddesses and godlings, the Hepatik host were the only ones who got along with each other, except for their cousin Bilious, the god of hangovers, whom they avoided by the simple expedient of staying in an inebriate stupor.

Fights, such that they were, lasted briefly. Altercations might arise, if someone had spilled another's drink. However, the skirmish was an embarrassingly short affair with one combatant missing a swing, only to land on his immortal face, and the pair crying into their respective drinks, while others of their tribe practiced projectile puking.

No longer amused by the quarrel between Eh? and Bonar, the other gods of war joined the drinkers. The patriarch of war slithered around the vomiting contestants, but not before he had been nailed by one of them. He raised himself to full height on his ten, tentacled legs, making his inflated son look like a dwarf. The offender, the god of cider, exploded with a thought.

*

Where peace dominated, the people capered, hopped and leapt in the streets celebrating the flare until...

Kabam. Kablooey.

Volcano and geysers erupted, from pole to pole, north to south, in the habitable strip. Waves crested in the once-frozen tidal pools and collapsed into troughs, hitting the beach with the force of Total Annihilation. In the desert regions and the prairies, a faint drizzle began to fall despite the still brilliant sky. Lightning streaked, vying with the resplendent sun and causing the short, black trees to explode into splinters. People stopped dancing, stared at the heavens adorned in a myriad of rainbows, and wondered.

In Eh?'s realm, bruised men rubbing their ears erupted from houses. The pace of husbands and their wives armed with household weaponry faltered and they stared at a sky where both sun and rain appeared as one.

Even on the field of battle, combatants paused and glanced up at the boiling rain in a sunny sky, only to attack again with renewed vigor.

*

General Disorder raced up to the Big TA, lifted him from the slippery floor, grimaced and wiped his hands on his shirt.

"I'm sorry. I'm sorry," said Oops, goddess of mishaps.

Her apologies annoyed TA. He raised his thunderstick...

Crack!

*

Another boom of thunder echoed across the mortal sky. It reverberated off the walls of home and hovel until the most fragile dissolved. The ground trembled and heaved. A woman slicing vegetables for that night's repast cut off her fingers. She kept slicing. Elsewhere, men and women prostrated themselves, praying to the great multiplicity of divines. Rather than placating the gods, their imprecations only added fuel to their ire.

The heavens opened wide....

*

Inlimine deflated. If he had had any, his shoulders would have drooped. His gavel dropped to the floor.

"Order?" he bleated.

"Order yourself, or I'll show you what to do with that gavel."

"Try it, fat head," said Lively Debate, who often enjoyed the halls of jurisprudence, "and I'll turn you into an ill-conceived argument."

Then the group disintegrated into chaos again. Horns, hooves, elbows, knees, shoulders - or whatever passed for such - dug into the flanks, front, side, backs, proboscis, or viscous ooze of his, her or its nearest neighbor.

"I cannot see. Give way!"

"You give way."

"No, you..."

"Will not..."

"Will too..."

"Make me."

Xdqtjljlhtkdlffft moaned and wiped his face with his hands, rattling both beads and rods within the abacus frame.

Arrrrrgh, god of fright and startlement, began wringing his fronds. "Oh, dear, oh dear."

"Shut up, wuss!" hissed Mildly Belligerent.

"Such negativity," said Nobb, goddess of enthusiasm. She began to weep.

*

Rain poured in sheets literally against a backdrop of blue. Linens hung out to dry in this rare glimpse of sun flew from the lines. Man-made rivers swelled as damns were clogged. Coupled with the sun, the sturdy buildings of Qeplurwonatesxef began to melt. Homes were washed away. In colder climes, precipitation came down as sleet, hail, even chunks of ice. Glaciers rolled visibly to the sea and the oceans began to freeze despite the warmth of the solar flare.

The countries devoted to the gods Hepatik had a deluge of spirits, each according to the predominate god, goddess or godling, Wine, Tequila, Rum, Vodka, Whiskey, Scotch, Bourbon or Gin. Husbands dumped the buckets of drinking water and filled them with the precious fluid bestowed upon them by the heavens. They hauled the receptacles into the house. After a few days of drinking the bevy of her choice, the wife joined her spouse in his efforts to collect divine bounty until they passed out dead drunk on the floor.

The land of Annuria had another of its not infrequent rain of frogs while the entire country felt a need to micturate, which lead to fist fights and no few embarrassing incidents in front of privies.

The adjacent country of Mezcal saw worms dropping from the sky. The frogs chased the worms, and the once pacific Hepatik kingdoms were brought to the brink of war, as one divine symbol devoured another.

Elsewhere, people quaked in their beds, unwilling to face the mix of sun and rain, while temperatures rose to a hissing height. Meanwhile the ground shook beneath them. When the lightning streaked across the sky again, it might have been noted that the mountains waved from side to side, if there had been anyone sober enough to witness the spectacle.

And many wished for the return of the comforting clouds and the sound of weapons' fire when the sky was rent by crackling light and perpetual thunder...

*

Dammit, the goddess of terrifying aspect who had her faces permanently fixed in an expression of rage, joined the fray. Unlike other goddesses, she was not content to have priestesses attend her. She would have men who must deport themselves in women's dress.

Dammit had few followers outside her temples, although she had a surfeit of priests. The faith was surprisingly popular among men. She brought some of the priests back the realm of the gods to attend her, granting them immortality if not godly status.

Next to her, Salacious made an obscene hand gesture at *Inlimine.* Her demigods did the same.

There were any number of fertility gods, almost as many as there were spirits of alcohol and war. Humanity was a randy lot.

The goddesses took advantage of that, but each had her male counterpart.

Ai-apece's followers showed his reverence by drinking large quantities of water. As a result, Ai-apece was not invited to many parties. Xdqtjljlhtkdlffft glanced down at the growing puddle of water beneath him and rolled his eyes.

One god slipped on a pile of steaming dung.

Xdqtjljlhtkdlffft searched for the gods of agriculture. His shoulders relaxed. The most important was busy counting his chickens. Then Xdqtjljlhtkdlffft checked for the rest of the menagerie. The contingent was loosely scattered, occupying a single quadrant of the circle. They neither spoke nor glanced in the direction of their nearest neighbor, which was for the best, since their deputation consisted of those gods, goddesses or godlings who were associated with animals or the divines of the animal kingdom. The latter were the most talented shapeshifters in the immortal pantheon.

The gods and goddesses often kept company with a given animal. Poppycock had his peacocks and Maurya his peahens. Some held hawks, lions, tigers, geese, doves, bunnies, kwirels, mice, spiders. In other words, they carried various species none of which got along with the others.

It was eat or be eaten in that crowd. The animal gods prowled among the rest, switching forms from predator to prey, which ever suited their fancy.

Only Ee-i-ee-oh eschewed the restless pacing of the others. Instead, he ran with purpose, chasing down not one, but dozens of animals, for he had brought the lot – not just a beloved pet or two, but the entire damn barnyard – the chattel, the whonkies, the pigs and the pugs. Ee-i-ee-oh followed the chickens, trying to count them. Achmun the maize god led the poultry in a merry chase, giggling every time a hen swiped a kernel of corn from his person.

Ee-i-ee-oh skated across their feces and fell against Bgsht, who in turn stepped on Adictus.

"If you step on my foot one more time," Adictus bellowed. She/he was a hermaphrodite. Her/his body was cleaved in twain, straight up and down, right half woman, left half man. He/she made an interesting dance partner.

Goddess Bgsht, once raped by a demon, stood in an iron chastity belt of her own design – she would not be taken from behind again – and rattled the lock at the androgynous god.

"Go fuck yourself," she said. "You don't know how lucky you are."

"Lucky?" Fanny ejaculated. "You are lucky. How would you feel if you had every social disease on the planet named after you?"

One of the attendants of Dammit hit Bgsht with his purse. Others joined in the fracas, with their bags swinging and skirts flying. Some actually hit their mark. Then the incredibly lethal Bawbell entered the skirmish. This goddess of gems and jewelry wore her armory. She was draped in chains of heavy precious metals, on necks, ankles, arms and wrists, from which hung stones of gargantuan size and incredible sharpness.

The battle turned bloody.

*

Women who had yet to cool after the defaming of the One Who Listens But Is Deaf slammed their husbands with baskets of wet laundry, poked them with wheedles and awls, or used cutlery to their best advantage. Men were sliced, diced and left to bleed and later to be scraped into the cooking pots of Qeplurwonatesxef for supper.

In steaming market squares, housewives pelted fishmongers with their wares. Women vendors clobbered male members of the public with whumpkins and squash. Any hapless man who had accompanied his spouse to the fair found himself surrounded, while wild women battered him with whatever they had on hand. In the farms and fields, female workers chased after their mates with shovels, rakes and hoes.

The wives of the wealthy, all followers of Bawbell, ripped into their husbands with their jewels, gauging out eyes and severing tongues, while prostitutes turned on their clients who had uncomfortable implements inserted in embarrassing and highly inconvenient locations.

All around the globe, the doctors and lawmakers vanished, often pursued by droves of wrathful mothers. The male population was left hanging, literally, from a tree limb or had their throats slit for every placating word they ever spoke and never meant...

*

In the immortal courts, Decimation sucker punched the god of disease and allergies. K-k-k-Ah-chu looked more like a demon than a god and would have scared anyone if they had stumbled upon the immortal realm still living. His body was thin, with every rib exposed. His skin was a sallow grey, his eyes rheumy and his cheeks red. His hooked nose ran continually into his mouth.

"Ooph," K-k-k-Ahchu said.

The first one growled – "You sneezed on me" – and proceeded to smother the offender with his own handkerchiefs. When that didn't work, Decimation knotted them together and began to throttle the lesser god.

Sparks began to fly from extended fingertip to trident and back again. The fine costumes of the immortals burst into flame. Death got caught in the crossfire and expired in a fiery blaze. Even his lovely pink tutu sizzled and flashed into a funeral pyre. A fittingly spectacular end for an old god.

Xdqtjljlhtkdlffft did his best to remain nonpartisan, but when another god slid on the effluence of the animals, it was just too much. He stood with the clatter of wooden beads and bawled: "Everybody with livestock get out! All the livestock, out!"

Abeona, who appeared to man as a hippopotamus, was the goddess of safe passages and childbearing. She took umbrage at the name. She yawned threateningly, exposing her great tusks, and stomped off to join the rest of the animal contingent.

*

In the mortal realm, the mountains toppled onto the bloody field of battle to crush friend and foe alike, and in the immortal realm the two war gods who represented their respective countries vanished in a cloud of dust.

Meanwhile the followers of the god Ai-apece drank a large amount of water and pissed on the debris of collapsed cottages.

Koy stared at the carnage, shrugged and returned to collecting the sacred herbs. There was naught she could do for these. Besides, war was not her provenance. The treating of wounds was.

When her script was full, she decided to head for home. She was unaffected by the sizzling heat, born of rain and sun. Instead, she lifted the veil from her face to reveal the last vestiges of beauty

The spirits of the dead, having lost their abode and, with no Death to guide them thence, began to fly about her head. She batted at them. They circled her with a high-pitched whine of woe. Koy tripped on the body of a newly dead, one who had made his way from the killing fields to the Hepatik Empire.

She swore. Above her head, sun and rain hissed at the other. The droplets stung her eyes as no Qeplurwonatesxef's tainted water did.

Koy licked her lips. *Tequila.*

She bent backwards on creaking neck and spine to drink deep. Then she soldiered on at an erratic angle. When Koy entered the next kingdom, the rain changed in character, color and quality again, even if the sky remained the same turquoise.

Beer.

The tequila had left her feeling dehydrated, so Koy paused to slake her thirst, and staggered on.

After crossing the next border, she found whiskey. By this time she ricocheted from boulder to dark stubbly tree, that had turned an alarming emerald green, until she entered the land of the vine. There she tarried to partake of the lovely grape.

Koy suddenly noticed her sodden script. The items inside had bloomed under the broiling sun. It weighed her down.

What was she doing, seeking treatments for the injuries of war? She was sick of this soggy land.

Koy tossed it away. "Sod it. I'm going to take the day off."

She slept where she fell, only to wake up sputtering. She had exposed her all-too- human nostrils, mouth and lungs to the rain. She wished for gills. Her head throbbed. She crawled over to the script she'd discarded with not – she winced – a very mighty throw.

Koy grabbed a handful of the desired herb, shoved in her mouth and chewed, not noticing that the leaves had changed from black to green. The taste reminded her of something, and her mind drifted back to a time when food tasted sweet and grass was green.

She stretched out upon the ground and slept the sleep of the young.

When she next woke the sky was orange. Not the brownish, burnished orange seen during those rare times when the rains would cease, the clouds blew away and the ruddy sun would scud dully along the horizon.

Koy recognized the vestiges of fire. Who didn't? It was a necessarily tool, and war bestowed upon the strip lands more than its share of conflagrations. Koy slowly spun upon her heel, absorbing the full three-hundred-and-sixty-degree view.

The sky was orange everywhere.

Curse the gods, she shook her fist at the heavens; the entire world was on fire.

It had begun.

*

The elder gods, except those of the war clan, who remained, stood aside, unwilling to be squashed by the mêlée.

Ai-apece urinated continuously, muttering under his breath, "No, no, please, no more water."

The elder gods sidled away.

The gods of commerce, who had pushed their tables of wares against the wall at the first sign of trouble, grunted and moved their tables a second time away from the flood. Then they took a defensive stance. Aequitas leaned more heavily on the scales of commerce. The Aladugyamum became vaguer. P'lfr scratched and pecked at the ground more intently, and Eksjequer twitched his scorpion tail at any who dare approach.

Even the more rational of the gods became rattled – nerves frayed by the ongoing assault – and gods showed their powers.

Xdqtjljlhtkdlffft gnashed his beads and began to dismantle his throne. Thread by thread, he unraveled it. Then the god tore at the lovely red tape with the teeth he showed to so few.

Inlimine scrambled under the many thrashing feet, tentacles and claws until he located his gavel. He dived after it with a cry of triumph which soon transformed into a gurgle of disgust when he realized he had plunged face first into a suspicious looking pool of yellow water.

Discordia, wife of *Inlimine,* egged the fighters on. She appeared as a head with a mouth so wide that she could have swallowed herself. Discordia was the sister of Death, her followers few and far between, because they were inevitably beheaded as part of their sacrifice to her.

Inlimine erupted, dripping, and gave his wife a resounding smack. The head bounced and rolled into the puddle. Then *Inlimine* he began to run along the outskirts of the battle, hitting any moving part he could see.

*

On Qeplurwonatesxef, men – those few who had survived the onslaught, the clerks, the shopkeepers – emerged from behind their desks and abandoned their counters. They rose to stretch their legs and exert their authority.

One, returning from a particularly rough day at the office, grabbed an axe from the shed and decapitated his wife. When the skull spun to gaze at him with shocked eyes, he decided to chop it up. He chased it around the room, swinging and hacking. Then he proceeded to cut the body up, butcher it and dress it as if her remains were a prize of the hunt.

Others searched out their employers or any particularly annoying co-worker and tore them apart with their teeth.

The first man sat to lunch upon a stew made of his wife's thigh while another roasted a confederate. Yet another concussed the controller and feasted upon him raw. One astute supervisor overcame his subordinate and punished him with the torture of a thousand paper cuts, from which he died.

There was pugilism all around; any man who had a fist to swing, swung it. In one lonely office, a clerk with conflict issues bludgeoned his boss and then attempted to put him back together again with red thread and wept when his efforts began to unwind.

*

Koy strode swiftly through the forest. Gone were the aches and pains of old age. Amazing, she thought, what good ol' fashioned green leaves will do. She flung the stick away, it only tangled in her legs, and paused to rue her decision. What if the herbs lost their efficaciousness?

All the more reason to hurry.

The trees powered by the sun had grown overly large until they towered well above her head. The landmarks vanished under leaf and bough. Soon she would not be able to keep to the path.

Time grows short. Time. Time. Always time, a day's a year, with neither night nor day, just the oppressive gloom of dusk.

Koy broke into the clearing and stopped short, for there ranging before her hut were all the rulers of the nations. She pulled the veil over her face.

All stood tall at regal height, a handspan below her chin. "What is happening? Have we angered the gods? What must we do, fair lady? What must we do?

"Fair lady, hah! Angered the gods, have you? Angered the gods, indeed," she barked, "You've done something far worse. You have angered me." She thumped her breast.

"I have cried it in the streets and in the market places. I warned you. You breed too much. You fight too much. You kill too much. Begone," she shooed them away.

Then catching the fear in their lizard eyes, she relented. "Don't worry about it," she mumbled. "You won't be around much longer. Have fun. Get drunk. It did a world of good for me."

"Huh?"

"Now bugger off!" She slammed the door to her fragile abode in their stunned faces.

*

The animal contingent barked, growled, mewled or howled as was their fashion. Some wishing to join the brawl; others crept away. All resented their quarantine, just because a few could not hold their bladders.

What about Ai-apece? Was he not a menace?

The wolf king bit any buttock that presented itself. Even the normally placid Ee-i-ee-i-o stood facing the roiling mass of goddesses, godlings and gods, with his pitchfork in his hand, ready to poke any combatant who drew nigh.

The flames of contention leapt higher and higher. Fur, feathers, scale and skin curled in the heat.

In the other three quadrants of the circle, tempers once frayed were now shredded.

As much as he hated to admit it, Xdqtjljlhtkdlffft knew *Inlimine* had been right. Mortals' eternal battle had spilled into their fair realm, which was usually not subject to the silly whims of winds, rain and fire. One fed another and back again.

Xdqtjljlhtkdlffft's gaze swung to the mêlée. Until now...

Thunder cracked; lightning shattered the purple sky; fire spat under the sudden torrent, and the dyes in his lovely throne were running scarlet, pooling like blood at its base.

Now he was *pissed*.

This was mankind's fault. All of this. The heavenly host never asked that all puny mortals worship a single god. His eyes flicked to the ungodly affray before him, sensing a flaw in his reasoning. He thrust the thought away. Even if the gods argued over precedence and real estate, it had never before come to this. The immortals had decorum; they had class; they had style. One even wore a pink tutu until he died.

Xdqtjljlhtkdlffft dodged a lightning bolt.

Without puling humanity, there would have been no need to call this forum. Death would still be alive. The gods would not be drowning under the mortal souls of the dead every time a battle commenced. Although, the god noted that many no longer could find their way into the immortal realm since Death had passed.

"Good. Without humans," Xdqtjljlhtkdlffft clapped his hands over his mouth. He had not realized he spoke out loud.

The other gods, goddesses and godlings gaped at him, followed his train of thought, forgot their origins as gods and took up the refrain.

"Without humans," one said.

"Without mankind," said another.

"Without mortals," said a third.

Until all voices spoke in unison. "Without humans. Without mankind. Without mortals."

The chant even penetrated the hive mind of the combatants and they added their voices to the throng.

"Without humans. Without mankind. Without mortals."

Nobb interjected: "How lovely the world would be."

They repeated this incantation three times, in the great magical tradition.

"Without humans, without mankind, without mortals, how lovely the world would be."

"Without humans, without mankind, without mortals, how lovely the world would be."

"Without humans, without mankind, without mortals, how lovely the world would be."

Something niggled in the back of Xdqtjljlhtkdlffft's mind. A stab of fear. A word of warning. A sense of impending doom...

*

The sun flared brighter, burning off the rain, beverages and all. It sparkled on verdant, rain-soaked grasses. The fields gleamed. Birds began to sing. Crows landed upon the shoulder of the dummy built to scare them and plucked at the cloth eyes.

The remaining dwellings crumbled into dust. Temples disappeared with a whoosh. Large vines of unmorning glories and grape overtook the towns, obliterating them in less than an instant.

Rabbits, rats and mice – or their Qeplurwonatesxef equivalent – emerged from their dens. They awaited the shriek of a homemaker come to chase them away from the fields. The crow cawed and took flight when the stuffed manikin became undone.

Flocks of brilliant birds rose and circled the sky. Bees buzzed lazily.

Wheels fell off wagons in the blinking of an eye; the boards returned to the earth and grew spontaneously as trees.

Horse and floxin freed from human servitude galloped gleefully over the grassy knoll.

Thus, the makings of man on Qeplurwonatesxef were wiped off the face of the planet, and virgin land appeared as it had before the first ship landed to disgorge its once-human occupants upon the unsuspecting world.

*

Xdqtjljlhtkdlffft realized first, or perhaps it was last, what they had done. Without man, there were no gods, and without gods, no man.

"Oh, no," he moaned, as he vanished in a cloud of smoke and his throne disintegrated to bits of sopping red cloth.

The empty forum rippled with blackened and singed stone, the mark of the aftermath of battle. Water dripped and dribbled in the courtyard, but there was no one left to listen...

*

Koy stepped from her shanty and breathed deeply. She walked to the pond, with a strong firm step of the young and bent over to watch as the years fell away.

Her skin smoothed; her hair – once straggly – straightened and untangled. Her tresses changed from silver to the original green. Her eyes were clear and sparkled back at her from her reflection. She was now as she once was...

Koy. The first, the one, the only.

Mother Nature rolled up her sleeves.

"Right," she said. "Let's try this again, and this time, let's get it right."

Jack and the Giant

Once upon a time, not so very long ago, an old woman and her son lived in poverty. They were unable to find two coins to rub together. Her son was by everyone's estimation useless. He had no skills and no one was willing to employ him.

Finally, the old woman realized it was time to sell the family car. It was a junk heap and didn't work all that well. One had to give it the boot to get it started, and she had injured her foot kicking the damn thing.

The old woman limped her way to the car and placed a sign on the windscreen. "For sale. Needs work. Make offer."

As luck would have it, the old woman was not home when the offer came. She had hobbled to town to pick up food; but her son, Jack, was.

An old man who often passed their hovel stopped, stuck his hands in his pockets and began to walk around the car.

Jack was ready. He considered himself a stern and skilled negotiator. He exited the house and headed for the curb.

The old man kicked one of the tires, and the car sprang to life.

Jack cringed and backed away – probably not the best way to start a sale – the image of himself presenting money to his mother fluttered away. The deal was surely lost.

He spun to return to the house when the man, with a surprisingly strong voice, shouted: "Hey, you, is this your car?"

Jack pulled his shoulders back and turned. "Mine," his voice dropped low, "and my mother's."

"Interesting form of ignition, but great for those nights when you have had a bit too much to drink, or visiting someone else's wife," he elbowed the young man, "and you can't find your keys."

"Ah, er," Jack stammered. "Yes, it took a long time before we got that option to work properly."

"How much? I'm a little short of cash right now."

"But obviously you are a man of good taste," said Jack.

The man preened. "Would you consider a barter? Means we can keep it off the books where you don't have to pay income tax."

Jack scratched his head. He'd never heard of income tax, but his mother was always grumbling about how much she paid in taxes, so not paying them must be a good thing.

The man extracted his hands from his pocket. Something small slipped between his fingers. The old man swore, bent over and picked it up. Then he extended his hand. "I've got these," he groped for the right word, "beans... that's right... beans."

Jack stared at his hand. "They look awfully small."

"Oh, they expand. You put them in water and they get bigger. All beans are like that." The old man glanced at the youth's perplexed expression. "I guess if you live with your mom you don't do much cooking."

Jack shook his head. The car started to sputter, and he realized it was about to run out of gas. Then the deal would be lost.

He seized the beans and held them close to his breast. "Better take your car then."

The old man threw the sign on the ground, climbed into the vehicle and steered onto the road.

He gave Jack a jaunty wave and shouted as the car chugged away: "Sucker!"

Jack hurried into the house and examined the beans in his hands, wondering how much water he needed to make them grow. He grabbed a tumbler from the splintered counter, dumped the beans inside it and filled it with water. The more, the better.

Then he waited

… and waited

… and waited.

He studied them. Were they getting larger? He hoped so. His mother would kill him if they couldn't even get a decent meal out of them. Still, they didn't look like any beans he had ever eaten – not lima, not pinto, not navy – and he couldn't envision them ever getting that big.

He heard an unearthly howl outside. His mother was virtually flying up the street in great loping strides, propelled by the crutches.

Jack ran outside.

"Where's the damn car?" she shrieked at him.

Jack puffed up. "I sold it."

She deflated and groaned. "I was afraid of that. How much money did you get for it?"

"I got something better. You don't have to pay taxes for it."

She dropped the bag, that night's meagre ration, and abandoned one of the crutches. The other she used to swing at him. Powered by anger, she chased him inside the house.

He clasped the glass and proffered it as a peace offering.

"You fucking idiot. What the hell is that? Water? You sold our car for a glass of water?"

"No, beans. Magic beans like the ones in the story you told me as a child. That turned out okay. They lived happily ever after."

"Those ain't no fucking beans." The old woman swung again. The crutch connected with the glass and it went flying out the back door. Jack went scrambling after it.

"No!" he wailed. "Why did you do that? They were just starting to grow, but they are so small now I'll never be able to find them."

"That should'a told you that they warn't no beans."

The woman gave her son a whack upside the head; he passed out.

Night painted the sky black when he awoke. She snored softly. Jack crept outside. The scene was if possible darker than inside. The streetlight had burned out and the town's people never fix it. The houses next door were empty and they stared at him with hollow eyes. Jack never ventured outside after dark voluntarily, but he had to find those beans. On his hands and knees, he felt the ground, trying in vain to locate the beans. He cut his hand on broken glass. Soon his hand became covered in thorns.

Weeping, the youth leaned against the trunk of a tree and nursed his bleeding hand. He sensed movement behind him. He swung around. Belatedly it dawned on Jack that they had no trees in their yard. Prickers and stickers yes, but nothing else grew in their yard but weeds.

His eyes glittered in the darkness. A beanstalk. He knew this tale. He knew how it ended. *Happily ever after.*

A branch unfolded beneath him and carried him up, up, ever up. Jack wrapped his arms around the trunk and began to shinny toward the heavens.

Perhaps he could make his mother proud of him after all.

The sky grew bright before he emerged to see a grand castle in front of him. He was not surprised to see a woman sweeping the stoop.

Success, he thought, and he swaggered toward her.

"My name is Jack," he said, "I've been climbing all night and I'm very hungry."

"If you knew my husband, you would just fall back down whence you came. He eats the likes of you."

"Pleeeease," he intoned. "I could help you around the house."

Jack eyed the enormous broom. "Not sweeping, though."

The woman snorted. "Not anything. You're so small you'd have trouble capturing a mouse."

"Please?"

She stepped aside, a bemused expression on her face. "This reminds me of something."

Jack darted between the broom and the woman's feet before she changed her mind. A pot was bubbling on the hearth. She plunked a huge bowl in front of him and ladled some porridge into it. He crawled onto the tabletop so he could reach it. He blew and blew, and when it cooled enough he plunged his hands into the gruel, eating until he was fit to burst.

She sputtered. "You sure you are a messy eater." She threw a cloth on top of him.

A voice boomed above his head. "Feigh, figh, foe, fum, I smell the blood of an American."

Jack began to shake. The woman grabbed the cloth and stuck it in her pocket.

"You should be so lucky," she said. "Americans, very succulent. Lots of nice marbling."

"Well, what have we got?"

"Porridge, but if you bring me an American, I'll cook it up for you."

Jack dosed off and on as he rode around the kitchen in her apron. He jolted awake when he heard a loud smack.

"Okay, woman, I've eaten my fill. Bring me my hen."

"Get it yourself. Haven't you heard of women's lib?"

The giant snarled.

"Okay, okay, hold your horses." She halted and snapped her

fingers. "Now I know what I'm going to serve for dinner, horse roast, but you'll have to go out and butcher a horse."

The woman strode from the room. She squatted down and released Jack. "You can go now. He'll be asleep soon enough; he ain't the man he used to be, but he'd kill you soon enough."

She grabbed the hen and returned to the kitchen. Jack watched through a crack in the door.

The giant took the hen from her arms and shook it. The bird squawked indignantly and shat in his face. Jack's mouth dropped open. The giant plucked shiny pieces of gold from his cheeks. "I think her aim is getting better."

He poked and prodded the hen. Each time, the bird defecated with a metallic patter.

Jack gaped when he realized that it wasn't the golden eggs of the story, but it would do.

The giant tired of his amusement, laid his head on the table and began to snore.

The woman busied herself somewhere else in the castle. Jack crept from his hiding place between broom and wall, wrapped one hand around the bird's beak and the other around its neck.

"Awk – *gargle.*"

Jack took off, running for the beanstalk, dragging the bird behind him. He leapt from one great limb to another while the hen protested the rough treatment by pecking his cheek. The sun was setting by the time he reached the shanty.

His mother turned on him. "Where the hell have you been?"

She thrust her chin at the enormous chicken. "Where did you get that?"

She rubbed her hands together. "I don't care. It'll feed us for a week."

The bird clucked indignantly.

He put his finger to his lips and raced inside their cottage. As soon as she entered, he slammed the door shut. Jack lifted the hen up to the table.

"You're gonna clean it. I don't pluck no damn chickens." She dug her finger into its ribs. It shat, hitting Jack square in the face.

"Ow, that hurts."

"Serves you right. You stole it. I know you did."

He opened his mouth to object, thought about the giant, and his mouth snapped shut. He scraped the crap from his face. "It's gold. Here, feel."

"I ain't touching that shit."

He washed it off. "It's metal, see." He thrust his hand under her nose.

She sniffed. "It don't smell bad." She poked at it. "It's cold." She picked it up. "It's metal. Okay, you take it to the bank tomorrow and see what we can get for it."

By the following day, the golden pellet had crumbled into dust, but it still sparkled in the thready light. Jack scraped it into a bag and went to the bank. The tellers behind the counter hemmed and hawed when they saw him and refused to look at what he carried in his filthy sack.

The bank manager came around his desk, ready to throw him out, but Jack poured the contents into his hand. An expression of wonder crossed his features. "Just a second."

When he returned he was all smiles. "That's gold, gold dust. Where did you get gold dust?"

"It rained down from the heavens," Jack said.

"Right." He looked the young man up and down, opened the door and handed him a wad of cash.

After Jack left, the manager signaled to the security guard to follow. "See where he goes," the banker hissed. The guard left without a sound.

That night they ate handsomely.

The bank manager tarried outside bank after it was closed. "So?"

The guard shrugged. "He went to the market and home. At least, I think that's his home. Little more than a shed really. We hold the mortgage on it but decided against foreclosing. That land isn't worth much, although the old woman tries to make payments when she can."

"Gold?"

"Not unless one counts the dandelions."

The banker shooed the guard away.

The next day the battle with the bird began anew. Jack shook it, careful to point the hen's tail at the wall. It lifted its bottom and... splat.

He peered at his mother. She shook her head no. "Uh, uh. Scrape it off yourself. That's your job."

She poked the bird. Scowling Jack gathered the warm pellets until no amount of prodding or threats could produce the desired results.

The following day, he returned to the bank. The bank manager confronted him. "I understand we own the note on your home. It's overdue. I demand payment in full. We've let you ride long enough."

Jack sighed. His body was covered in bruises where he had been pelted by the bird.

The banker's face turned sly. "Unless you tell me where the gold is."

Jack shoveled the previous day's take onto the desk. "Is this enough?"

The banker scurried away, weighed it and returned. "Almost."

"I can bring more tomorrow," Jack said. "I'm pretty sure."

The banker raised a brow. "Okay, get out of here."

That night there was no princely meal, but they had plenty of leftovers. He explained their plight.

"You stay with that bank manager man when he leaves the room. You can't trust them. You come home and tell me how much it weighed. Don't leave him alone again."

Another day and another battle with the avian adversary that came from someplace lower than heaven. Mother and son soon learned to dance for the bird, startle it and dodge away.

And so it went until the bank manager told Jack that their debt was paid. Both mother and son noticed him lurking in the shadows.

The old woman chuckled and muttered: "If he only knew."

Meanwhile, they fed the hen, hoping to improve production, but there's only so much excrement that any creature could make and the bird was starting to develop a weight problem.

Then one day as they darted around the room avoiding the projectile pellets Jack's mother fell breaking her hip. Unfortunately, she fell on the hen. They had collected just enough to pay for a shiny new hip.

The bird fed them for a week, as long as they didn't mind picking feathers from their teeth.

"I told you it had to be cleaned," his mother said as she spat a plume onto the floor

A few weeks later, mother and son were worse off than before.

"I'm gonna have to go back up," he said.

"What? Go back where?"

"Never mind."

After checking to make sure the bank manager was not standing in the shadows, Jack clambered up the tree. It was harder to climb this time, for the stalk had grown and the tree had sprouted pungent flowers. As before, he started in the night and arrived the next day when the sun began to set. The woman was shelling beans the size of boulders. When she saw him, she grabbed the broom and chased through the fluffy cloud. He slipped inside the castle. The old woman paced back and forth in the barnyard, scratching her head.

The giant appeared at the door. "Feigh, fie, foe, fum, I smell the blood of an American."

"Chance would be a fine thing. You get a basic fry-up, and when you bring me an American, we will feast," she groused.

Hiding in a corner, Jack could hardly stay awake. The cloying sweet aroma of the smoke from the hearth seemed to go straight to his head. He drooled when she served the bacon, for he had eaten nothing for several days.

"Bring me my money bag," demanded the giant.

"Bring me, this. Bring me, that. One of these days, I'm going on strike," she muttered, but she went dutifully to the cupboard and pulled out an envelope.

Jack blinked. *Wasn't this supposed to be a bag?*

Acrid smoke twined around his head. He rubbed his eyes. They were beginning to sting. He waited. The giant went to sleep, and the wife took herself to bed. Jack began to giggle. He clapped his hand over his mouth lest he wake the huge monster.

He slipped from his hiding place, peered inside the envelope and almost burst out laughing when he saw the squares of plastic. Jack had heard of credit cards, but he'd never seen one.

When he accompanied his mother to the shops, the cards seemed magical things. The customer passed the slip of plastic to the shopkeeper and the bill was paid.

Jack didn't think twice. He shoved the envelope inside his belt, rearranged it so it didn't hit him in the balls every time he took a step, and scurried away.

The following day, he went to the store. "It's awful big," the merchant scoffed as Jack handed him a card as large as a poster, but the shopkeeper ran it through his magic machine and returned it all smiles.

Jack frowned. The man behind the counter resembled the banker, and Jack wondered if they were related.

The shopkeeper ducked his head in approval. "Are you sure that's all?"

Jack went through the merchandise picking out two house dresses for his mother and a brand-new duvet.

"Fine choices, sir. Are you sure you don't want anything for yourself?"

Jack chose new trousers, a shirt and a jacket.

"Ahem," the shopkeeper coughed delicately into his hands. "Some underthings?"

"What?"

Obligingly, the merchant plucked several pairs of underpants and some socks from the shelf.

"Oh," he said.

"The changing room is over there," the shopkeeper said.

When Jack emerged he felt like a new man.

The merchant swept the old clothes into a pile. "Shall I burn these for you?" he suggested.

Jack shrugged.

"You might want to consider some soap, maybe some deodorant."

"Better not. I'll ask my mom if she needs some," he countered.

"Of course, by all means ask your mother."

Then Jack went to the grocery store, stocking up on enough food that, should the cards shatter as easily as the bird had been crushed, they would still have enough to eat for weeks.

The next day, mother and son out to purchase a car, new bed and a refrigerator to keep their stores. Jack took her to the nice shopkeeper who fawned as they entered. He thrust deodorants, undies and women's unmentionables into their hands. They outfitted themselves, complete with all the soaps, perfumes and detergent that such large cards could buy.

His mother pranced around in her new finery. She begged the next day to go to the store again. This time, the greeting was not so friendly. When they proffered the card, the merchant seized it, took out a chainsaw and cut into pieces.

"This card was reported stolen." He brandished a bill, waving it under their noses. "You are expected to pay this now."

And they were worse off than they were before.

"Now what are we going to do? We just got out of debt." She put her hand on her hip and fixed him with an accusatory stare. "Where do you keep getting these things? Are you stealing them?"

"Well, you smashed the hen," he noted. "If we still had the hen, we could pay these bills off."

That night he approached the tree – studiously ignoring the shadowy figures of the banker and the shopkeeper. Jack sidled around the trunk of the tree and realized with a shock that there were several stalks twined together. He could no longer wrap his arms around its circumference and shinny up it as he had before.

No matter it had to be done. So, he climbed and climbed and climbed.

When Jack's head emerged above the clouds, he found the old woman plucking flowers and leaves from the tree and shoving them into her mouth.

She saw Jack. She stabbed her finger at him. "It's you! Again!"

She deflated. "Go on in, my husband is already home. He's mellowed. He doesn't go out and terrorize villagers, do battle with ogres or trolls, or even hunt. Can't get him to do a damn thing since you first appeared."

Jack scuttled in the door while the wife continued to tick off on her fingers the things her spouse did not get done. "... get rid of those frigging fairies, butcher meat. Just sits on his fat ass, eats and sleeps."

Jack spied the giant where he sat holding a large, white wand clenched between his fingers. He placed it to his lips, inhaled and began to cough. Without thinking, Jack scrabbled up the table leg and thumped the giant roundly between the shoulder blades.

The giant clutched the youth between forefinger and thumb. "Oh, it's you. My wife told me about you. Jack, isn't it?"

"Yes, sir,"

"Stole the hen, didn't you? Can't say I missed her, she was an ill-tempered creature. Then you took my credit cards." The giant shook Jack. "Do you know how much trouble it is to cancel credit cards?"

"I am sorry. My mother and I are poor. You have so much and we have so little. I thought you could spare a little something for us."

The giant began to laugh in great whooping guffaws, and dangling from his fingertips, Jack began to wave about like a flag in a wind.

"You wanted riches? You shouldn't be called Jack. Your mother should have named you jerk. Don't you realize what you have under your feet?"

Jack glanced beneath him. Was this a trick question? "Ah, the floor?"

The giant blew smoke in Jack's face. "No, what you climbed to get here?"

Jack stared the giant, feeling on firmer footing. "A tree."

"No, you idiot." The giant threw up his hands and Jack bounced helplessly from his fingertips.

"It's marijuana. Hooch. Do you know how much this sells for in Colorado?"

The Die is Cast

The good and much-beloved queen strolled through the gardens. Somewhere within the confines of the castle, a dozen servants prepared the rooms reserved for her lying in.

This was her last day of freedom before her confinement. She resented the seclusion but understood the need to protect the unborn child. The queen saw a winter rose, grasped the stem to pluck it and pricked her finger. Blood welled from the cut, dripping to the ground. A raven cawed overhead. The woman queen saw the deep red in the pristine snow and blue-black feathers of the raven and prayed to God that her daughter might have all three.

Wishes should never be squandered or worded imprudently, for when she was born, her daughter sported black feathers instead of hair. She also had snow white skin and the ruby red eyes of the albino. As the little girl grew, she developed a taste for blood.

Snow White was kept locked in the castle lest any see her, and the king and the queen prayed fervently for another child. This one, maybe, a little bit more normal.

To avoid distressing the princess, servants were ordered to wear a cap of black feathers. The parents lavished education upon her, if not love. She learned her letters, and her embroidery and needlepoint were wonders to behold.

The queen pitied her daughter. No child should be caged for the crime of a foolish mother and imprudent words spoken in a moment of passion.

Finally, the queen called the huntsman. She instructed him that he was to blindfold Snow White and take her deep into the forest and set her free. He was not to touch her, except to drop a hood over her head. When the huntsman left the girl, she would remain covered until she chose to free herself. The huntsman was not to look back.

The man was one of the few old enough to remember the princess. One day she was feted and the next she vanished. No funeral. Nothing. The girl must have had a serious deformity to be imprisoned and now abandoned. He had been in service long enough that he was not surprised, especially when the good queen offered him a handsome stipend and early retirement for his silence.

The huntsman prepared a rope to bind the girl's hands, for how else could he lead her if he could not touch her? He considered his route carefully. The queen must see them enter the forest, but he who had lost both his wife and his child to the deep woods did not have the heart to leave the girl completely alone.

In his time as huntsman, he had run into the dwarves, as they worked their mines. He had even supped with them. They seemed goodly if not overly bright. The huntsman could introduce them to his charge. Secluded as the dwarves were, the seven brothers were not familiar with the female form, so unless she was truly hideous, they would accept her. They would feed her.

It was, the huntsman decided, the best he could do for the princess.

The next day, he packed a script with food, pheasants' eggs, sweetmeats and anything else he could find to tempt the royal palate. He slipped sideways into the tower room as the servants exited. He saw a flash of blue-black hair, but before he could examine the princess closely he slipped the hood over her head.

"You must not remove that," he said. "The orders come from your mother, the Queen."

He slid the loop over her wrists and tightened it. "I will lead you and, if need be, tell you where to go. You will not misstep."

But the huntsman misspoke, for he had not the knowing of how to guide one blind, particularly one that had to be led on the end of a rope.

"Oops, there's a root..." She tripped. "And a hole." She fell.

Each tumbled was punctuated by a series of expletives. The huntsman's face grew red to the roots. He had no idea the princesses knew those words, and wondered if he had taken the wrong child, the daughter of a stable hand, mayhap.

"Mind the gap," he cautioned.

The huntsman carried a lamp on the end of a post so that the queen could watch their progress. He had got far enough away from the castle, but he was pretty sure the queen heard all.

"Low-lying branch."

Wap.

He decided he would be judicious in following her instructions and never to return to the castle again. He valued his head.

Snow White made a grab at the hood and would have torn it off, but he gave the robe a hard jerk and then had to run after her as she rolled down a hill.

The huntsman squatted beside her, waiting patiently for her to regain consciousness.

"Princess, I am sorry. I have been given certain orders. I durst not disobey. I am not to lay eyes upon your pretty face. Neither can I touch you, even to steer you along the right path nor carry you over the pitfalls of the forest. But our goal lies close at hand. Little men who will take care of you and see you safe and sound for the rest of your life."

*

Sir Waldo of Dafney was not well-liked among the fairy folk or the woodland creatures. When he sanitized their tales, he had effectively castrated them, diluting their supernatural powers and belittling the dangers inherent in many species until humans believed all they did all day was dance and sing in weak and wavery voices

He was wrong most of the time. The six of the seven names provided by Dafney were not correct. Instead of Sleepy, Dopey, Bashful, Sneezy, Doc, Happy, and Grumpy, they had been named for other less-savory traits. Creepy, Mopey, Snootful, Sleazy, Pox, Crappy and, of course, Grumpy.

The dwarves generally avoided humanity, but they greeted the huntsman warmly for he normally brought food with him - fine hind or buck or perhaps a well-fatted boar. The brothers froze mid-step when they observed the creature with lumps, bumps and bulges that they had never seen before. The package squirmed and foul language issued from beneath the hood.

Dumpy poked the creature. "A bit underdone, don't you think?"

The huntsman tore his feathered cap from his head. "I'm sorry I have not come carrying gifts, but to ask a boon. This child needs protection."

"Doesn't sound like it," said Pox.

"This is the princess. I was to leave her in the forest, but raised in a castle, she knows naught about the wild wood. She needs your help," the huntsman said.

"Why should we help?"

"It'll cost you," said another.

"I can bring you venison and meat." He wrung his cap in his hands, crumpling the feather. "It is just a girl."

"A female, is it?"

The seven dwarves formed a huddle. "Does she cook and clean?"

The huntsman shrugged. "I'm sure she could learn."

The next thing he knew he had sold the princess into slavery. He patted the sack of diamonds on his belt, cheered by the reassuring weight, and bid the dwarves *adieu*. "Nice, ah, er, doing business with you," he said.

"Wait a second, aren't you going the wrong way? The castle is that way." The eldest pointed south.

"Um, no. I was going to retire anyway." He darted into the trees before they could change their minds.

The dwarves circled the princess. "So, what have we got here?" asked Sleazy.

"Snow White," said the hood.

"What?"

"Snow White. That's my name."

"Oh."

One of the dwarves stepped forward and whipped the hood from her head.

The jet-black feathers cascaded half-way down her back. She spun, and they viewed the sickly white skin and the ruby red eyes.

"Passing strange these female creatures are," said Pox.

"It's nice to have one, though."

By the end of the week, the brothers realized that they had been rooked. The woman had no idea how to make a bed or do laundry. She'd swish it around inside the horse trough and slop it down to the ground, so their clothes were stiffer with mud than they had been before they were washed, and her cooking tasted like leftovers from the laundry.

The dwarves sat around the kitchen table one night wondering what they could do with her.

"I know," said one, with light dawning in his eyes. "Pa told us about women. They make children."

"This one can't even make a stew. How do you expect her to make a child?"

The first winked and elbowed his brother. "You know... make children."

Snow White didn't know what they meant, but she was pretty sure that she wouldn't like it. She didn't like cooking, cleaning or anything else, until she learned she could ride a broom. Then that chore, sweeping, became fun as she zipped around the room, although it did little for the crockery.

"Oh, Snow? Snow?" Pox crooned. "Let's go over how to make a bed one last time."

He slammed the door behind her as soon as she had entered the bedroom. He told her to lay down flat and seeing how she was so tall, she had to stretch out across seven little beds.

Snow White gaped at the dwarf. Hadn't it been him who said that making the bed could not be accomplished while lying inside it?

The dwarf proceeded to climb into bed beside her. He hopped up and down, jumping from bed to bed to bed. The wood creaked and squeaked.

Beyond the door, Snow White could hear the sniggers of the other dwarves.

One by one, the dwarves entered the room to have their wicked way with her. They leapt and hopped from here to there, there to here. One actually clambered onto her stomach and rocked back and forth, moaning.

Snow White screamed, and the twitters in the main room turned into whoops, applause and guffaws. They left her alone for the rest of the night. Eventually, she worked up the courage to join that night's repast. The youngest grumbled that he had to cook again.

The eldest stabbed his spoon at the pan and then Snow. "Consider the alternative."

Crappy boasted, "I think we made a wise investment."

Snow resented them bouncing around her night after night when she preferred to sleep, and she hated that they would spend the rest of the evening, thumbs latched in their belts, swaggering.

The dwarves were happy; she was not.

As days blended into nights into weeks, months into years, it dawned on Snow that she was bigger than they were, and the dwarves could not hold her against her will.

However, the huntsman had convinced her that the woods were no good place for a princess to be. Yet, it seemed safe enough during the day. Snow began to take walks in the fields around the dwarves' cottage. Eventually, she realized that her journey could be far less harrowing, less painful, without the blind fold.

She started hoarding food and tried to recollect the path she and the huntsman had made, although Snow White did not expect a warm welcome at home. She was ruined, no longer marriageable now that she had lived with the seven dwarves.

For Snow, there would be no handsome prince. She snorted. Even before her ruination, it had been exceedingly unlikely that she would meet a prince, handsome or otherwise, since she had never been introduced to court.

When she checked her precious store of food, she found it had grown fuzzy. She tasted it, gagged, vomited and spent the next three hours hallucinating.

The following day Snow crept out the door as soon as the seven brothers disappeared into hills. She sat, waiting until she could no longer hear the ongoing argument that accompanied them wherever they went.

Then she returned inside long enough to fill her tattered skirts with gems. She knotted the cloth carefully, so they would not spill out. By the time she was finished with the procedure her legs were exposed to the thigh. Unfettered and free she ran, away from the dwarves, away from their cottage, away from the hills and away from the castle she used to call home.

Eventually she reached a wide spot in the road. Women shrieked, grabbed their children and covered their eyes as soon as they saw her. They herded their young indoors. The men exited the houses to watch her and gave her a leer that she had come to know too well from the dwarves.

Snow White screwed up the courage to inquire after a boarding house.

"I know just the kind of house you need," said one man.

Another interrupted, "The bordello is over there."

The two pointed to a ramshackle building at the edge of town.

Snow White scratched on the door. A large buxom woman opened the door with a bang. "I told you we're taking the night off," she spoke to the air.

The woman glanced down. "Oh, I thought it was one of these horny devils. What *can* I do for you?"

"I need a place to stay. I have been walking for ever so long," Snow said.

The woman stepped down to ground level, with a great jouncing of bazooms, and circled Snow White. "Your legs are good, and I always say it pays to advertise. Eyes, a bit odd, but most men are too drunk to notice." The woman patted the younger woman on the head. "I dig that crazy hat with all those lovely feathers. Where ever did you find it?"

"It's my hair," replied Snow White.

"Yeah, sure it is, honey. Keep your beauty secrets to yourself. That's okay by me."

Lastly, the woman spat on her hand and wiped it along Snow White's cheek. "You'll clean up nicely. You must stay."

"Well, I can pay for bed and board." Snow White stuffed her hand in her pocket and extracted a large sapphire she had kept out for just such eventuality.

The madam's eyes widened. She seized it and slow grin spread across her face. "Hell, for this you can buy the whole damned brothel, including the women."

"But my lady, I have no such need."

"My lady? Boy, do you have the wrong end of the schtick. You seem a bit naïve." She draped a meaty arm across Snow White's shoulders and drew her inside the building of garish red velvet. "See, no one will notice your eyes. They'll just think it's reflected light."

"Huh?"

The madam pushed her gently into a large overstuffed loveseat. "What we have here is a business opportunity. I know this is a small burg, but it's on the crossroads. We get a lot of traffic and we are the only, ah, um, hostelry for several counties, and we provide other services."

Snow White's eyes narrowed. "That wouldn't be cooking and cleaning?"

The madam dismissed the thought with a wave of her hand. "Hell no, we have servants to do that."

Snow White nodded. "As it should be."

"No, this is the kind of services that gentlemen savor. Gentlemen," she chuckled, "farmers, shepherds. Anything with three legs."

The woman flopped down on the loveseat and elbowed Snow White. "If you know what I mean."

Instantly, Snow White was on guard. "This doesn't have anything to do with dwarves bouncing around on beds."

"Dwarves? Whatever turns you on, I say."

"I hate dwarves."

"Good then, no dwarves." The old woman scratched her chin. "There may be some bouncing."

Snow White stuck out her chin. "Bouncing? No way. Not interested."

"But that's the beauty of this deal. You don't have to do any bouncing. That's the girls' job. You'd be the boss. You'd tell what girls had to, uh, bounce with what gentlemen, but I've found it's better to let the john and the girl do their own negotiations. Make sure you listen, so you get the right cut. Then all you have to do is rake in the dough."

"Dough?" Snow White thrust her chin out stubbornly. "I told you, I don't cook. I most certainly won't bake."

The woman rose, rubbed her backside and extended her hand to Snow White. "I can see training is going to take a little longer than expected. Let's go into the kitchen and I'll explain. Better yet, I'll keep your little bauble with me for the bordello and I agree stay with you for a month until you know the ropes for another one like this." She winked. "You'll have a place to stay. You'll get fed."

When Snow White opened her mouth to admonish the woman, the madam hurried on. "No cooking, and if you don't like it, you can move on. I get the baubles and you are free to go."

Snow White ducked her head in assent.

The learning curve was long and arduous. It took a week for Snow White to grasp the difference between a boarding house and a bordello.

"I mean, if you want to take in travelers, dear, that is entirely up to you, but bouncing is where the big bucks are. Besides few women would stay here, and men? You know all about men, even those of the vertically-challenged variety. They're all the same."

So, Snow White became the madam of one of the largest whore houses in four counties. She was lenient with the women. If they didn't want a man, they were not forced, although any woman who lolled around for too long found she had to pay rent, work in the kitchens or do the laundry.

Within a year, Snow White realized she had remained intact - a virgin still - despite the best efforts of the dwarves. She thought briefly of returning to her mother who had rejected her so, but soon discounted the possibility as foolish.

Her triumph was complete when the seven dwarves came stumbling into her establishment, seeking employment. They had lost most of their fortune when she left, and the silly creatures spent the rest looking for her. They did not even recognize the woman standing before them. She took them into her quarters where she could watch to make sure the women kept their clients happy. She hid her smile behind her hand when she heard the dwarves' exclamations as they witnessed the actual act.

"Why I never..."

"You mean you're supposed to do that..."

"Disgusting..."

Snow White shook with mirth. It seemed the dwarves had been no more educated than she herself in the ways of the flesh. All the dwarves knew was they were supposed to bounce up and down and make the bed creak. They took it for granted that she was supposed to wince, scrunch up her face and turn away while it was happening.

Snow White sighed.

If she had known she might have saved herself, but the die was cast.

Signs and Sigils

Calleigh sat in the black castle of *Cill Mhantáin*. Years ago she had retreated indoors. No *rí* of any worth was without a sorcerer or a mage. Few, though, could lay claim to a god who must remain free, and no one would dare hinder a goddess, much less a hag.

It was her duty to bring the winter's chill to Ireland, but she didn't have to like it. Calleigh preferred a cozy fire, with walls around her and a roof over her head. Some of her kind settled in crystal caves, but she learned long ago that the ventilation in a grotto was crap and the acoustics lousy.

Here she had hot and cold running servants to do her bidding and no one, not even the king, would gainsay her.

As more of the enchanted moved indoors, communication became sporadic. Communal sabbats upon the moors were rare. While humanity used the tools available to them to communicate, vellum, feathered quill and human runners.

The fey refused to do something so primitive. They did not relish calves without their skins or ducks without their plumes.

Instead, the fairy used the tools they had on hand. For some this was a bowl of water or a reflection on a lake. For others it was cast beads or clay runes. Calleigh used clear crystal, so like ice.

The caves of stone became the hubs where messages could intersect.

Calleigh placed her crystal on the hearth and watched the flames dance within its heart.

She heard the soft trill of a bird, cut short and then repeated several times, a click and then a voice. Calleigh opened her mouth to speak and was cut short. Figures formed inside the crystal.

A disembodied voice intoned:

Please listen carefully to our menu, for our options may have changed.

If you would like the name and address of the coven nearest you, press pentacle.

If you need supplies, press cauldron for the sales department.

If you would like to schedule a ritual, press six-pointed star.
If you need inspiration, press Awen.
If you would like to do a blessing, press the triple-teardrop crescent.
If you would like to invoke cycles, press deosil.
If you need information about male magic, press the god symbol
If you would like to discuss infertility, press the maiden symbol
If you would like to invoke women's power, press the mother symbol
If you would like sage advice, press crone
If you would like to contact the spirit world, press soul.

Calleigh pressed the six-pointed star, ritual, as it came flitting across the crystal, and she waited for the next set of options.

If earth magic, press the statute of the voluptuous mother.
If northern tradition, press Valknut.
If Anglo-Saxon paganism, press Seax Wica.
If fertility is an issue, press horned god.
If planetary magic, press the appropriate planetary sigil.
If moon magic, press the phase of the moon.
If drawing energy, press spiral
If banishment, press widdershin's spiral.
If capturing or isolating negative energy, press labyrinth.
If you would like to return to the previous menu, press circle.

Calleigh became confused, her rite entailed both moon magic and fertility. When she listened to the options three times, she pressed circle to return to the previous menu.

Then she heard an option that suited her needs

If you would like to speak to an operator, press Hecate's wheel.

Calleigh stabbed at Hecate's wheel before it could scurry away, escaping out the crystal's base.

The bird's trill sounded several times.

We are experiencing unusually high call volume, please hold.

Her temperature was beginning to rise and outside the snow began to melt.

The trilling bird call ceased, and she heard a new voice. Calleigh grabbed the crystal, nearly scalding herself on the super-heated stone.

"Hello, hello, hello!" she bellowed into the point. "Is someone there?"

In order for us to better assist you, please provide your Social Insecurity Number.

If you don't remember it, your Social Insecurity Number consists of:

your numerological rank for your name, or destiny number.

your numerological rank according to your date of birth, or life path number.

If a master number, please use the master numbers 11, 22, 33.

This is followed by the appropriate symbol for your age - maid, mother or crone.

Along with the destiny designation of your familiar.

Next add your heart's desire, personality, and growth numbers.

Therefore, if your birthday is a five; your name is an eleven; you are still a virgin; your cat's name is Fluffy; your heart's desire is nine; personality number, three, and growth number is eight, then your Social Insecurity Number would be:

5-11-the maiden sigil-1-9-3-8.

She swore and went tearing through her drawers trying to find a quill and the appropriate charts.

Calleigh hated numerology. She didn't keep track of such things. It smacked of arithmetic, and she'd flunked the maths in fairy school. Never even achieved her Oh-levels, much less Ah-levels.

As far as she was concerned, life was what is was – and right now it sucked – no odd conglomeration figures was going to change it. If anything, numerology's predictive nature fixed one's fate in stone. Overall, boiling life's essence down to a number was depressing. She preferred to let life surprise her.

It always complied.

With her tongue sticking out of the corner of her mouth, she matched runes and numbers. Biting her tongue in agitation, she came up with eight as a destiny number.

Stability, a life that never changed. What a surprise.

She tapped in the appropriate symbols, numbers, sigils and what not – lots of what not.

The sun rose in the sky and she was still listening to trilling birds. Calleigh had to suppress the impulse to kill the little suckers.

The next voice she heard had the hollow quality of a facsimile. She stared at the crystal suspiciously.

"I'm sorry, your request for a rite is denied. You have used your quota for ritual magic this year."

"Horse pucky," she roared. Calleigh threw the crystal against the wall. It shattered and reformed.

She banged through the door and rampaged around the castle, freezing every piece of the crockery she could find, even if it was attached to someone's hand. No few servants froze that day.

A *Tiarna* came whistling down the hall, happy with the respite that winter gave the warriors of the kingdom.

Calleigh zapped him and watched in satisfaction as a frog bounded away.

The Pied Piper of Hamelin

The people of Hamelin trailed after the piper and his parade of cavorting rats. They didn't trust him, not since that first kerfuffle. Okay, then they refused to pay him, but he stole that which was most precious, their children. Everyone remembered the childless years. The grief and the loneliness, but with fewer mouths to feed the town prospered and new babies eventually came.

And the rats returned. The citizens wondered if the pied piper had turned them loose again within the city. So, the populace followed him each year to ensure he left with the rats.

The crowd stopped when they reached the wooden wall – not that any wall could keep such vermin out – and waited until the last animal exited the gates. Then the guard slammed it shut tight. The city fathers made sure the entrance was well guarded against him should he try to re-enter the city.

No one questioned how the guards were supposed to identify the man. His garb was gaudy; he was easily recognized. The pied piper wore a black mask. No one had ever seen his face or knew his features. If he wore the rough-spun cloth of the commoner, who would distinguish him?

This ritual of slithering, slinking, creeping and cavorting vermin had become an annual affair, an anti-carnival, and the mayor commented that each year's batch of rats looked fatter and sleeker than the last.

The rat man's rates went up each year when he presented them with the bill citing: "Overages. The price of the replacement staff killed by the plague, and the recruitment and training thereof, to the tasks of clubbing, poisoning, and disposal of product..."

Many whispered that the raw recruits came from adjacent villages, divested of their children, as Hamelin had once been. Some said the job description included the clubbing of recruits who complained and the disposal thereof.

The pied piper added the cost of poisons, the replacement of clubs deemed unfit. The city people believed the rat man was padding the budget but could do little to stop him.

Many believed he was the black death itself. The populace would have happily seen him hanged from the gibbet.

A guard climbed down from his post atop the tower. "He went into the Forbidden Grove."

The words traveled from lip to ear. "He did it again. The rat man must have terrible magic indeed if he dared enter *the* grove."

Seen from a far, the coppice was beautiful, seductively so, with the long, willow-leafed, pink-tipped fronds waving gently in the breeze, as if beckoning to those who came close to enter.

When people walked abreast magical forest, the grove smelled sickly sweet, with a heady, but lethal perfume. Those who succumbed to the grove's invitation, did not return, or if they did wander beyond the confines of the trees, they shrieked and screamed and flailed as if to ward off evil spirits, and the individual died, the sooner the better for all were as mad as a hatter.

No one entered the Forbidden Grove and lived.

*

The rat man paused long enough to stop his ears with cloth. He took a deep breath before reseating his mask and ducking into the wood. He exhaled one long, low note as he hurried past the trees. He kept his elbows close, lest they brush either branch or leaf. The mask served a duo purpose, protecting his eyes and breath from the heady perfume and disguising his visage.

The fairy wood was infested with wee ones, who lead the unwary to their demise. The Forbidden Grove was lousy with them. The piper sensed more than heard their entreaties.

"Candy, little boy," one said.

"Take a bite of the sugary flowers," said another.

"Let me tempt you..."

"Sweets for the sweet."

The wee ones buzzed around his head on their dragonfly chargers.

"Let me tempt you..."

"Sweets for the sweet."

"Just a little bite of our fairy fruit."

The rat man batted at one. The dragonfly tumbled head over heels, its wings getting tangled with its tail.

"Goddamn you..." shouted its rider.

He stomped on it.

Splat.

Neither were the rats impervious to the toxic plants. Those that tarried got drunk on the aroma and some scampered after the wee ones.

He heard an answering note to his trill. His bride awaited him.

Beneath the mask, the pied piper smiled. His bride. He loved her and marveled that he had found such a one, a woman who wanted to wed the rat man.

Others may not find her pretty. She was, after all, a vertically challenged troll. In other words, she was short. Man height. She had small eyes, obscured by heavy brow-ridges, thick cheek bones and a broad nose. She was strong. She could crack nuts with her teeth.

She was a boon to his business and the brains of the operation. Their home life presented the picture of typical domesticity. He hastened his pace and strode from the grove. His lips brushed the craggy cheek.

The music stopped for an instant. The creatures froze. A few had enough wits about them to escape.

The piper led the creatures to the cave behind their cottage. The vermin hopped, jumped and twirled at his command. His wife was prepared for his homecoming, with the doors of the unoccupied cages left wide open.

The piper stepped aside, the rats split into groups and boogied into the crates in twos and threes.

He piped, the rats skipped in place. She slammed the doors shut. She smiled and returned to the grove.

The rat man fed the rats with the leavings of yesterday's pies. He went inside their cottage. He set the pipes aside and hid that day's gold. Divested of his pied garb, he donned the simple clothes of a farmer.

Then the piper went to survey their lands. The air above the far ovens rippled with heat. Their gardens were extensive, each lined with neat little rows of root vegetables.

She crept up behind him. "A good harvest," she said.

She scooped carrots, turnips, parsnips and swedes into her skirt. He followed her into the kitchens where she chopped up the meat, bones and all, until it was mince. She added vegetables and wrapped the mixture into the crust made of fine white powder and lard.

His income had doubled since he had wed, and the costs of their operations were pared to nearly nothing with only the couple to minister them. Nothing went to waste since they had started recycling. Her idea.

Heretofore, he'd released the rats before he entered the Forbidden Grove. It was good for repeat business, but vermin were always abundant and happy to inhabit the city left empty by his piping.

Now his wife maintained a stand in the city, and the couple wanted for nothing. The townsfolk accepted her as any other raucous-voiced, ugly-faced ale-wife touting her wares.

Her meaty hands formed the breads and the sweetmeats she sold in the market square.

It was said that her crust and her breads were the flakiest and her pies were to die for.

The elders boasted that their bones strengthened after they ate her cakes and her pies. The families complimented the shopkeeper saying that their sires remained robust. Until, of course, they died.

The next day he helped carry her wares into the city. He wore his hood pulled low. The guards greeted the wife and her spouse as regular visitors to the city.

When the rat man entered, the guard salivated. "More pies, missus?'

The rat man flipped back the cloth to expose their wares.

The guard breathed deeply. "I will see you later, missus," he said.

"Nay, not later." She gave him a fresh pie. "Fresh baked last night."

"What is that sweet smell?" he asked.

"Oleander."

"Heavenly," he said.

The husband covered the pies. He was a man of few words having developed a lisp after years of piping.

The rat man kissed his wife farewell and took the long way back to their domicile. The piper fed the rats again and marked the cages of the long-term residents for slaughter.

He grabbed a basket to harvest more vegetables. When he got back to the stores, he found a rabbit clad in white gloves leaning against one of the bushel baskets. He crunched on a carrot. "Ah, what's up, doc," it said.

The rat man seized a hoe and struck the creature.

The hare wobbled a bit. "Jeez, picky, picky." It wandered away.

The piper darted into the cottage to get his gun. When he returned, the animal had fled.

Still fuming, the piper killed the rats for that night's pies with relish. He made a mental note to set traps in the shed.

"Wascally Wabbit."

Briar Rose

Briar Rose followed the sweet notes of a siren's song to the turret. Somewhere in the back of her mind, she recalled that the King and Queen waited in the Great Hall to welcome her back home after an absence of nearly sixteen years. But she had managed to slip away from her fussy fairy godmothers, relishing her freedom before the onus of royalty descended on her shoulders, and she reveled in their cries of desolation.

Briar Rose *had* to locate the source of this enchanting music or die trying.

*

Elsewhere in the castle, Rumpelstiltskin wound his way through long-forgotten passages toward the rhythmic sound of the spinning wheel, as enticing for him as the dulcet song was for the young princess Briar Rose.

Occasionally he would dig between tunnels, opening new routes in the castle walls...

*

The princess, who had a more direct path, but no less arduous, arrived in the tower chamber first. She stared at the wondrous face of a woman older than time itself, but beautiful none-the-less. The girl's brow wrinkled, for the visage seemed somehow familiar as if she should recollect it.

Then her attention was captured by the spinning wheel.

Tapokita. Tapokita. Tapokita.

Around and around it went, spinning.

Hypnotized Briar Rose advanced hand extended to the wheel.

Tapokita. Tapokita. Tapokita

The old woman's eyes narrowed. She would be the unnamed, unacknowledged sister no more.

Tapokita. Tapokita. Tapokita

The king and queen would remember her name forever, as long as they lived.

The girl's fingertips grazed the spindle, and she deflated like an empty bladder.

There was a loud clatter deep within the walls of the chamber.

Bang, bang, crash!

"Halt. Who goes there where their presence is not desired?" screeched the old woman, with arms raised, the spell of banishment forming on his lips.

*

Rumpelstiltskin stumbled out of the secret passage. His eyes flipped from lifeless, recumbent figure of the princess to the witch.

"Oops, sorry. Wrong fairy tale." He vanished into the cavity and a door swooshed shut behind him.

*

Seven pairs of hands battered at the door.

"Ouch, stop..."

"Don't push me."

"Give way..."

"Me first! I am eldest you know."

"I'm eldest," shrieked the wicked sister from her perch near the spinning wheel.

"Hey, these nails are iron, you know. They burn."

The self-proclaimed eldest leaned against the wall and waited for her sisters to get sorted.

"Get out of my way."

The door burst open, a hole seared through the center of it, and one of the seven arrowed into the circular room while the rest clustered around their sister who cradled her blistered and burned hands against her breast.

"Too late, sister. The deed is done."

Esmeralda spun, grabbed the sleeping princess and thrust herself through the chimney to the secret passageway she had prepared earlier. Except... someone had dug between the passages.

The previously neat holes went willy nilly, hither and thither – and yon!

And made a balls-up of the system to boot.

Instead of moving forward to a known route, the good fairy and Briar Rose fell.

They fell and fell and fell and fell, and they fell some more.

Through a portal created when the dwarf disturbed the magical ley with his incessant digging.

Outside, a forest of briars wrapped itself around the castle.

The triumphant expression on the fairy's face melted and her mouth formed a small o.

Princess and fairy godmother landed with an oomph. She had just enough presence of mind to embrace Briar Rose and roll before the great iron beast bearing down on them crushed them under its squealing wheels.

HOONNNNNK!

The sound seemed to go on forever. *HO-O-N-N-N-N-N-K!*

The fairy bundled Briar Rose into her arms and flew to the tall spires of this strange new citadel. Esmeralda glanced from side to side, both dazed and amazed.

Men did not dress as men were supposed to dress in peacock feather and stiff, flouncy collars, while the women here dressed as men, in tights and trousers.

She gasped and tried to cover her eyes, nearly dropping Briar Rose, so she might not see the woman who was strode bare-legged up the street, tarted-up worse than the most blatant doxy of yore. Not that Esmeralda knew a lot of trollops.

The castles here had neither turrets nor towers. They were towers – single narrow structures that rose high into the heavens and were designed to sway hypnotically with the tearing wind. The walls glittered, blinding. She became dazzled by the reflections of sun, cloud and blue sky all around her.

Esmeralda flew – *thunk* – into the side of a building.

Then the two, fairy godmother and fairy-tale princess, plummeted.

Gritting her teeth and wings beating frantically, Esmeralda finally reached the summit of one of the smaller towers. The others loomed all around her.

The fairy stood stunned. She lowered the princess to the roof, sat beside her and drummed her fingers against the tacky surface.

She must think.

*

That night she toured this dark, grey, dirty land searching for a clue of their whereabouts. She watched as humanity voluntarily entered the great open maw of an iron dragon which rode on the back of a metal snake. Its path twisted both above and below the belly of the earth.

Surely, they must die.

Or these mortals rode in the streets on metal steeds that spoke not in snorts, soft wickers and righteous nays, but in growling, blasting, blaring of horns.

Around her, lights without fire sprang to life, pushing the darkness aside so that it was forced to hide in small niches. It seemed these people had captured the magic of the spark and of fire, without incantation and the waving of hands or wands.

She found a sign and puzzled over it. "Manhattan Borough of New York."

She frowned. Her people could not exist in this tangle of iron and glass, but she was here and not dead. Yet. The presence of steel was starting to wear on her, and her body ached. She could travel no more this night, but she had marked her trail and soon she stood at the bottom of the tower where Briar Rose lay, wondering how she could make it to the top.

The door man sauntered up. Glittering braids adorned his shoulders.

The fairy studied him. She had seen him, or persons of his ilk, in the past. He wore a bright red coast and a black cap, feathered and furred. A short, unsheathed blade hung from his waist band.

He extended his hand. "What can I do for you? You look lost."

"I am wondering how to get to the top."

"Well." He stared at her. "You could always take the elevator."

"Elevator?"

The man thrust his hand under her nose and waggled his fingers. "Big box. Goes up and down."

He dropped his hand. "That is... if you have any business being in this building at all. Who are you visiting?"

"Briar Rose."

A crease formed between his brows. "Rose, Rose, I don't think I remember a Rose unless you mean Ross. Do you mean Ross? We have a Ross."

"Ross, Rose, what is the difference? I need to get up there," she pointed to the top. "Knave."

"Knave." He snorted and opened the door. "You some kind of professor? The elevator is down this hall at the back. You'll see two lighted buttons. Hit the arrow that points up."

"Hit it? Why? Has it done something wrong?"

"You're crazy. Yup, you must know the Rosses. They have a strange sense of humor." Again, he extended his hand. "A tip is customary."

"Tip?" The fairy faltered for a moment trying to think of something sage to say.

"Sharpen your blade."

*

Esmeralda tended her charge. What else could she do? Meanwhile, her powers waned. She used them rarely and she flew not at all.

The fairy rode the box, and her skin crawled inside this tomb made of metal. She spent her time observing humankind. She learned their ways and adopted them. She lost the accoutrements, marks of her status and her craft. Gossamer gowns and wings tended to get tangled in revolving doors

The city was like the belly of a metal beast that the people rode daily, and she planned her strategy.

Her first priority was to find shelter for the maiden Briar Rose.

Their island atop the tower was less than ideal. While those down below sweltered in the summer heat, the fairy and her charge were belted by roaring winds. Nights alternated between baking hot as the heat rose from the street below or chilled to the bone as the fog rolled in from the sea she learned was called the Atlantic.

The weather was at best fickle. Rains, when they came, were fierce. Lightning bounced between the towers. Briar Rose began to fade.

The continuous singing of the wires and the street noise was driving the fairy mad. The fumes made her ill.

After a particularly nasty storm, Esmeralda began to hollow an area inside a metal hut. It housed little more than wires and green boards.

She got a nasty shock, but she persevered, setting herself on fire several times and blowing herself up twice.

When night fell, Esmeralda noticed that the magic lights-without-flame weren't working. Their tower was dark while it was surrounded by sparkling illumination.

A trap door clanged open. A curved bar followed by a floor emerged from the building.

Her eyes lit up. An elevator without a box.

Heads like mushrooms appeared in the opening. The fairy had barely enough time to grab Briar Rose and drag her behind the shed.

Men, with mushroom heads and a single glowing central eye, clambered onto the roof.

They halted when they saw the open door to the shed.

"Damn wind. Wiring must 'a' got wet."

One mushroom man examined the interior. "Not winds. Look at that. No wind could do that. It's almost empty. Something tore it apart."

"Gremlins?" suggested the other.

The mention of her fey cousins caused Esmeralda to gasp and stiffen.

"Did you hear that?"

"Hear what?"

"Something."

"Who's going to be up here at this time of night? We shouldn't be. This isn't a simple flip of a switch or the tightening of a few wires."

The other man stared at the pieces and parts strewn across the roof. "This place is creepy."

The bizarre beings headed toward the lift. Esmeralda seized the limp, frail princess and leapt sprightly onto the moving floor before the mushroom men could lumber back. The controls dangled on the chain. She pressed the down arrow.

"What the hell?" said one mushroom beast

She waited. The blackness was absolute on the lift. Doors screeched open. At the end of a long hall, a single red box glowed with the words "fire escape."

She pulled the flaccid form onto a solid floor inside the building. She let her senses stretch beyond the darkness, beyond the walls, and heard the sound of movement. Half-dragging the princess, Esmeralda thudded down the stairs.

She let Briar Rose slide down the wall, arranged her limbs with some semblance of decorum and scratched on the door.

A woman opened it with such force that it banged against the wall and the princess bounced. Esmeralda made an adroit sideways step, to prevent Briar Rose from gliding face-first onto the floor.

"Are you meals on wheels?" the woman demanded. "I didn't get my meal today."

"The lights are out, and the elevator is not working. We are stuck, my friend and I, on this floor." Esmeralda peered inside the apartment. "If you have food, I could fix something for you to eat."

"I have food. Someone comes in the morning and cooks breakfast and dinner. I ate those hours ago," she wailed. "I am supposed to get meals on wheels for lunch. I'm hungry."

Esmeralda stooped and looped her arm around the girl's waist. The fairy godmother staggered under the slight frame, and arm in arm the two lurched for the door.

The old woman gaped. "Good Lord, she's crocked."

"No, no, she's sick."

"It isn't catching, is it? She's not patient zero."

"Catching? No, I don't think so."

"The kitchen is over there. Don't know how you are going to prepare anything without lights. It's a gas stove, so you can cook. Maybe use one of the other burners like candlelight."

Esmeralda examined the stove. "Twist the knob."

She heard a click and circle of flame exploded on top of the unit. The fairy flinched.

The woman watched her fry eggs and ham with a slab of butter.

"You don't care much about cholesterol, do you?"

"Cholesterol?"

"I like you. Maybe I can get rid of the part-time help and keep you. Eat what I damn well please. It's not like I'm going to live forever."

Esmeralda leaned over and blew out the flame.

"No, no," The old woman sprung forward and twisted the knob. "You could have blown us up."

She ate her platter of ham and eggs with a great smacking of lips and finished with a sigh of contentment. "It's the first time I've been full in ever so long."

A slight lightening of the atmosphere indicated the dawning of a new day.

The woman snoozed, and the fairy clasped her charge's hand and sent as much energy she could spare.

A blare of human voices thrust Esmeralda from a light dose. She sat bolt upright to gawp at tiny human figures darting around inside a wide, but incredibly flat box.

The fairy marveled at the kind of things humankind fit into boxes. Chariots that went up and down. Human voices, human shapes that raced across a glass and shouted. Boxes that dived underground and others that ran along the street.

"Power's back," said the old woman. "But elevator's not."

The woman, who introduced herself as Nettie, turned up the volume. "I suppose we must watch the news. It's always depressing, but it's the only way I keep up."

Esmeralda eyed the box. People sat in chairs. Pictures of huge faces hung over their shoulders. Sometimes the window exploded in fire, wars and battles.

This was the future, Esmeralda surmised. No good future either. She must get back with her small charge perhaps to derail this future to one much more pleasant. She wondered if the castle was safe, and if the thicket covered it from prying eyes.

Nettie dosed again, mouth ajar. A small amount of spittle slid from the corner of her mouth down her chin. Esmeralda stirred.

"I'm sorry," Nettie said as she sat up. She eyed Briar Rose. "She sure does sleep a lot. Are you *sure* she is not on drugs?"

The remark led to much repositioning of the body, rearranging of limbs, and painting of eyes on lids.

Seeing her second guest awake, Nettie's questions began anew until Esmeralda was forced to intervene.

"She is deaf and dumb."

"Dumb? I'll say," remarked the old woman.

"Pardon."

The television blared. Suddenly a man in black robes materialized on the screen.

A wizard?

A man of magic?

Esmeralda sat at attention as he bellowed at the unseen viewer: "Why bury your loved ones when you can save them now to spend an eternity with you later? Don't lose a loved one to some disease. Come to Fly-by-Night Cryogenics, 567 Bowery, where you can have them frozen until science finds a cure, or forever if you would like."

The fairy bounced up, expression taut. She patted the old woman on the shoulder and thanked her. She clasped the princess around the waist and lugged her to the elevator. Esmeralda propped Briar Rose against the wall. People got on and off the lift. Faces sour with disapproval as they rode the metal box down to the street.

Esmeralda flagged a taxi and tossed the princess into the back seat.

The driver pursed his lips. "Drunk?"

Esmeralda glowered at him. "No sick. Take me to..." she recited the address.

The driver cast nervous glances at the hunchback woman and the young girl. He steered this way and that, taking the old bat and the drunken woman for a real ride. Esmeralda slept once more. She awoke startled when the cab stopped in front of a brownstone.

"Oh, this place. I've seen it advertised. Don't waste your money. You can freeze them, mebbe, but can you thaw them out again? That's what ah says."

The fairy thought of giving him a piece of her mind and decided against it.

Seeing her expression, the cabbie relented and helped her with her burden. She thrust a coin at him.

"This is gold," he exclaimed, and he bit the soft metal to confirm his assessment. "I can't give you change for this. How big is it? I don't even know what it's worth."

Esmeralda magicked up a sack of gold and thrust it at him. "Keep it."

"Wow! I can take you back if you would like." He glanced at Briar Rose dangling from her arm. "Maybe not."

The wizard from the magic box appeared. He handed her brochures which she ignored as he repeated by rote the benefits of cryogenics. He explained the chemistry and the procedure for resuscitation.

"Of course, there are fees, for maintenance and care. It costs a pretty penny, but who can put a price on a loved one's life. We have two options. Time payments, or if money is a problem, we have a special discount rate. All you have to do is sign a release that would allow this fine lady to have, ahem, visitors. We have a lot of well-paying clients who would love to meet someone as lovely as her."

The good fairy expanded in her anger until she towered over the salesman. "No, this lady must remain untouched for a hundred years."

"Yes, yes, whatever you say."

"How much?"

"Well, there are maintenance fees, chemicals to preserve her as she is now, and physicians to care for her." He listed his price and expected the woman to fly into a rage.

"What's a dollar?"

"Money, deary, you could say coin of the realm."

"Oh, gold, I have gold."

"Oh, gold will do quite nicely," the clerk said as he rubbed his hands together. She waved her hands and coins dropped from the air. The man scuttled sideways to keep from being buried.

The good fairy handed her charge over to the mage. Then she contemplated her best course of action. The maid was protected, and the castle covered in spiked vines. Esmeralda decided to return to the portal and back to her own time where she could stand guard lest some knight errant fall into a time not of her choosing.

She watched as the mage and a ghostly looking man in white put Briar Rose in her cylindrical coffin. Esmeralda kissed the cold glass. Fluid filled the cavity. The rosy face turned blue.

"There," he clapped his hands together. "It is done. It will take a little bit longer to revive her."

He spun, expecting the look of relief that usually flooded the mark's face, but the room was empty.

For Esmeralda was already gone, back through the portal to the tower room. Exhausted, she stretched out on the floor and slept. Her snores soon resounded throughout the halls of the castle joining those of the royal family and the staff.

*

Years passed and many a knight tangled with the thicket. Most did not survive, for the bad fairy also kept guard, setting fire to all those who came too close. Few chose to confront the evil dragon coiled between castle and briar woods. Those who did were eaten.

The bad fairy would then resume her own shape, lean back, sated, and belch.

Summers came and went to the dawn of a new century, and Briar Rose's beauty was legend while the riches of the kingdom became inflated.

The thought of gold insinuated itself in the mind of Prince Fürst. He would be the one to save the princess and claim her wealth and her person as bride. He would rescue her, and he would save his family, who had descended into poverty, at the same time. For the regal bloodline held true. Surely the castle kept its riches safe. After all, what did the old king and queen have to spend wealth on as they slumbered? Fürst reasoned that the king and queen were old, possibly dead, making the princess wealthy in her own right. His kingdom would truly be powerful, unlike his father's kingdom with its castle that crumbled around their ears.

Fürst knew he cut a fine figure in his armor; the armorer's art had advanced much from the tin buckets they made a hundred years ago. So, the idea, planted by his mother – "God rest her soul" – when he was young, grew until it became an obsession.

His father tried to stop him. It was foolish, a story for silly girls. A fairytale, but Fürst would not be denied.

Prince Fürst headed unerringly toward Tanglewood, singing a little ditty he had written to seduce the lovely maiden.

"Do wah ditty, ditty, dum ditty do," he intoned.

When he confronted the wall of thorns, he chanted, "Do wah ditty, ditty, dum ditty do."

The briars parted at the sound of his voice.

The prince reached the serpent and he slew her in a single blow. "Do wah ditty, ditty, dum ditty do."

He entered the great hall. The members of the court stirred one by one and then disintegrated into dust.

"Do wah ditty, ditty, dum ditty do. AWK!"

He struck a sour note, for everywhere he went the human occupants dissolved into piles of powder made of dried bones and desiccated flesh.

The prince did not care about the girl's family or their staff. Fürst came for her, Briar Rose, and he had what she needed. A kiss. His step faltered. Maybe a little nooky before the kiss.

"Do wah ditty, ditty dum ditty do."

The good fairy yawned as an off-key voice penetrated her slumbers.

"Do wah ditty, ditty dum ditty do."

This must be it, she thought. Esmeralda shook her head. The idiot was singing. Who would sing in a dragon's lair? He *must* hold true love's kiss.

Fürst entered the tower chambers and froze.

"But, but, but... you, you're an old woman," he stuttered.

"Yes, I am the one left behind to guide you to your true love's kiss."

"Where is she?" he said. "I long to see her. She is my heart's desire."

The good fairy pounced on the prince, wrapped him in her arms and carried him through the portal.

The words of his song echoed through the castle with its little piles of dust and bone.

"Do wah ditty, ditty dum ditty do... argh."

The good fairy had prepared for this moment. She had maintained the portal and changed its path, so it opened beside the metal cocoon that made the princess's bed.

The prince stood aghast before this coffin. Briar Rose maintained a cold blue beauty and he was smitten despite the sapphire hue.

He wielded his sword, sheering the lock from the door.

"No, wait," the good fairy clawed at Fürst to stop him.

The door creaked on its hinges.

"We must defrost her first," the fairy finished lamely.

Too late.

The prince planted his kiss on her ice-cold lips.

And stuck.

The Idiot King

Rumpelstiltskin moved the stone aside with a grinding noise.

A voice boomed from the darkness. "Halt! Who goes there?"

Rumpelstiltskin cringed against the wall of the cavern where not even moonshine could find him. He heard the clatter of metal-shod feet. The bouncing flame leaped across the walls of his cave

Another pair of metal-shod feet advanced. "Do you see anything?"

"No."

The footsteps retreated. Rumpelstiltskin held his breath. Silence. He stuck the pick through the opening. When no sword descended to slice it in two, he poked his head outside the opening.

What luck. He was in the courtyard. During the day it would be a busy enough place, but at night it was quiet. No one dared go abroad during the witching hours.

Good, it was a castle. It had turrets, towers and what-not. He spied the tallest tower and slipped from the opening. He hesitated long enough to restore the stone, leaving it slightly askew in case he needed an emergency exit. Rumpelstiltskin dissolved into the shadows.

But is it the right castle? he wondered as he vanished inside the building.

Rumpelstiltskin shrugged.

Only time would tell.

*

Cinderella sat among the cinders where she had been dumped by her fairy godmother. A girl was taught to believe in happily-ever-afters. Particularly if something as magical as a fairy godmother attended. Cinderella learned otherwise.

Oh, she had married the handsome prince and found him to be a royal pain in the ass. A brat who thought more about the cut of his cotte than his princely duties – especially his duties to his wife.

His parents had encouraged him to spread his seed far and wide among the courtiers, assuming even an illegitimate royal get would be better than the spawn of a commoner, a former servant, of dubious parentage.

When the fairy godmother had spirited her away, the parents breathed a sigh of relief and chose the most prolific of the prince's paramours as his wife. The second was never seen and the wedding hidden from the public, for Cinderella was a popular queen. To the people Cinders was still the monarch and the second wife did not exist. Thus, the transition was smooth.

Cinderella was left to live among the cinders, but her stepmother and her stepsisters followed the old woman's example and were deferential. They whispered how best to profit from Cinderella's presence. Perhaps a stipend from the king for their silence that the one-time legitimate queen had been imprisoned in their cellars.

The stepsisters stayed away from the deposed queen, whose memory they had discovered was long indeed. Forsooth, she scared them to death. At night she wept and moaned.

The stepsisters never slept. Cinders would roam the halls. In the morning, Cinderella stepped up the horror. She stalked them, made dire signs – like a quick slash across the throat – and the sisters were sore afraid. It was as if Cinderella had gone to the castle happy and full of hope and then returned as mad as a hatter.

Oft-times, Cinderella would visit the prince and his new bride. While she still lived as a bride, her loneliness led her to explore the entire castle that was no longer her home. She poked and prodded into nooks and crannies until she located every door that took servants, lovers and administrators between rooms without being seen. She found his clandestine bedchamber where the prince would meet his lovers of both genders.

Eventually, the ousted Cinderella spent more time within the walls of the castle than in the halls where no one would ever see her. The court turned their gazes away from her when she did appear. The courtiers whispered among themselves how foolish the prince had been to wed this mad woman because he had a foot fetish and had been distracted by her glass slippers.

Thus, after the first wife and the idiot king had separated, Cinderella would materialize like an apparition beside the profaned bed of her marriage to extend her arms in a gesture of open invitation.

"Return to me," she would murmur, and the newlyweds screamed and screamed, until they decided to sleep apart.

The prince had no other children even after he married his royal whore, but he had already adopted one of his illegitimate offspring as his own, as indeed they were, so there was still a surfeit of heirs, even if he never bred again.

Sometimes Cinders would visit the royal nursery to rend the children's dreams. Soon all his progeny sported a nervous tic, as did the prince and his parents until the latter died.

Hereafter, the idiot prince became the imbecile king.

In the end, she outlived them all. The ersatz queen preceded her spouse to the grave. Her death was deemed a mystery until the king decreed that his wife had strangled herself with her bare hands.

A few years later, the profligate prince turned king followed his mistress to the tomb. The children took over for but a short time, their twitches and maniacal laughter, becoming more pronounced each year they reigned. Until one day, they vanished to be caged inside the oubliettes.

Meanwhile, Cinderella wandered the empty manor of her childhood during the day and the castle of her debasement at night. For there was naught here left to haunt with her wails of despair and shrieks of terror. Sometimes she did it, anyway, when she was feeling sad and lonely.

More often she felt the presence of the dead, in a slight breeze, like the wave of a hand close to her cheek, that would waft across her face.

Cinderella sensed the slight buzz of human conversation inside the empty home of her stepsisters where surely none must be. Cinders dismissed it as her imagination, but she remained in the basement that had been her domain and the upstairs fell into rack and ruin.

Then one day Cinderella unfurled from her bed of ashes, wondering what had brought her here. She had purloined many pieces of furniture from the main floors, before they had collapsed. She exchanged transport of the heavy items, including her stepmother's bed, for womanly favors from the village youth, who only knew her as the mad woman in the manor, and the kitchens were now sumptuously appointed.

Cinderella rubbed her eyes, which felt surprisingly squishy. When she pulled away, she viewed her legs along with her body that lay stretched on the ground in an attitude of death.

Her sisters flitted into the kitchen to order her about. "I want this… Give me that…"

Cinders opened her mouth in a banshee screech and the sisters exploded into little papery tatters.

She exhaled and blew them away.

"You forget who rules here. I am the one and only true queen of this land. I've killed them. I've killed them all."

Cinderella sought to get her body under her control. When she sat, she had been half-asleep, but now she was fully cognizant of her situation, and she could not figure how to coordinate her post-mortem body and limbs.

Once she thought of movement, the less command she exhibited over her incorporeal frame. Cinderella cupped her hand under her chin, and she gave a little shriek of joy. All she had to do was think of the act; and her ghostly corpse followed.

She thought hard about getting upright, and the next thing she knew her head smacked the ceiling with surprisingly realistic pain. Frantically Cinderella thought of down and found herself neck deep in the floor boards, peering eye to eye with a mouse.

She closed her eyes and visualized herself sitting cross-legged next to the hearth, finger tapping her chin contemplatively, and she was in that posture, floating above her body. Cinderella had to concentrate on solidity to keep her backside firmly planted on the floor.

She spent the rest of the day learning how to operate this not-quite-flesh. It was easy. By nightfall Cinderella, or what was left of her, could zing here and zip there with little more than recall of motion. Cinders could climb nonexistent stairs to the turrets whose floor, steps and structure had crumbled long ago. She could stride across a memory of a floor in the upper bedchambers seeking the ghost of her stepmother.

The sun set in a crimson glow, silhouetting the castle. A smile unpleasant to behold crawled across Cinderella's features.

It was time to visit her husband dearest, for she had no doubt that what passed for a mortal god would not permit the prince's entry into heaven. His sins against the kingdom and man were too grievous, too great and too many. His children may still be jittering across the bailey to the dismay of the courtiers.

She concentrated on the secret passage inside the walls and found herself embedded in it, nose to the proverbial grindstone. Cinders imagined the roominess of the dank halls, and she rematerialized.

"Now it's time to go greet my husband."

As she traversed the long hall Cinderella tried to keep her feet firmly on the ground. It consumed a lot of energy and concentration, so she passed the royal chambers before she realized she had arrived.

She gave up. It was so much easier to hover, flit or fly. Soon Cinderella stood abreast the queen's chambers. The place of her humiliation. She tapped along the wall till she located the secret entrance and then she drifted through the door.

Her husband lay naked upon the bed with a slender wraith draped over him.

Cinderella cleared her throat. The wraith gave her a sloe-eyed look and wrapped her legs tighter around his waist.

He moaned.

"Husband, so you would dishonor me in this life too?" she said.

His eyes opened wide and he stared at her. "Wife?"

"Yes, your only true wife," she said, "and this time you will not find it so easy to get rid of me."

The wraith undulated upon his person, and the idiot prince forgot about her presence.

"Not this time," she snarled. She reached through the ephemeral figure of the wraith and clawed at him.

He screamed.

The wraith rose above him and sniffed her displeasure. Then she floated to the door, squeezed between the boards and glided up the hall to find a mortal who might appreciate her talents.

"You aren't, uh, going to stay, are you?" he stammered. "You have your sisters. Surely, they must miss you."

"They are dead,"

"I'm dead too. So, what's the difference? Can't you leave me in peace?"

"Too easy," Cinderella countered. "I've already taken care of my sisters, now I plan to take care of you."

The apparition gulped and floated off and away from the bed. The former king zipped through the door. She maintained a leisurely pursuit. Never quite catching him, but always in visual sighting.

He howled; she shrieked.

He begged for forgiveness and cried for help.

She cackled.

He protested his innocence and she scratched at him. Non-existent blood welled from wounds that could not, should not, appear on a ghostly form.

*

Rumpelstiltskin erupted through the tower door. "Ah, ha," he shouted. "Now I have you."

He froze as husband and wife spun in a deadly embrace.

Cinderella bellowed at the dwarf. "Get out. Get out! GET OUT! You have no right to be here."

Such was the strength of her oath that Rumpelstiltskin was ejected from the tower and sent spinning through space.

"*Goddammitttttttttttt!*"

So, Cinderella and the Idiot King remain to this day – errant husband and vengeful wife streaking through the walls of the castle ruins – while the dwarf orbited the planet.

The Reception

Glinda picked up her skirts and she ran. She ran as if her life depended on it.

The hoop skirt blew into her face, temporarily blinding her. The witch tripped over a root. She leapt to her feet, cursing. The words issued from her mouth as little flowers, little tormented flowers, for they wilted as the intent of the curse attempted to break free.

With the hoops clutched in one hand, the other braced to hold her skirts down, she moved at a more sedate pace.

Damn, damn, damn, damn, damn. She had to beat the animals to the Wizard's celebration.

But she could hear their continuing refrain just up ahead. "Oh, woe, oh woe, cursed by an evil witch. Oh, woe is me," frog and elephant chorused.

Glinda gained time, walking as they slept.

The following morning, the refrain returned.

"Oh, woe, oh woe, cursed by an evil witch. Oh, woe is me," one croaked and the other trumpeted.

They soon overtook her; the frog rode astride the elephant's broad back. *"Oh, woe, oh woe, cursed by an evil witch. Oh, woe is me."*

She beat at her ears in an attempt to rid herself of their pleas, which were drawing her back. Just then, they broke through the forest, and she was racing at their heels. The plain opened before them. The Emerald City glittered in the noonday sun.

They kept pace with each other, the witch, and the frog astride the pink elephant. Together the three lifted the great door knocker together and pounded on the door. The doorkeeper was greeted by an angry looking pink elephant ridden by a toad, and the missing witch herself, Glinda the Good.

He backed away from the door, dug the flask from his trousers, studied it as if looking for inherent truth, and then emptied the contents down his throat.

"Right, pink elephant, pink witch and a frog. Perfectly reasonable. Yes, it happens all the time in the merry ol' land of Oz."

The doorkeeper wandered into the celebration. Glinda fumed. The elephant tore the door off its hinges.

The crowd howled. Some fainted. Others took the pledge that day and haven't had a drop since.

Glinda hailed a taxi, and when the driver did not go fast enough, she threw him over the side of the wain and seized the reins.

"Follow that," the frog squinted into the distance, "purple horse?"

All around them, people scurried to get out of their way – the enraged delirium tremen and the deranged witch.

Glinda sprung from the carriage before it came to a complete stop. She gathered her skirts as best she could and took the stairs two at a time.

The Lord Chamberlain announced her arrival. "The late Glinda the Good."

She hurried up the aisle, scolding the wand most severely. "You behave unless you want a new mistress. I'll take you to the repair shop and have you taken to bits before I am demoted. I promise you that."

Dorothy stormed down from the dais. "Where have you been? This is my celebration and you're late." Dorothy stabbed a finger at her.

"Yes, and a very nice celebration it is if I do say so myself. How many years have you been with us now? Eighteen?"

"Oz celebrates this day because I rid them of the wicked witches, no thanks to you."

"Very well deserved. Well deserved. I must say." Glinda curtseyed. "I apologize for the delay. My wand. Well, my wand is, ah, er, indisposed. I must take it into the shop. I had to walk all the way from the south."

At this moment, the pink elephant thundered into the room. The court scattered. Dorothy stood her ground.

Glinda cleared her throat. "A funny thing happened on the way to the palace. Just a little mishap really."

She untangled the wand from her cloak. "And I must fix it."

"Remember," she mumbled. "Remember what I just said, wand. I'll grind you under my heel if anything happens."

She chanted a few nonsense syllables for effect and pointed the staff in their direction. There was a whirring noise and a moan. Light issued from the wand, not the more typical lighting, it waggled like string blowing in the breeze; but it was enough.

The elephant changed into a uniform grey while the frog busily peered into his privates.

"It's done. It's done."

Then she flung the pair into the heavens, flying them whence they came without benefit of bubble.

The elephant and its hitchhiker collided in mid-air with a flying dwarf. *Smack!*

They plunged to earth. A third figure appeared, wearing a costume of red and blue, its scarlet cape flapping in the breeze. The crowd marveled. It might have been mistaken for a flying monkey, but it flew without benefit of tail. The man caught the three, and forming an arc in the sky, vanished as quickly as he came.

The courtiers applauded. Dorothy glowered at the good witch while Glinda tried to retreat inside her gown

Grandma's House

The wolf arrived before Little Red, as he expected. The beast paused just outside the cottage and groomed himself. The door flew open, bouncing him down the stairs. He yelped.

The old woman jangled in a cacophony of amulets and trinkets. She had attempted to makeup her face, with a ludicrous effect. The eye liner made her look like a raccoon. The rouge mimicked a fever.

The wolf eyed her. This lady was puttin' on the dog.

"Tom? Tom? Is that you?" She peered owlishly at the steps. Finally, she conceded defeat and seated her spectacles on her nose.

"You? Who are you?" she said.

"I'm the wolf."

"You shouldn't be here," she said, glancing nervously up and down the path.

"I come from Little Red," the wolf ventured.

"Ridiculous name. I never liked the child or the name. She's a nuisance."

The wolf scratched behind his ear, uninterested in family history. "She wanted me to tell you that she's on her way here, but she's running late."

The old woman stood with her feet splayed and her arms akimbo. "I don't have time for a visit. I've got things to do. Just because someone is retired doesn't mean they aren't busy. First, there's the bingo and lunch at the community center, and I have a date. Why in Heaven's name is she coming here?"

"She thought you were sick."

"Well, I am sick, sick unto death of her. I only told them that, so they'd stay away."

"She'll be disappointed."

"Who cares? You stay here and wait for her if you want. I got to go."

"Aren't you afraid of me?"

"No, you look pretty toothless to me," the old woman said.

"Afraid that I'll eat you?" The wolf gave her a wide grin showing all his teeth.

"Me? Why eat me?" She plucked the empty sack of her skin. "I'm old; I'm stringy; I got no meat on my bones. Why don't you wait for Little Red. She's fresh, young and plump. You can eat her with my blessings."

"You hooo! Cooey!" Grandma whipped the spectacles from her face and waved at the woodsman. "Tom! Tom!"

The wolf went inside. He sniffed around the floor until he got a whiff of food. The wolf followed the scent to a cupboard. He clawed at the curtain and knocked a large pot off the shelf. It broke. The wolf took a mouthful of food and promptly spat it out. "Ptui." The lid rolled over and hit his paws.

He read the note. "With love, Little Red."

No wonder the old lady didn't like her. Big Bad tried to clean the taste off his tongue. He didn't know what it was, but it was bloody awful. It was elder abuse, pure and simple! The Hoods should be reported. He wouldn't feed that even to his young'uns who didn't seem to mind that the meal was second hand.

The wolf wandered around the room trying to evade the smell. He stared at the mess. No way he was going to lick that up.

The wolf located another curtain. He poked his head behind it. A bedroom. He ran to the window and pawed at the shutters. They opened with a spring. Fresh air. Big Bad inhaled deeply. Then he climbed onto the bed, curled up and went to sleep.

Bang, bang, bang.

The startled wolf leapt to his feet, snarling.

"Grandma. Grandma. It's me, Little Red. I've brought you goodies."

The growl descended from his throat to his chest.

"Goodies?" he barked. "What goodies?"

"Your favorite, offal stew," the girl replied.

The wolf clamored down from his perch and bounded into the kitchen. "Awful. You admit that it's awful and you still feed it to her."

Little Red entered the house, pointed down at the broken crock and scolded. "Did you do this? Bad! Bad doggy. Bad!"

"I'm no damn dog, and yes, I am bad." He puffed up his chest. "Big Bad. You may have heard of me. Wait a second, you sent me here. You should remember."

"If you made this mess; you should clean it up."

The wolf shook his head. "I'm not cleaning that up. It's horrible. I wouldn't even feed that to my children and they eat what I've sicked up."

"Bad," Little Red muttered. Then she set about mopping up food and pottery.

"She's not here. Your grandma is not here," the wolf informed the girl. "She had a date."

"I bet she's out with that no-good woodsman," Little Red said. "My mother doesn't like him."

Big Bad noted: "Well, your grandmother likes him, but she's not overly fond of you."

"What?"

"Oh, nothing. I don't want to get involved with family squabbles."

Little Red frowned at him. "Was it the woodsman?"

"Sorry, didn't see him. He was standing behind ah, er," the wolf gave a gentle huff "a tree."

"Yeah, right," she said.

She dumped the slop on the back stoop. The flies rose in a thick swarm and made a beeline away from the goo.

Little Red wiped her hands on her apron and pursed her lips. "I guess the chaste berry isn't working? I'll have to think of something else. Mother will be disappointed."

"You are poisoning her?" The wolf's tongue hung from his mouth.

"No, it'll just slow her down. Women her age shouldn't be out cavorting with woodsmen. It's unseemly." Little Red turned to the wolf. "Did she say when she'd be back?"

"No, she didn't seem in any hurry to return," he said.

"Then let's see what we can cook up for her."

The wolf settled on his haunches as Little Red stuck her nose into every nook and cranny and prodded items she found in the cupboard.

"I guess, I'll just tidy up a bit," she said. She grabbed the broom and began sweeping with vigorous strokes, raising a cloud of dust.

The wolf sputtered and coughed.

She extracted dishes from a bucket, spat on them and began drying them with her apron.

The wolf found himself wondering where else that apron had been and what it had wiped. It seemed to be an all-purpose piece of apparel Big Bad soon learned as she took it off and used it to swipe at the dust and the dirt she had raised with her sweeping from the furniture.

Little Red stepped back to survey her work. The wolf followed her gaze. Everything appeared uniformly grey.

She hefted the basket onto the table. "You want some?"

"Ah, no thank you, I'm over, ah, stimulated."

"Suit yourself," she shrugged. "What else can I do?"

"Don't you think you have helped enough?" he said.

Little Red continued her search. She flicked aside a curtain to reveal a closet and began shaking out the clothes. She gave a cry of joy when her finger hit something hard wrapped in linen. She pulled a blunder buss from the cloth. "I knew she had one."

"What are you going to do?"

"Clean it," she said.

"The same way you cleaned everything else?" The wolf felt slightly nauseated.

"Of course." She spat on the barrel and began to rub it down.

"What does your grandmother have that for?" He gulped.

"Troublesome wolves. Now keep quiet."

"Um, maybe I should go feed my kids. The missus will be wanting a break."

"Go ahead, don't let me stop you."

As he existed from the cottage Big Bad noticed that the flies avoided the pile of offal.

He nosed around to see if he could find anything edible. He did not. The wolf trotted back to the den.

Inside, Little Red stared down the barrel of the gun. She tore a piece from her petticoat. Then she searched under the bed for the powder. She measured a few of the black granules and then poured it down the barrel. She rammed the cloth into it, followed by the shot.

She shrugged out of the cloak and used it to cover the blunderbuss. Little Red scanned the garden, looking for the pesky woodsman.

It was getting dark when Big Bad was freed from his domestic duties. He returned to the cottage, burning with curiosity. He watched as Little Red crept from the door, carrying what appeared to be a long stick and dived into a clump of bushes next to the path.

He smelled the acrid stench of death. The wolf tracked her to where she was lying in wait.

Silently he retreated and went back to the cottage. He entered, saw the basket on the table. He seized the handle with his mouth and dragged it down to the floor. Swearing through his teeth, he followed her trail. Then he too waited.

Stars dotted the sky when there was a commotion on the path. Little Red's grandmother and her suitor – linked arm in arm – stumbled down the path from the public house, singing off key.

Little Red lit the cloth fuse and leveled the gun at the woodsman.

The wolf stirred as he swung his head around. She spun to face him and wallop, he hit her a glancing blow on the head with the crock, and her nose was forced into her brain pan.

The shot went wild. Little Red dropped and granny dropped simultaneously. The wolf bounded to check the old woman.

He was sniffing her wizened frame when he felt the soft swish of air as the ax came dangerously close to his neck.

The wolf leapt to his feet. "No, no," he begged, "I have children. If you must kill me, cut off my hands and my feet too."

The woodsman obliged and kept chopping in a frenzy, severing all four paws. He vomited and then ran home to his wife.

The wolf emerged from the empty sack of his skin, as the tale foretold, but not as a prince, a wolf still. Famished by this reformation of flesh, he devoured the remains of Little Red and then went to share this repast with his young'uns.

The next day at the tavern, the woodsman regaled the clientele with his heroic exploits, how he tried to save the grandmother from the wolf, but the creature had eaten her. The woodsman freed her from the beast's stomach, but too late, she was dead, as was Little Red Riding Hood.

No one went to check on the grandmother, for if they had, they would have found her shot through by a blunderbuss.

For the woodsman, the story was worth a few drinks at the local, and it didn't matter that it wasn't true. He was the hero of the hour until the barman ejected him from the pub.

Three Little Pigs

The animals in the barn gathered around the antiquated television set. The action was going to take place outside their door, but the animals could not be fussed to go to the pens. The risk was too great that the observer would suddenly become the participant in the contests.

Safe inside the barns, the horses had their nosebags; others had to carry their snacks in whatever conveyance they could cobble together. The chickens routed among the detritus of straw and hay. The sheep nibbled absently at the nearest bales.

The screen before them flashed from a lively commercial about feed to black. The first strains of the national anthem, *The Farmer in the Dell*, began to echo inside the large building.

The gathering shifted ready for the games to begin.

"Hiss," said the cat.

The other animals fell silent.

Two names appeared in white letters on a black background, with translations to sheep, cattle, horses and pig.

In Memory:
Peter Cottontail (2015 to 2017)
Keith Uberduck (2014 to 2017)

Voices murmured in the background. The cat laughed.

"Did you hear that?" she asked.

"Hear what?" said the milk cow.

Cat indicated the television with a jut of her head. "Someone said: 'They were delicious,' and another voice said – 'I thought they were a bit stringy myself.'"

"I don't think that's so funny," the cow said.

"I guess you had to have been there." The cat gave the heifer a sidelong look. Her tail swished rapidly back and forth.

*

The two announcers, a parrot and a kestrel, sat comfortably in a roost in front of the microphone. Parrot preened, making sure every feather was in place.

Behind the camera, a coyote began to count backwards. "We're on in: ten, nine, eight, seven, six..."

Rather than repeat the final numbers, coyote pawed the air – *five, four, three, two, one.*

A fox held up a sign and pointed at them.

Parrot stopped fiddling with his plumage and mugged the camera, but it was the kestrel who got to the microphone first.

"Welcome to TWDL, Twaddle television. This is the two-hundred-and-forty-fifth annual match between the Three Little Pigs and the notorious Wolf..."

Parrot interrupted his cohort. "Notorious, awk, I'll say. His reputation has grown ever since that incident with Little Red."

"Coming back to life is no mean feat," the kestrel snapped. "He's had some bad press, but I believe the reports about his appetites have been greatly exaggerated."

"Just ask Little Red about that." The parrot chuckled. "But you'll have to address your question to his stomach."

"Which brings to mind the history of this match. Predator and prey, domesticated versus the truly wild. Who is superior?" The Kestrel puffed his chest out. "That is what this contest is all about. Nature versus nurture."

"Nurture," Parrot declared emphatically.

The kestrel fixed the other bird with a hard glare. "*You would.*"

Kestrel persisted, "Did the wolf commit a crime when he followed his natural instincts, all within natural order as noted in natural law? Or, are the pigs the offenders – guilty of committing unnatural acts in building their houses and in laying a trap for wolf? Some would say the swine did not act according to natural instincts. Did the pigs violate the natural order implied by the laws concerning predator versus prey? Did the wolf break the law or did the pigs?"

Parrot fluffed himself up. "Natural order is reflected in the domesticated animals who tamed man and showed him that life could happen another way, and there is that whole vegetarian versus carnivore thing too."

"The topic is hotly debated to this day. No other sporting event in the animal kingdom has had more influence on society, except the Great Race where the four-legged competed against the two-legged for preeminence of the species."

"That was a balls-up, for sure," squawked Parrot.

Kestrel conceded. "The race was fixed. The Great Race is recreated every year, and everyone knows who is going to win; but this is the real thing. A real battle. We meet at the location where the first event occurred, and we await the final verdict, a definitive outcome which will decide our fates forever. Will it be lupine or porcine? Predator or prey?"

"The match itself has been contested throughout its history," said Parrot, "And the pigs have been truly inventive in the defense of their lives and their homes."

Kestrel rose and flapped his wings. "Their creativity has been a source of contention and resulted in a number of rulings. For example, the year the pigs used steel as beams and studs. Now how could the wolf be expected to huff and puff and blow their houses down when they are reinforced with steel? All the same, wolf showed his strength, for he did manage to knock down the shells of straw and wood to reveal the pigs' violation."

"Wait a second," protested Parrot. "Be fair. It wasn't a violation when it happened."

"It became a violation once the deception was exposed, the match's board decreed that the supports must be made of the same material as the structure," Kestrel said, "And the victory was conceded to the wolf."

Parrot argued: "The following year, the pigs made sure their supports were up to code."

"Yes," Kestrel countered. "By building solid structures. The house of straw was a solid block of bales. The wood house was filled with tree trunks, and the brick house... well. The sports' board made the correct decision when the pigs lost the game and ruled that the home must hollow, by definition able to house somebody."

"You can hardly call wolf defenseless. He's got those teeth and those claws," and the parrot mimicked the wolf by snapping at the air with his beak. "He's undermined their foundations any number of times."

"And he won each time," Kestrel noted.

"Wolf," said Parrot, "has also lost by default when he went into overtime as he tried to chop through the shutters of the brick house."

"Yes," said Kestrel. "The pigs objected to his use of tools. That sparked a lengthy debate. If I recollect correctly, the board ruled, if the pigs were permitted to use tools to build their houses, then wolf could also use tools in dismantling them."

"He *still* lost that round," Parrot noted.

"Well," Kestrel spat, "Pigs won once because they made their homes without windows or doors. Wolf would have been forced to go down chimney or quit."

"And he quit," the parrot said. "He refused to go down the chimney, missing the whole point of the games. You remember what happened next?" chuckled Parrot.

Kestrel began to laugh. "Sure do, that was when wolf demonstrated his species didn't just act on instinct to rip and rend. He used tools."

"Yes, but a bulldozer?"

"He won, didn't he? All three houses fell, and the pigs nearly lost their lives."

"Still the win was taken away from him and the board decreed no motorized tools were allowed on either side."

"It still shows creativity on the part of the wolf, and I have long contended that this contest is biased and unfair. I mean, really, three against one?"

"Ha!" Parrot jeered. "The very next year, wolf tied mice to a wheel to power a roller. Three mice were crushed during that incident."

Kestrel tried to look nonchalant, picking between his toes. "Yes, and they were delicious."

"My money is on the pigs," said Parrot.

"It would be. You are a domesticated animal after all," Kestrel said.

"All our sports fans want to know is who will win this year," Parrot said. "The pigs' team captain is here to discuss pre-match training."

Hawk flew down from a bough to land on the platform. Parrot skittered away. The kestrel tried to fluff his feathers as much as possible and took a deft step sideways.

Hawk ignored them both, taking over the microphone. "Our team is always ready. We have been training. Of course, Orville is the brains of the operation. Egbert the brawn. Herbert has been fattening up all year and will be more than a mouthful for the opponent."

"W-W-W-We have some video clips," stuttered Parrot, hiding behind the kestrel.

The screen behind the commentators glowed, showing Herbert snorting down food; Orville drawing the house plans on a blackboard while Egbert hauled bales of straw to the build site.

"What is their strategy?" said Parrot.

Hawk bristled: "To construct the sturdiest houses possible, to stymie the wolf. One must have sympathy for the pigs. They are forced to rebuild their homes each year."

Kestrel spoke up. "Do you think the pigs will build this year without violating the rulings of the board?"

"Of course." Hawk glowered at the kestrel.

The kestrel sidled around the microphone until it stood between himself and the larger bird.

"Let's bring in the team captain for Wolf," Kestrel said.

"Team, ha," said Parrot. "How can one animal be a team?"

Hawk bridled. "Being a predator is hard work."

Kestrel screeched. "Parrot, you make my point. How *can* one animal be a team? The contest is prejudiced against the predator. It takes place on your turf and not in the wild, where the domesticated would not survive for a minute."

"Exactly," hissed Parrot.

Before an argument could break out between the two commentators, a great horned owl waddled onto the platform. He stopped, yawned and scratched his stomach with his foot.

"Ungodly hour, this," he grumbled. "I need coffee."

A miniature horse, carrying a tray on his back, stepped forward. Owl hopped onto the tray. "Coffee, that's the ticket. You wouldn't happen to have a mouse hidden somewhere, would you? I'm hungry."

The horse shivered and twitched his tail, nearly unseating the owl.

"Back to the games," Kestrel said. "What do you think the wolf's chances are this year?"

Owl shook himself awake. "Very good, he has done extensive frittering away the hours, while the pigs worked on their homes, and loping as is required in the prelims."

The image of the pigs working industriously on their house faded away and the wolf appeared, back leg extended, licking his crotch.

"I believe he is seen here frittering," said Owl as he dunked his beak in the coffee mug a second time.

"Awk!" screeched Parrot as he made a swiping motion with his wings. "Not good for the kiddies."

"Who? What?" said Owl.

*

A goat in the barn snorted, jumped up and fainted dead away. Another herded her kids in front of her, leaving the stands and the television behind, with a bleat of disgust.

*

The picture changed to Wolf scratching behind the ear while the three little pigs argued about construction standards.

"I'd say he's got this frittering thing down pat," Owl said. "See how he keeps an eye on his opponents, planning his strategy."

"What is his strategy?"

"Lunch." Owl winked at the parrot, who nearly swooned.

"See how Wolf has maintained that lean, mean physique. He's been running every day and howling at the moon at night. He's fighting fit."

Behind them the picture changed to Wolf racing through a field of flowers, chasing a butterfly.

Hawk and Owl returned to their perches. Kestrel shouted up at them. "Don't you think there's a conflict of interest to have you not only as team captains, but also as umpires?"

Hawk and Owl exchanged glances.

"Why?" said Hawk. "There are two of us. If we have biases, they cancel each other out."

"Two, two," hooted Owl.

The commentators turned back to face the camera.

"Our players have pedigree," Parrot said. "The pigs are fourth-generation players, with ties all the way back to the beginning of the games. They have been bred specifically for this purpose and they have trained for it all their lives. The pigs have both the will and the determination.

Kestrel countered, "Yes, but the wolf has it up on them in sheer cussedness, and he's got them on lineage too. His family goes back to the first, the original combatant, in an unbroken line of descent." He paused for effect. "Don't forget early-on in the games, the entire porcine population was wiped out after that unfortunate accident in the sausage factory. The current contenders are distant cousins of the originals who agreed to take on the challenge because of the perks."

"What about the rumor that Wolf, the current contender, was whelped of a shepherd bitch?" snapped Parrot.

"Go pluck yourself!" Kestrel rose to his full height.

Parrot strutted his stuff. "I'm colorful, not dull like you. I get to go inside the house, where it's warm and dry."

"Grey and brown is utilitarian attire," Kestrel said. "Perfect for every occasion. Great camouflage."

"I don't need camouflage."

"Froo-froo."

"Frump."

*

The close-up of the two announcers faded to a commercial about tractors. A voice came over the speakers into the bay: "Psssst. Wait, should we be showing that? Tractors are against the rules."

The tractor vanished and there was a glimpse of the kestrel and the parrot circling each other around the microphone with wings flapping and feathers plumped for maximum effect.

That picture was replaced quickly by a black screen – the call letters, TWDL – and another rousing rendition of *Farmer in the Dell*, until Wolf reappeared, cleaning his private parts.

*

Parrot yielded the game of flying feathers to the kestrel to announce the next notable. "Well, what have we here? It's Farmer John, lord mayor of Dell."

The bird forgot himself and flew up to sit on the farmer's shoulder.

"Farmer John, we are honored," he chattered.

The old man spat. "Don't be. I'm only here to tell ye' that there better not be a mess like was left for me last year. Pig shit all over the place. That's why we have pigpens fer 'em critters," he added.

"Yes, sir." Kestrel eyed the farmer warily.

"Yes, sir," parroted Parrot.

The kestrel bent over and began drilling a hole in the table top as a protest.

"Git off, Parrot," the farmer shooed the bird away. "I don't like bird shit any better'n I like pig shit."

The tune *Farmer in the Dell* followed the old man up the hill. Kestrel nodded to a couple of crows who rose in a flurry of wings. They hovered above the farmer, aimed and cut loose.

The farmer shook his fists at the birds. "Goddammit."

The camera zoomed in for a tight shot of the commentators.

"We have a great half-time line-up," chirped Parrot. "Of course, half-time wouldn't be complete without the lovely Twinkle Toes."

"In her lovely pink tutu," interjected Kestrel.

A hippopotamus materialized on the screen behind them. She did an ungainly pirouette. The tutu bounced up in back, revealing the wide, tough bottom. She peered over her shoulder, batted her eyelashes and giggled.

"And the equally lovely Silky Bantam Sisters, as back-up dancers," Parrot added.

Eight hens high-stepped into the farmyard. Their soft, downy snow-white plumage blew in the faint breeze waving from the tip of their heads to the top of their curly toes. They faced away from the camera and wiggled their tails at the audience.

"Dig those crazy feathers," crooned Parrot.

Kestrel groaned and forged ahead. "Another half-time must is cheerleaders and their traditional accompaniment, the barnyard marching band."

At that moment, several geese wandered onto the field while a variety of animals – sheep, ponies, donkeys, roosters, turkeys – tried to form a line behind them.

Kestrel elbowed Parrot out the way. "We have the fabulous, Lady Gagh, fresh from an appearance at Old McDonald's."

A dainty little filly, wearing pink-dyed mane, pranced across the staging area to swear at the road crew.

Kestrel hurried on, "She will be singing her own adaptation of the ever-popular 'Goosey, Goosey, Gander,' and she will premiere, for the first time ever on Twaddle TV, her most recent hit single: 'She Thinks My Plough Horse Is Sexy.'"

*

The cheerleaders waddled forward, bottoms waggling. Occasionally the geese got distracted. They stopped and began to peck at something tantalizing on the ground.

The barnyard band trailed in the cheerleaders' wake, tripped over the animal in front, with a great braying, gobbling and cock-a-doodle-doo-ing. Each species lent its voice to the cacophony. The noise was further disrupted as the animals froze to avoid treading on the grazing geese.

"'Scuse me…"

"So sorry…"

Ram head-butted one of the cheerleaders, and the gaggle ran, honking, from the field.

*

Inside the barn, there were roars of laughter, and the horse almost inhaled his feed bag.

*

Fox trotted around the side of the building to cue the contestants. "Places everyone."

The three pigs lined up and walked onto the playing field, one each to stand beside their respective houses. Wolf materialized next to the wood pile.

Orville advanced to Wolf and shook his paw.

Wolf tried to take a bite out of the pig. He gasped, pulled away from the wolf and shouted.

"Foul. I call foul."

The geese entered the field. "Yes?"

Wolf loped off.

"This is it," Kestrel shrieked. "The games are about to begin."

The marching band did their best approximation of a drum roll.

"The scene is tense as the opponents size-up each other," squawked Parrot.

Kestrel rolled his eyes toward the heavens.

A rooster crowed.

Orville and Egbert rushed to join their brother Herbert next to the house of straw.

Wolf ducked behind the pile of wood.

"Hey," said Egbert, in a forced stage whisper, "What's he playin' at?"

Orville shook his head, no, while Herbert chewed happily on the straw.

"Hey." Orville punched Herbert in the ribs. "Don't do that. You're eating your house."

"I'm hungry."

Across the field, Wolf reared back into view.

"Hmm, he seems to have developed some kind of growth on his back," Parrot said.

"It looks like this year Wolf has a bag of tricks ready for us," Kestrel noted.

Wolf stood on his hind legs and propped the short tube on the woodpile. The tube had a strange conglomeration of handles and hoses that attached the pipe to the bag.

Wolf squeezed the trigger and flame engulfed the three pigs and the straw house.

Orville opened his mouth to protest but no sound came from his lips. The hog was transformed into a flaming candle of roast pork. Herbert and Egbert squealed and dashed for the pond.

Parrot jumped up and down. "Hey, not fair. Not fair."

From his perch, Hawk thumped Owl. "Look what your man did."

Owl blinked and yawned. "Wha- wha- Who?"

"Call foul," insisted Hawk. "If you don't I will. I call it."

He paced along the limb, nearly knocking Owl off.

"Foul. Foul!" the red-tail screamed.

"I didn't see anything foul," said Owl.

"What's wrong with you?" Hawk blustered. "Are you as blind as a bat?"

Owl turned his wide-eyed gaze upon hawk. "I have excellent night vision, better than you." He shrugged. "During the day, well, I was napping."

Hawk pointed at the inferno of straw and roasting pig. Wolf adjusted his position slightly and pulled the flame-thrower's trigger a second time. The stream of fire extended beyond the blazing bales to the house of wood. It exploded.

The animals inside the barn screamed.

Orville writhed in the foreground while his two brothers tread water in the nearby pond.

Wolf dropped the cylinder, shrugged out of the backpack, stepped from the tangle of hoses and grabbed another tube, far larger and far longer than the first. This one had not one, but two handles.

"Gun, gun, gun," shouted the parrot.

Parrot, Kestrel, Hawk and Owl flew away. Wolf squeezed the trigger mechanism and they dissolved in a flurry of green, blue-grey and tawny feathers.

Wolf leered at the camera. "I'm tired of this game."

Coyote and fox dropped down on all fours and began to sprint for cover.

Wolf stuffed something long and thin like a stick into the tube. The other end ballooned out and then tapered to a rounded point. He hefted the device onto the wood pile to steady it and blasted the brick house from its foundations.

Chunks of brick and stone rained down upon the barnyard. The animals inside the barn stampeded. One nearly intact brick landed on the parrot with a sickening splat.

Wolf shoved a second rocket into the launcher, swung on the pig pen and fired.

He advanced to the abandoned camera. "Now we have a definitive ruling. Predators rock. The wild world rocks. The farmyard stinks. Pigs are food." He turned the tube toward the animals as they existed the barn. "Anyone object?"

They froze as a unit. "Ah, er, no."

He swung the tube in the air and then leveled it at the barn. The farm animals thundered for the pasture. Herbert and Egbert emerged from the pond, squealing, and headed for the hills.

Wolf grinned at the stampede, pressed the trigger, and the barn was lifted from its foundation and pattered down on the barnyard in a hail of pebbles.

Farmer John came roaring down the hill. Wolf loaded again, shot, and the Farmer in the Dell rode the blast.

Wolf danced a celebratory dance around the flames. The public-address system kicked in to the soothing strains of Lady Gagh's latest hit...

"She thinks my plough horse is sexy.
"Got me wondering a lot about her.
"What can I say? What can I do?
"Gonna turn that hoss, turn it into glue.

"Once he was a proud papa, this horse of mine.
"From what I discerns and 'cuz' o' concerns,
"Into evil I fell and him I did geld.
"My lady's lust abates, which is fine.
"Still those children of mine look quite equine.
"While my daughters seem a bit bovine to me...

"Now she's a'eyein' the bull in the field.
"Big horny thing he is too.
"Now I is so sad 'cuz my lady's gone mad,
"I don't know what else I should do.
"'Cept kill the good lady too.
"Ooooh, kill the good lady too."

The Giant's Balls

Many years ago, the king had a son who knew no fear. The prince could have stayed at home safe and sound, but he decided to go out into the world to see what he could see.

One day the prince rested on a stoop, looking across the road where he spied huge spheres. Next to the balls stood nine-penny pins as tall as a man.

The prince began to play, pushing the balls around and knocking down pins fully as big as himself.

The clatter and clash in the courtyard caught the giant's attention. He emerged from his home to observe this tiny mortal playing with his balls, but he was intrigued by the man's strength.

Finally, he spoke: "How dare you diddle another's balls?"

The prince spared nary a glance. He was not afraid. It made sense that the skittle balls belonged to someone of great stature.

"I should eat you for your audacity," the giant growled.

The prince countered, "I wouldn't make more than a mouthful for someone like yourself."

The giant raised a furry brow. "How about a little wager then?"

"A wager? What sort of wager?"

"We play and if you lose I shall have you as an appetizer."

"And if I win?"

"You get my bride."

The prince peeked at the wizened old woman who was sweeping the giant's stoop.

"Uh, ah, er, no thanks."

The giant turned to stare at the old woman. "That is not my bride. She is just a servant. Nay, my bride is a beauty. A princess in her own right."

The prince looked dubious.

"Or I could eat you right now." The giant paused.

"Afraid?" he jeered.

The prince squared his shoulders. "I am a knight of royal blood. Of course, I am not afraid."

So the tournament began, but the prince was smart. He had been educated in all the arcane arts, like geometry, and he won game after game.

First it was two of three, then seven of ten, while the giant hedged on his bet.

The sun set, rose and set again. Still the prince won.

Finally, the giant had to admit defeat. Weeping, he called into his great mansion: "My pretty, little bride come meet your new husband."

A head as large as the moon poked through the door, followed by a body even larger than that of the giant. She just kept coming and coming and coming. She had a wart on her nose upon which trees grew.

The prince toed his way backward. "No thanks. I would not dream of separating you from your beloved. I'll just take these, though, as a souvenir of this match." The prince began rolling the balls away.

Thus, the prince learned fear of a bad match, and the giant lost his balls. The giant never had children, for his bride never spoke to him again, and the prince never wed.

The lesson, my dear children, if you have not figured it out yet, is never play with another man's balls. You never know what might pop out.

Hansel and Gretel

The children dawdled next to a stall while an older woman studied the wares. The woman was by marketplace standards one of the upper crust – a servant of a wealthy household or perhaps a middle-class grandmother shopping for the family.

Gretel clasped the woman's skirt just below the bustle, stuck her finger in her mouth. She gazed at the heavens with the soft, unfocussed look of the terminally bored. A boy loitered in the background. His leg swung back as he prepared to kick a stone, and the girl hissed at him. He stuck his hands in his pockets and scowled.

Together the three of them appeared like any other family, with a harried grandmother doubly burdened by the shopping and the children. She ignored both of them.

The children were neat and clean. Nothing in their demeanor suggested thieves set loose upon the town by parents too poor to keep them. Their mother and father had taught the children their skills and left them behind to move to the city.

They had been well trained in their craft. Hansel could pick a pocket before he could feed himself. Gretel surpassed her brother. She could steal a complete outfit from a clothesline before she had seen five summers. Meanwhile, she was still trying to teach her younger brother how to use a spoon.

To survive and to thrive the siblings had to appear innocuous – not worth a second glance. Each evening she took Hansel to the river, threw him into the shallows and forced him to wash. Clean but poor children were tolerated. Filthy street urchins were not.

The woman perused the produce while Gretel stuffed her apron with apples, for she was well hid by the old lady's bustle and her bulk.

Hansel stared at the crowd. He noticed a milk maid with a full loaf of bread swinging in a sack that she had slung over her shoulder. Hansel crept up behind the girl, cut the bottom off the bag and let the loaf slide into his grasp. He side-stepped, vanishing between two stands. When he reappeared, one leg was decidedly wider than the other and he walked with a limp.

Gretel loosed her hold on the woman's bustle. The release in pressure caused the woman to spin around so fast that Gretel goosed her.

"Well, I never. Go away," the woman said.

"Oops, 'scuse me." Gretel bobbed in a curtsey.

The merchant spied the apples in Gretel's apron. "Oi! Look, missus, you're going to pay for those."

"What? I will not," the woman replied. "The children have nowt to do with me."

Gretel clasped her brother's arm and sprinted away from the stall with the merchant lurching behind. Seeing the disabled boy, a couple passed Gretel a coin.

Hansel stumbled and tripped. The loaf of bread slipped from his trousers.

"Oi, stop thieves!" bellowed the shopkeeper.

The old woman snatched the coin from Gretel's hand and attempted to catch the girl, but she was no match for two youths fueled by terror.

The merchant halted beside the couple, winded and gasping for air. The children rounded a corner and disappeared, leaving the noise of the market far behind them.

"What did you get?" asked Hansel.

She shook out a sleeve and an onion fell to the ground. She dug around in the other sleeve and pulled out two potatoes. Then she emptied her apron of apples. "With the bread, we will eat well tonight. I wonder what the professor has for us."

The children reached a distant section of the bazaar where merchants of more dubious repute hawked their wares. Many could not afford to pay the fees and licenses required to lease a stall in town center. Others sold goods of questionable quality and even more questionable origin.

Professor Thingagummy was demonstrating one of his inventions for another shopkeeper. "You want to mash potatoes or you want a smooth broth made of fine vegetables without all the slicing and dicing, cooking and straining. If you make cider or mill grain, this, milady, is the device for you.

"Saves work; saves time."

The professor hooked his thumbs under lapels. "It's my invention. I call it the musher."

"Musher? Looks like a hammer to me."

"A mallet to be precise, but it's been repurposed for the busy cook." He placed a melon on the table and smacked it, and the two were covered in pulp and rind.

The professor took off his spectacles, cleaned them and reseated them on his nose. The woman wiped her eyes, whirled around and stomped away.

Professor Thingagummy noticed the children. "I thought it was a pretty good idea myself."

Gretel nodded.

An old hag had been lingering in the shadows, with toe tapping, and a black cat clawing at her face.

When the prospective customer stormed off, the second advanced, brandishing the howling feline at arm's length in front of her.

Gretel grabbed her brother and told him to stay put. The girl slinked around the woman and attempted to pluck her money from her purse.

A hand snaked out and seized her wrist. "You'd better not, or I'll turn you into a toad."

"Come, come, children," said Professor Thingagummy. "Go inside. We have all this lovely melon for dinner."

He wiped bits of melon from his shirt.

Gretel hung her head in feigned shame at his reproof. The professor had befriended the pair, and she had developed affection for him. He was a funny old goat. He made stuff from other stuff, sometimes changed, sometimes not so much. He made clockwork toys that whistled and moved as if they were alive. Most, though, still resembled the clocks from which they were made.

Inventions, he called them, and he sold them to the unsuspecting public.

He had an unpronounceable, foreign-sounding name. The girl had dubbed him the professor because he was smart, and Hansel had supplied the moniker, Thingagummy.

The problem was that most of the items Thingagummy created didn't work, at least not as planned, and not for long. Sometimes the unhappy client discovered another use for the whachamacallit, as a butter churn or a bucket used to slop the hogs.

"What do you call this?" the woman said while cat squirmed in her grip.

The professor peered down at a bundle of feline fury incarnate. "Well, I don't know about you, madam, but I call it a cat."

"You told me it was an exterminator." The irate customer shoved the cat into the professor's arms. "I tell you it doesn't work. It doesn't hunt. It's defective. All it does is eat and shit, so you take it back."

"I don't want it." Thingagummy gestured vaguely at a placard with squiggly lines on it. "All sales final," he said, and he thrust the cat back into her arms.

"I can't afford to feed it." She held it out again. By this time, the cat was fed up with being switched back and forth between one angry individual and another. It clamped onto the old woman's arm with tooth and claw.

"Ow." She released it, but the cat hung suspended from her arm.

Thingagummy stepped back. "I don't want it. I sold it to you. So, you keep it."

"Look, I came here because I'm being eaten out of house and home by rats. This cat was supposed to catch them. It doesn't. It's just another mouth to feed. You got all sorts of gadgets and gizmos. Don't you have something for me to rid my house of vermin?"

"I don't know. What seems to be the problem?"

Her mouth dropped open. "Are you deaf as well as stupid? I just told you," she said through clenched teeth. "I'm being eaten out of house and home. I've got mice; I got rats. They have fleas. Then there are the termites. I don't know how many times I've had to rebuild my home."

"Oh, if it's vermin you got, that's simple. Poisons. Any good witch should be able to fix a poison up for you."

"I am a witch," she growled.

"Not a very good one, I gather," the professor mumbled.

A furrow formed between her brows. "You want a tail? Then you'll see how good I am at my craft."

His arms swept over all the displays on the table. He pointed at one. "I've got alarms, useful against highwaymen and robbers."

"That's an owl," she said.

"Yes," he replied, "but turn it loose on a robber and he won't be dashing away with your purse."

The woman considered the bird. "Don't owls eat mice and rats?"

He examined the bird. "I suppose they do. I never asked."

"I'LL TAKE IT!" she shrieked.

Thingagummy flinched.

A few measly coins and some beads changed hands.

The woman strode through the marketplace, clutching the owl to her breast.

"Hey, wait, you forgot." He glanced at the cage and shut the door. "I guess she doesn't need it. What a horrible woman."

The other shoppers scrambled to get out of her way, the mad woman who had a cat tap-dancing on the top of her pointy hat and an owl trying to rip her face off with its feet.

Gretel's gaze followed the witch's progress, the glint of speculation in her eyes.

She hauled her brother behind Thingagummy's stall where they had made their bed.

Gretel indicated the woman with the cat shredding her hat. "There's money to be made."

"How?"

"Remember when Mum brought home that cake shaped like a house she'd lifted from the baker?"

"No."

"Sure you do," Gretel said. "She broke a tooth on it."

"Oh yeah, she was pissed, said we'd never use that baker again."

Gretel snorted. "Quite right too."

She pushed Hansel down on the cot.

"What are we going to do?" he asked.

"I don't know yet. All I know is owls don't eat termites, so she will still have problems with her home." She pulled a wry face, tore a chunk off the loaf and began to chew.

*

The next day, the old woman returned. "I want my money back. That bloody bird flew off."

"You needed the cage. Of course, it's flown away. The whole device doesn't work without the cage. You open the cage door when you are waylaid by a highwayman, and Bob's your uncle, your attacker doesn't have any eyes."

110

"What good would that do me? I fly. I don't run into highwaymen. I wanted the owl to catch mice, rats and other small critters. The predator needs to be free to hunt."

Professor Thingagummy looked down his nose at her. "I guess you don't have as many problems with vermin as you thought. With plenty of food around, why would the owl leave?"

"How the hell do I know? But I think there is a clue. That damn bird was yelping when it buggered off, with its toe wedged between a rat's teeth."

"Then it got rid of one rat, didn't it? No refunds."

She glared at him. "Right."

Gretel shivered, sure that the next thing Thingagummy said was going to be 'ribbit'.

The woman spun, nearly tripping over the child.

Gretel tugged at her skirt. "Maybe I can help you."

"Kids! I don't need kids unless you know how to catch mice."

The girl could barely maintain a straight face. She watched in fascination as the cat, still perched on the top of the witch's head, minced what was left of her pointy hat.

"Prevention," Gretel explained.

"What?"

"Rather than getting rid of pests, wouldn't it be better if you never got them in the first place?"

"A little late for that," the witch groused.

"The baker makes gingerbread houses as hard as rocks. Even mice and rats break their teeth on it. If you had that kind of house, they'd have nothing to eat, no place to burrow and no home. Without mice and rats, you have no fleas, and since your home is not built of wood, no termites."

"Hmmm. Not bad, where do I find this gingerbread?"

"I have the secret recipe, but it'll cost you."

"How about if I don't turn you into something nasty?"

"Well, you could, but you'd never get the recipe."

Professor Thingagummy emerged from the tent. He recoiled when he saw the witch. Tea splashed over the side of his filthy cup. "Get that, that, *thing* out of here. She doesn't know how to use a perfectly good invention without losing it or breaking it, and then she comes to complain to me."

Gretel winked at the old woman and lowered her voice.

"Meet us at the fountain tomorrow and I'll show you a sample?"

"Well, the owl was as useless as the cat is." She nodded at the professor and stamped away, losing none of her dignity despite the enraged feline hissing and spitting on top of her head.

"What was that all about?" asked Hansel.

"Tonight you steal the house and we show it to her tomorrow."

"What if it breaks?"

"It won't." She grabbed him by the scruff of the neck. "We could make lots of money from this, so don't screw up."

*

The witch paced back and forth in front of the fountain. She had rid herself of the cat, at least temporarily, by latching it to the side of a tree. She chuckled as she thought of the startled expression as the cat dangled from the trunk by hook and claw.

Gretel and Hansel approached. The girl blinked. Only the rim remained of the witch's once proud hat.

Hansel carried the display in his arms.

The witch towered over the boy. She squinted. "I've seen that in the marketplace. You stole it from the baker, didn't you?"

Gretel thrust out her chin. "Borrowed," she corrected. "The baker is a friend of mine. He lent it to us for the demonstration. You can follow us and watch when we return it."

The witch settled to her normal height, mollified. "It's a bit small."

"This is his display. Notice it has an ingredient that makes it so it never dissolves."

Gretel dropped the cake into the fountain.

The witch cried out and reached to rescue the gingerbread house.

Gretel stopped her.

Minutes passed. The witch bent over, yanked the house from the water and tapped it.

Thunk!

"What makes you think I can't get this special ingredient from the baker?"

"Do you think he would share his secrets with just anyone?" countered Gretel.

An expression of suspicion flitted across the old woman's features.

Gretel sighed. "Professor Thingagummy is a nice man; he's sort'a adopted us, but a lot of his things don't work. This cake would solve all your problems. You'd just need to make the house bigger."

"What's the price?" She shoved the display back into Gretel's arms.

"That depends. Do you want us to make this special cake or do you want to make it yourself?

"Both. You make; I'll watch, and maybe, I'll help."

Gretel passed the gingerbread house to Hansel and shook the witch's hand. The children veered toward the town center.

"Is she following?"

"She is, at a distance."

The boy and the girl paused at the edge of the square. "I don't like this. I shouldn't be here," said Hansel. "I could lose a hand."

Gretel cuffed him, seized his ear and towed him across the bazaar to the baker's stall. "I caught him and brought him back to apologize. He saw me looking at the pretty cake and decided to get it for me. When he gave it to me this morning, I brought him right back. I knew he didn't have the money to buy it."

She released Hansel's ear and pushed him into the baker's arms.

Gretel fussed with the display. "I, ah, washed it for you."

The baker held Hansel by the shoulders and shook him. The boy stood, one toe rubbing the other. His head hung low. "I'm, uh... *shake...* uh... *shake...*uh... *shake...* sorry, mister."

Gretel intervened. "I will take him to the priest for confession. He will be punished. My brother will be saying Hail Marys until Christmastide."

She clipped Hansel's ear again.

The baker glared at the children. "Little lady, give me one good reason why I shouldn't turn you both over to the guard."

"I didn't do anything wrong," she said.

"Well since you returned it... Send your brother to the church."

"Yes, sir," she said. "Go."

Hansel scarpered before the baker could change his mind.

The man dried the display with his filthy apron. "Haven't seen this thing this clean in a long time."

He peered up at her. "You seem like a good girl. How'd you like to learn how to make the real thing?"

Gretel pointed. "Something that is hard as a rock?"

"No, gingerbread, the kind you can eat. It's a slow day."

It wasn't what she needed, but it was a start. Gretel memorized every ingredient and succeeded in making a lopsided house. He praised her. It crumbled in her hands.

"What turns it to stone?"

"Concrete. Been used since Roman times." He leaned over and whispered in her ear. Her eyes widened. "Stone?"

"What if you were cooking for the king and wanted to make a gingerbread house the size of your stall?"

"Oh, my, you'd have to multiply everything by a hundred weight. Maybe more. A cup of sugar would become a hundred cups of sugar or a thousand, but I won't ever be cooking for the king. He has his own staff."

While the recipe was still fresh, she went to Thingagummy. "Where does she live?"

"Who?"

"The witch?"

"You mean that dreadful old woman? How would I know?" he said. "She always leaves that way." He gestured north. "But I have no idea where she resides."

Gretel grabbed Hansel. "Come. Bring the musher, but don't talk to me." She recited the recipe under her breath as they hastened up the trail. She saw a little-used turn off, and she took a chance, towing her brother behind her.

The witch was stirring something in her cauldron. She jumped as the children approached.

"I need to give you the recipe before I forget it," said Gretel, "It's for a house the size as the sample you saw. The baker says it would take at least one-hundred times that amount to make a house as big as yours."

A stick floated into her grasp. The old woman began writing what Gretel repeated on the dry soil.

Hansel peered into the cauldron.

"What if it rains? Won't it wash away?" Gretel protested.

The witch gave a wave of her hand, and flames danced across the ground, until the words were seared into the earth.

Hansel gulped.

"My brother and I cannot buy the ingredients, my lady. We do not have the funds," Gretel said, keeping one eye on the scorched earth. She was beginning to wonder about the wisdom of her plan.

"How did you do that?" Gretel indicated the crystallized recipe.

"You saw. Fire. I can get the ingredients." She gestured toward the heavens and sacks of grain fell from the sky.

Gretel swallowed hard. "The fire will aid in the drying process."

The witch put the children to work. They dumped pounds of sugar and flour that she produced from thin air into the cauldron and it seemed there was always a little bit of room for more in there. The children added the ginger and the other spices.

They slaved long into the night; both too afraid to stop. Gretel made the old woman turn her back when she threw in the secret ingredients – ground rock, sand and lime.

Their hands formed slabs of dough into bricks until they bled. The witch bathed each batch with flame.

The next morning, Gretel explained that the walls were glued with frosting, similarly seared until it hardened, and then she asked if they could rest.

When the sun dipped low in the sky, the children awoke to find the woman erecting her home, floating pieces together and then, riding her broomstick, she forced each section to its allotted location.

The children huddled together for warmth.

"Let's go," complained Hansel.

"Not until we're paid," Gretel hissed.

"You are not leaving, and you are not getting paid until it's survived its first rainstorm." The witch grabbed the children, dragged them into the newly completed kitchen and threw them in a cage.

She fed them. She fed them well and the children grew fat. Days passed, but eventually the wild wald yielded a harvest of torrential rain.

The gingerbread house held.

A rumor spread throughout the village that the wicked witch had built a home of gingerbread. The people descended upon the hapless woman like locusts to gnaw at the walls.

"Right," said the witch. She confronted the children. "I've got half the town chewing on my home."

Gretel stuck out her chin, which was difficult to do since she had developed more than one. "We didn't guarantee it against incursions of people. Does it still stand?"

"We-ell, yes."

"We lived up to our end of the bargain. Set us free."

Instead, the witch fired her ovens. Gretel trembled.

Hansel challenged her. "What are you going to do? Eat us?"

The witch sliced onions, carrots and mushrooms, and placed them in the pot. She seized the musher and proceeded to mash the children. She added them to the vegetables and shoved the lot into oven.

Soon the townsfolk grew tired of chewing on a house that never yielded to their teeth. The smell of roasting meat made their mouths water.

"I have a pot roast, here. One farthing."

Professor Thingagummy pressed forward until he was at the front of the queue. "Ah, professor, to what do I owe the pleasure."

"I was wondering what became of the children."

"Not here. Not anymore. Feel free to go inside and see for yourself."

When he returned, she thrust a bowl into his hands. "This is for you. Free of charge," she said.

Thingagummy ate, grimaced and plucked a bone shard from the stew.

She grimaced. "Sorry, my poor old eyes don't always catch everything."

He finished the rest of his bowl without comment. Around him, the townsfolk ate until they were stuffed.

"Now," said the witch, "leave my little house and do not return or I will curse you and your entire town."

The crowd dispersed.

The old woman grinned.

That night she danced widdershins around the cauldron to summon the horned god. Her pace was frenetic; her shriek deafening and shrill.

Few slept that night in the village. Some felt ill after that day's repast, and all shuddered in their beds. Many clung to each other fearful they may awaken on the morrow in another form.

Their terror augmented her powers. Her sorcery reverberated back and forth between the villagers and herself. The branches in the forest whipped round, as if something battered at the heavens. The ground before her opened, raising a cloud of dust.

The witch heard a muffled voice. It said, "Blah, blah, blah, blah, blah."

She scratched her head and continued her dance. Knees up, knees down. Knees up, knees down. Eldritch screaming accompanied each step.

A spinning shape appeared, lifted from the earth by magic. The witch fell to her knees. *Her Lord approached.*

The whirling stopped.

She gaped.

The horned god who materialized before her was quite unlike anything she had seen at a village fête. The mummers that accompanied their costumed counterpart goaded the green man to randy capers. His outfit included the antlers of a hart, a face painted green and a cloak of the finest fleece, which not only displayed fine thighs and an oversized codpiece to emphasize his sexual prowess.

The creature she had summoned was something quite different. He was completely covered with thick, brown fur, except for his face where the pelt lightened to tan. The dark fur was thickest at the crown, tangled and twisted to form two curved horns.

This beast appeared two dimensional, flat, like a child's drawing. He did not have the thick thighs or the mask with the pointed muzzle of the buck. The face was flat; the eyes ringed in back. The mouth was open, big and wide. It was filled with the pointed teeth of a wolf rather than a ruminant.

Her god was shaped like the whirlwind that had borne him to the surface. He was tapered at the bottom with teeny, tiny bowed legs that were ill suited to support his barrel chest.

He spoke. She leaned forward, eager to hear the words of her god.

"Blah, blah, blah, blah, blah!"

She blinked. Carried away with the spirit of the occasion she repeated his words. "Blah, blah, blah, blah, blah."

The creature noticed the old woman for the first time.

"Blah?" He began to spin, picking up speed until she could no longer see his features, just a brown blur. She tried to emulate him, but soon became dizzy and fell.

Her eyes tracked him as he wrought a path of destruction through the woods. The horned one mowed through everything. He created a broad corridor, eating his way through the brush and devouring all that stood in his way.

"Blah, blah, blah, blah, blah." He felled trees and pulverized rock and stone, turning all into sand.

The witch stared at her hands, wondering what she had raised, and decided mayhap it was time for a holiday.

Seven Brothers

A couple had seven sons, but the wife wished desperately for a daughter. Her wish was granted, for the eighth child was a girl, and the wife was content.

But as things often happen, the woman was killed in a drive-by shooting. The man was devoted to his children. He worked long hours, so they wanted for nothing.

Yet he did not like leaving his children alone. He invited the mother's evil stepsister to come live with them where she could care for the children.

The stepsister moved in gladly, but she didn't think she should work.

"Come on," she shouted. "Quit texting and do the dishes."

The girl set her mobile aside, but the boys did not listen.

Every day, the boys texted and played their games while the sister worked.

The mother's wicked stepsister ranted and raged at them, but they did naught. One day, she seized their phones and tossed them in the garbage disposal.

"You go outside," she told the boys, "and mow that lawn."

The eldest stared at her in defiance. "Make me," he said.

The evil stepsister began to speak in a strange tongue while they laughed at her.

With a great wiggling of fingers and a waggling of eyebrows, the mother's wicked stepsister spat on each of them.

"Yu - baa, baa," said the first.

The second bleated and one after another they were transformed to sheep.

"Now," said the stepsister, "you will mow the lawn if you are going to eat at all." And she turned them out into the fields.

"I am sorry," she said, "that I had to deal so harshly with your brothers. You have always been an obedient child."

"That's alright," said the girl. "I never really liked them anyway. They were always picking on me."

The two went out shopping, and that night they served mutton for dinner.

Gilda and the Bears

Once upon a time in the far-off land of Toronto, there was a little girl named Gilda. She was not a good girl. In fact, she was quite a bad one. If her parents said black, she would say white. Nothing they did or said influenced her. Gilda did as Gilda wanted, and no one was going to gainsay her.

One summer, the parents decided to go on holiday, but they could find neither a baby sitter for Gilda nor lodging for the three of them. Gilda's reputation as a holy terror was renowned. The frantic parents set their sights on small rental cabins near Mill Lake.

When they arrived, the family was warned not to go into the forest, which the owner said went on for two-hundred miles without break.

Hearing this, Gilda headed for the woods.

"She doesn't obey very well, does she?" the owner said.

Her mother stared at her feet and mumbled: "No, she doesn't."

She called for Gilda, who moved further way from her parents.

"Well, she's your problem," the owner said, "but..." he raised his voice so Gilda might hear "... little girls who don't obey get eaten by bears."

Gilda chuffed with a sharp exhalation of breath. Bears, bah! No bear would eat her.

The father shrugged. "They'd probably get indigestion if they did."

The owner took out a piece of paper and shoved it into the father's hands. "You have to sign this. It's a release of responsibility for anything that might happen if you or anyone of your family enters the forest. Don't come running to complain if you lose your daughter."

The parents signed the document, unpacked the car and discussed plans for the week. They shouted for Gilda to help with dinner, but she had vanished into the wild woods.

"Now what?" grumbled the wife. "What if she gets lost?"

"We couldn't be that lucky," he said. "She's probably sitting at the edge of the woods waiting for supper. She'll be back."

But the father was wrong. Gilda was doing the very thing she had been warned against. She went for a walk in the forest. She came upon a house in the trunk of an ancient tree. The door was open wide. She entered without knocking, for the way she figured it if they didn't want visitors they should keep the door closed.

The place stank. Gilda sniffed the air. It smelled like – she wrinkled her nose – wet dog. She knew because when a neighbor's dog had annoyed her, Gilda had tried to drown it, and when her parents pulled the terrier from the water, it had smelled just like this house.

Otherwise the place was tidy.

She came upon the kitchen table where she found three bowls of porridge. Gilda was hungry because her parents would not stop at a drive-through no matter how she fussed.

Gilda tasted the porridge from the first bowl and pushed it away. "This porridge is too hot!" she exclaimed, waving her hand in front of her mouth and exhaling in short little bursts.

Then she tested the porridge from the second bowl. She dropped the spoon into the bowl. The cold porridge soothed her scalded tongue, but it too lumpy to be eaten.

Finally she tried the last bowl. It was just right, neither too hot nor too cold. She ate it all up.

Gilda wandered into the living room where there was a huge television. She turned it on, but the reception was lousy. All stations were snow except the fishing channel.

She saw three chairs. One was big and fluffy. Gilda climbed into the first chair, thinking it would be nice and soft, and was immediately suffocated by the cushions. "This chair is too big!" she said.

She sat in the second chair. It was as hard as rocks.

So Gilda plopped into the last chair. "Ahhh, this chair is just right," she sighed. She snuggled deep, but the chair broke into pieces.

By this time, Gilda was angry. She didn't particularly like porridge; she would have preferred a hamburger, and she didn't like fishing anyway. She stormed around the house, picked one of the chair legs and threw it at the television.

It exploded.

She clambered up the stairs to complain to whoever owned this establishment, but she was quite alone. Then she noticed the beds. She flopped down on the first bed, but it was too hard.

Then she lay in the second bed, but it was too soft. Then stretched out on the third bed; it was just right.

Tired from her exertions, Gilda fell asleep.

As she slumbered, the family of bears returned from their morning constitutional with empty stomachs and ravenous appetites.

The mother bear skidded to a halt as soon as she entered their home. "Someone has been here," she said.

The father bear elbowed his way past her. "What do you mean?"

"Someone has been here. I told you. I told you to close and lock the door, but 'nooooo,' you said, 'who would bother us?'"

Mother and father bear paused to study the wreckage of the television. The cushions in the room were in disarray and the child's chair splintered to bits.

"Someone's been sitting in my chair," growled Papa Bear.

"Someone's been sitting in my chair," said Mama Bear.

"Someone's been sitting in my chair and broken it all to pieces," cried Baby Bear.

They tiptoed through shards of exploded tubes to the kitchen.

"Someone's been eating my porridge," growled the Papa Bear.

"Someone's been eating my porridge," said the Mama Bear.

"Someone's been eating my porridge and they ate it all up!" cried Baby Bear.

The mother continued to parrot Father Bear. "That's right, 'leave the door open. No one will ever disturb us here.'"

"Well, no one ever visits," he countered, urinating on one of the chairs, trying to get rid of the foul odor of human.

They decided to look around more and when they got upstairs to the bedroom, Papa Bear growled, "Someone's been sleeping in my bed."

"Someone's been sleeping in my bed, too," said Mama Bear.

"Someone's been sleeping in my bed and she's still there!" exclaimed Baby Bear.

Just then, Gilda woke up and saw the three bears. She screamed, "What are you doing here, you nasty old bears? Is that why this house smells like wet dog?"

The mother and father bear exchanged glances over the bed. It was just too much to have someone break into their den and insult their housekeeping.

Gilda jumped up, but the bears were too fast. They knocked her down, and they ate her.

"Excellent brunch," said Papa Bear. "Still mad about leaving the door open?" he asked Momma Bear.

The mother bear bared her teeth in a toothy grin. "No, I'd say let's leave the door open every day and see if we can capture another fine meal."

Back at the cabin, the parents waited for Gilda to appear. When she didn't, Gilda's mother griped because they had to go out and find her.

"Do you want to enter that forest while it's dark?"

Gilda's mother shook her head no.

"What's the worst that can happen?" the father asked.

"She won't come back."

Both gazed at the moon that was rising over the lake. It was so peaceful and quiet inside the cabin.

Then they gathered up their belongings and left before anyone could ask them any questions.

Maid Marion

Friar Tuck licked the bone clean, carefully removing ligament and tendon. He hefted his corpulent bulk from the log with a grunt. He lumbered through camp to the surrounding forest, tied the bone on a string and hauled it high beyond the reach of the average predator.

Early on, he learned to dry each bone before putting it in his belt. Placed in the sack too soon and the bone would start to grow fronds of mould, in black, grey and green, and develop a malodorous stench that repelled even the most seasoned collector of relics.

He kept numerous bags strung from his waistband – one for the finger bones of the saints, which saint depended on the punter's preference; another to carry the splinters of the true cross that often performed double function as toothpicks, and another for the sacred waters of the Savior.

The latter consisted of his urine collected, poured into clay flasks and sealed with wax. Each purchaser received a strong admonition not to disturb the contents. It was a sin. The malefactor would be sent to Hell. Tuck also provided lurid descriptions of the same.

Friar Tuck reasoned the water was holy enough. He had taken his vows, and he blessed each vial, for he had difficulty making water anymore. Thus, each piss was a blessing.

The friar also presented anyone who purchased his relics with a certificate of authenticity. It contained a poorly written Bible verse; the same Bible verse he had memorized to prove his ability to read and write required by his mendicant order. The customer didn't know the difference. They were as illiterate as he was.

Tuck lifted his cassock, placed a bowl under his cock and waited. He strained and produced a few drops of liquid tinged with blood.

The Blood of Christ, a big seller, but not a good sign.

Friar Tuck preferred to sell old rags and bandages used to treat wounds of the Merry Men as the kerchief of Mary Magdalene that had been dipped in Jesus's blood as he hung upon the cross.

The camp began to stir. Robin Hode arrived from his personal lair under the oak in Sherwood Forest. The leader did not sleep with the Merry Men. Friar Tuck did not blame him. The Merry Men were not very merry, an ill-tempered lot of buggers. Forsooth, even by Tuck's standards, they were a bunch of miserable knaves.

But it was a cushy job being preacher to the most notorious band of criminals in the county, who were despised by the king and pursued by the Sheriff of Nottingham.

Friar Tuck became celebrated by his order for his bravery. Renown came from afar, for he doubted they would have approved his lifestyle had they witnessed it.

Hode and the not-so-merry men had no wish to have Tuck minister to their souls. What they coveted was his cart.

And his ass. The friar chortled at his witticism.

The gang left him in peace to do as he will, and what better protection could a friar have against thieves than to live among them?

The longer he stayed, though, the greater care he must take. Those who desired relics were passionate about their collection, and it wouldn't do to sell the same item to the same individual twice. This required a good memory for faces and names, but his memory wasn't what it used to be. Neither was his vision. His eyes had grown dim of late.

Friar Tuck stretched and yawned. He decided to stay within the confines of the camp, rather than ply his trade this day. He wasn't feeling that well and he hadn't been able to make water today. He reclined against a tree and made ready for a nap.

Elsewhere the men gathered around the fire. Few spoke and those that did snarled at each other. The daily hangover did little to improve their tempers. Robin Hode held himself aloof from the rest. They supped well upon the leftovers from last night's dinner that had been cooked by the lovely Maid Marion – the hens pilfered from a peasant's stores.

With their stomachs full, the mood lightened, and they began to reminisce about the maid who ministered to their needs more than any friar ever could.

The men focused on their leader and teased him about missing last night's entertainment. Hode snapped at them and stormed off.

Tuck woke to find Hode looming over him. "We'll need your cart today, old man," he said. Hode did not bother with the honorific. He was the chief here. He made obeisance to no man. "We have work to do."

Friar Tuck shrugged. "Go ahead take it, but I won't be driving it this day. I feel ill."

"You don't look well. A bit sallow of face. Take care of yourself, old man. I for one would miss your larcenous soul."

"Blasphemy, lad. I have protected you, my son, and I will persist in doing so for years to come." The friar made the sign of the cross at Robin. "God's blessing upon you in your endeavor."

Robin stared into the forest and sighed. "Yes. Whatever. You see how I am blessed."

Friar Tuck settled back into the deep shade of the sacred holly and returned to slumber. Little time had passed, or so it seemed to the friar, when a toe prodded his side. He waved it away as he would shoo a fly. "Come, Robin, do not disturb a sick, old man in his repose."

The gentle poke became a nudge, more insistent, and then a kick.

"Ow!" Friar Tuck opened his eyes. The sun hit him full in the face. Something about this seemed wrong, that darkness should become blinding light, but muddled by sleep as he was, Friar could not remember what. He shaded his face and peered at Little John. The friar recognized the man by his stature rather than his features. He cast a long shadow and was silhouetted by the sun.

"Where is Hode? We have booty to divide."

"Try his camp." Tuck rolled over and raised his hood as a sign of dismissal.

Little John trudged through the woods, angry. He held little truck with the church and less with its representatives. He never could understand why Robin Hode tolerated the fat friar. Like many of his kind, Tuck was prone to inconvenient admonitions against sin and lewd behavior, but he did not practice what he preached. Everyone in the camp knew of his trade in relics.

*

Hode smeared his face with cerus to attain the pale skin of a lady. He pursed his lips and spread vermillion on them. He studied his reflection in the small glass. He swore. He should have been able to find a mirror larger than this with as many noble carriages he had robbed. The mirror was about the size of an egg and fit into his palm nicely; however, he could see little – just a small portion of his face at a time.

He used the costly vermillion on his cheeks and the powdered antimony around his eyes. Then he leaned back to apply drops of belladonna to give him the shining eyes of a maid.

The drops stung and his eyes watered. The young warrior had to restrain himself to keep from rubbing them for fear of smudging his make-up.

Branches cracked and crashed in the forest as if someone raced through the coppice to reach him. Hode struggled into his cotehardie.

"Tuck, where were you? You are late," he shouted. "You know I need your help to lace up the sleeves."

He swung toward the sound, but with eyes blurred by the drops of nightshade, he did not recognize the visage that stood at the edge of the clearing. However, he had enough presence of mind to throw on his headdress to cover his hair.

The action came too late, for Little John noticed the dark hair of their leader atop the face tarted-up like a prostitute. He stared. His jaw unhinged, and his hands dangled limply at his side.

Their leader wore a woman's vest, which accentuated a small waist, over his Lincolnshire green hose, the bulge of his member apparent despite the cote.

The continued silence unnerved this leader of men and he thrashed about as he tried to get into his skirts.

"Gah, gah, gah," stammered Little John. The color drained from his face. His stomach churned, and his jaw clenched. His fingers tightened on his quarterstaff, and he fainted.

*

The following morning Friar Tuck made his ablutions. He bottled the sanguine fluid from yesterday and blessed it. At least he had a use for it. He had not had the Blood of Christ in his stores for a long time.

"Old man, we need your services." Robin's voice interrupted the rite of sanctification and Tuck almost dropped his precious supply of blood.

The friar wound his way to Robin's camp to find Little John and Maid Marion in the shade of the old oak tree. The three spoke briefly.

"You know it's not legal," Tuck said.

Robin snorted. "Since when has that stopped us?"

A few seconds later, the three joined the Merry Men who had assembled around the fire.

Friar Tuck cleared his throat and began the rite.

"Dearly beloved we are gathered here today to join this man and this, um, er, woman in holy matrimony..."

The Tooth Fairy

The tooth fairy flitted into the bedroom on the first story and nearly collided with another of her kind.

"Sandman! What the hell are you doing here?"

"Language, language."

She began to fume, and steam rose from her person.

"When did you start smoking?" The sandman fixed her with an admonitory stare.

"That's not smoke," she retorted.

"What is it then?" said the sandman.

She sniffed her gown. "Miasma."

She lit a cigarette. "Now I'm smoking. Shouldn't you be long gone by now?"

"Yes, it's good that you are here now. This one presented me with quite a case. Toothache."

"Great. More miasma."

"Huh?"

"Never mind." The tooth fairy began to cough.

The sandman patted her shoulder. "There, there. You just take that nasty old tooth and she'll sleep well."

"Do you know how many germs there are in a human mouth? It's a cesspool. It's disgusting."

"We all have our jobs to do," he said.

"Right, jobs," she huffed.

"I must be off. The Jones kids next door are throwing tantrums. They should have been asleep hours ago." He checked his hour glass. "And I dare say there are no few adults that are in need of my services, including Mr. and Mrs. Jones."

The sandman leapt out the window, vanishing with a sprinkle of, well, sand.

The tooth fairy appraised the room; it was a mess. The offending tooth dangled on a string from the doorknob. Blood and some suspicious looking muck splattered the door's frame.

The fairy plucked a flask from her voluminous skirts and took a swig. She wiped her lips and then thrust it back into an unseen pocket.

She patted her skirts until she unearthed a pair of tongs. Her lips twisted into something worse than a sneer or a grimace. She stretched as far as she could without advancing and tried to hook the string.

No such luck.

The tooth fairy snapped her fingers. The flask meekly appeared in her hands. She upended it and gulped the last of the brew down. She closed it and heard the reassuring glug of liquid as it refilled itself.

A single step forward, another reach, another string of invectives and another drink.

Her next step qualified as more of a lurch. She nearly fell against the door knob. Bile and booze rose in her throat. The tongs closed around the string and she lifted it.

She added the nasty tooth to the growing necklace she wore. A symbol of her craft. She staggered toward the window and fell out, hitting the pavement with a faint slap. Sometimes she wished she could kill herself, but she was a creature of fairy, immortal, and she was doomed to do this till the end of her undying days.

She hopped to her feet and smoothed her skirts to make sure the precious flask had not absented itself.

"That's right," she muttered to no one in particular, "let your wand go on the fritz, just once, and you lose your wand, your crown, your name, your status and your pretty dress, even if it was frilly and pink."

Now she wore the rough spun cloth of the poor of no recognizable color

A rat poked his head from the skip, contemplated her critically with glowing red eyes and chewed on someone else's dinner. "Serves you right," it said.

"What do you know?"

"Everybody knows about the downfall of Glinda the Good."

"I'm not her anymore," she said.

The rat grinned, a piece of rotting meat dangling between his teeth. "I know. Dorothy took your place, right and proper."

"Watch it, buddy, I may not be able to turn you into a toad, but I bet I'm pretty sure I can still turn you into a furry pancake."

The rat skittered away as slime from her burden dribbled salva and blood between her breasts.

Rapunzel

"One... two... three... four... five... six... seven... eight... nine... ten... eleven... twelve... thirteen... fourteen... fifteen... sixteen... seventeen... eighteen... nineteen... twenty. Twenty-one... twenty-two... twenty-three... twenty-four... twenty-five... twenty-six... twenty-seven... twenty-eight... twenty-nine... thirty. Thirty-one... thirty-two... thirty-three... thirty-four... thirty-five... thirty-six... thirty-seven... thirty-eight... thirty-nine... forty. Forty-one... forty-two... forty-three... forty-four... forty-five... forty-six... forty-seven... forty-eight... forty-nine... fifty. Fifty-one... fifty-two... fifty-three... fifty-four... fifty-five... fifty-six... fifty-seven... fifty-eight... fifty-nine... sixty. Sixty-one... sixty-two... sixty-three... sixty-four... sixty-five... sixty-six... sixty-seven... sixty-eight... sixty-nine... seventy. Seventy-one... seventy-two... seventy-three... seventy-four... seventy-five... seventy-six... seventy-seven... seventy-eight... seventy-nine... eighty. Eighty-one... eighty-two... eighty-three... eighty-four... eighty-five... eighty-six... eighty-seven... eighty-eight... eighty-nine... ninety. Ninety-one... ninety-two... ninety-three... ninety-four... ninety-five... ninety-six... ninety-seven... ninety-eight... ninety-nine...

"One hundred." Rapunzel laid the brush aside. She didn't know why she bothered with the tradition – it wasn't like anybody cared about her appearance anymore – but then certain amenities must be observed. It was one of the few rituals her mother had drummed into her head that the princess still maintained.

Besides, it helped her kill time between loser princes.

And Rapunzel could count to one-hundred like nobody's business.

Absent-mindedly she twined a few strands that escaped the brush into an ever-growing braid. She plucked a curl from the bristles. Her eyes widened in horror.

A grey hair!

Rapunzel gasped a few deep gulps of air to steady herself. Princes, she decided long ago, were by and large a sorry and unreliable lot, more interested in their sword hand and what dangled betwixt their legs than heroism.

Just then, a voice drifted from the base of the tower. "Rapunzel, Rapunzel, let down your gold hair. 'Tis I, Prince Charming, come to save you from the dragon's lair."

She winced. There went a perfectly good day. She rose and kicked a skull out of the way as she walked toward the window.

"Rapunzel, Rapunzel, let down your gold hair."

The princess mouthed the next words: "'Tis I, Prince What-not, come to save you from the dragon's lair."

She gathered the extensive braid and lugged it over to the window sill.

Rapunzel glared at the young man.

He cupped his hands around his mouth and said: "Rapunzel, Rapunzel, let down your hair."

"All right," she muttered, "you asked for it."

Rapunzel steadied herself, with legs splayed and knees locked against the wall before she lobbed the braid out the window.

Prince Whossisname leapt out of the way before he was crushed by her hair.

"Hey, what you on about? You could have killed me." He brushed himself off and shook his fist at her. He thought a bit and clasped one hand with the other in a gesture of entreaty.

Then he grabbed at the plait and gave it a sharp tug, testing its strength against his weight. The rest of the braid descended to blanket the young man in its golden tresses.

She gazed at the tangle of braid that seemed to have sprouted lips at its center.

"Wat'choo playin' at?" it said.

For the first time, she poked her head, shorn of its locks, over the sill.

He clambered from beneath the mountain of hair.

"You, you, you've cut your hair."

"Long hair, pah!" Rapunzel said. "That's so... so... *sooo*... medieval."

"But –"

"What did you expect? That I should hang around here waiting for you and swooning at your feet after you damn near pull every hair out of my head trying to get to me?"

She paused. "Been there. Done that. Bought the bodice. It didn't fit and I won't wear it. If you want to visit me, bring a damn ladder, fercrissakes."

At that moment, a dragon came raging around the tower and expectorated fire. Prince Wossits expired with a sizzle and flash surrounded by the stench of burning hair.

Rapunzel plucked a clavicle from a stack of bones that had accrued through the years and tossed it to the dragon. The great wyrme caught it and waddled back to her den, happily munching her bone.

The princess slammed the shutters closed to block the smell of roasting flesh and flaming hair.

"I slay my own dragons," she said. "Male chauvinist pig."

Alice

As usual Alice sat with her sister along the river bank, for her family never left her alone since she told them about the white rabbit. Always a willful child, now they saw her as more than passing strange.

Alice's eyes were glazed, and her sister gave her a hearty poke in the ribs.

"Time to go," said Mathilda.

"Oh, can't I stay just a little while longer?" Alice pleaded. Her gaze strayed to the opening between the roots of the old apple tree.

Her sister put her hands on her hips. "No, most certainly not."

Mathilda grabbed Alice's hand and hauled her down the path toward home. "Come. We would not want mother to worry."

Alice pouted. "Why should I care?"

The girls approached the home. Their mother stood in the doorway, toe tapping, until she could shut the door behind them.

"How was she today?"

"Still the same," said Mathilda. "Dreamy."

Alice flopped down on her stomach and watched a spider spin its web in the corner.

"What is wrong with her?" asked her mother.

"I don't know. She's never been the same since that day when she says she fell down the rabbit hole." Mathilda averted her eyes. She had never confessed to her mother that she too fell asleep that afternoon. Perhaps Alice had gone somewhere else that left her irrevocably altered.

"I know she wants to go back there," Mathilda coughed into her hand. "Wherever there is."

"Alice?"

The girl sat up and faced her mother, although Alice's eyes remained soft and unfocused, as if she stared at a distant point beyond mortal perception.

"Whatever shall we do with her? People will start to talk and then where shall we be?" her mother hissed.

Mathilda placed what she hoped was a reassuring hand on her mother's shoulder and rolled her eyes significantly to the ceiling.

"The mad woman in the attic? Never! I could not do that to her."

"I cannot stay here forever, mother, and we cannot afford a nurse," admonished Mathilda. "Something must be done."

"Not today," said the woman. She patted the keys in her pocket. She locked the front door. "Come, child, time for a nap."

The frown line on Alice's forehead deepened. Alice's mother steered her daughter to her room, opened the door, gave Alice a gentle shove and locked that door too.

Mathilda stood her arms looped across her chest. "What is the difference? Attic or bedroom?" She indicated the locked door with a jut of her chin. "Between this prison, and making it permanent upstairs, so I can have some kind of life of my own? I would like to wed and have children of my own."

"Not today, you won't. Not today."

Mathilda retreated.

Alice sat ear pressed against the door. When sound of footsteps assured her that she was alone, Alice stole to the window. She had escaped in the past to find her way back to her friends, Dodo, Dormouse, Mad Hatter and the Cheshire Cat. The Duchess and the Queen of Hearts had fallen into disrepute since her first visit and were guarded by the cards they kept in servitude for so many years.

Alice missed the treats, the cakes, the sweetmeats, the redcap mushrooms and the sensations they gave her as she expanded and shrank. She liked that she could stomp her foot and residents of the rabbit hole quaked before her. She liked talking in rhyme even if sometimes the poems made no sense.

Today Alice was determined to escape. She had packed her clothes and wrapped them up in a cloak. She eschewed food. She would find plenty to eat below. She fiddled with the latch and opened the bedroom window wide. She grabbed the cat and threw her to the oak that grew beside her room.

Alice gathered her skirts, swung onto a branch, and with Dinah tucked under her arm, climbed down. "They are so mean about cats," Alice said. "Wait till they meet you, Dinah. They will love you as I do."

She raced to the river and then slithered down the hole. The mouse who stayed on permanent guard ever since her first visit shrieked: "Incoming. Huge human-sized person and what? Oh, no, it's a cah--"

Silence.

"Dinah! Spit him out."

The cat sat on her haunches with a self-satisfied expression on her face, belched delicately and groomed herself.

Alice opened her mouth to scold when her gaze fell on the cake atop the table. This is what she came for; this is what she craved. She pounced on the cake and gobbled it up. Her head hit the roots overhead so hard that she knocked herself silly. Alice stretched out and lolled on the ground.

Dinah hissed at her.

Alice began to cry with great big tears.

"What became of mouse?" asked Dodo.

"He's, ah, indisposed," Alice said.

Dinah mewled and bounded away.

A chorus rang out. "Cat, cat, cat, cat, cat!"

Alice gazed at them bleary-eyed. "Cat? What cat?"

She clutched her head and wept. The animals donned their water wings. The lake formed, and the animals swam to shore and began to dry themselves.

Alice found the bottle labelled 'drink me.'

This is what she needed.

She drank, and she shrank. Dinah jumped on her now mouse-sized mistress. Alice poked the cat in the eye with the bottle.

Dinah scampered away and climbed to a perch where she could watch the animals dance.

"Forward, backward..." Dodo sang.

Dinah's tail lashed in agitation.

"... inward, out–"

The cat swooped down on the hapless bird and sat on him.

Alice wiped her lips on the back of her hand. She crawled away, searching for rabbit's house where stones turned into cakes.

The Cheshire Cat greeted her. "Now the Dodo is truly extinct."

The body began to fade, first tail, then legs, body and stripes. Only the head remained, grinning at her. Alice didn't pay attention. She had seen this trick before. Instead she kicked it. It bounced about the garden like a football.

"That'll wipe the grin off his face," she said.

The Cheshire Cat's body reappeared and bounded after the head. Sightless, it bumped into trees, tripped over roots and fell into holes.

"Oops, 'scuse me, so sorry," the distant head said.

The drink had worn off. Alice began to grow, and with the predictability of a clock, Bill the Lizard pelted her with pebbles. She clutched at them and waited until she had attained full height. Then the greedy girl reached in through the cottage window and stuffed the cakes into the pockets of her pinafore.

A bird attacked her head. "Serpent! Serpent!"

Alice took a swipe at it. Then she popped one of the cakes into her mouth and rubbed her belly.

Dinah chased after the rolling head and batted at it.

"Oh nooooo!" shouted Cheshire.

Dinah pursued the Cheshire Cat, swatting its head across White Rabbit's pristine lawn.

"Alice, help me," Cheshire shouted, its grin turned upside down.

"Help yourself. You're all mad, you know."

She turned away, and Dinah chased the head into the forest.

"Time to find that damn caterpillar. I've got a bone to pick with him."

Alice followed her nose to the sweet smell of smoke where the caterpillar sat, fat and blue, his skin stretched taut over his long torso.

He sucked on the hookah and blew smoke rings around her head. "Who…" he puffed, "… are you?"

She coughed.

"Who... are... you?"

She grinned. He opened his eyes wide from half-mast.

"Oh, no, not you," he cried.

The skin on his back split and the wings of a butterfly unfurled. He flew away. Dinah became distracted from her treasured head, leapt on the butterfly and ate it.

Alice climbed to the top of the mushroom. She wrapped herself in the caterpillar's skin, seized the hookah she had coveted and inhaled deeply.

She became dizzy and almost swooned, but she discovered she had many feet to hold herself upright.

"Oh, my," she said, "isn't the view from here lovely? So many bright colors."

What had Caterpillar said, so many months ago? Alice snapped her fingers. "One side makes you larger; another makes you small."

She peered owlishly at the dotted mushroom cap. "But which is which?"

She could not remember, so Alice ate it all while Dinah darted after the bread-and-butterflies and scratched among the flowers.

In the world above years passed. Her mother aged and died. Her sister left the family home to have a family of her own.

Alice stayed in Wonderland, chewing her way through first one mushroom and then the next. Dinah passed away, sated.

Wonderland became a silent place, with every other species extinct, save Alice.

One day as she puffed away on her pipe, the mushroom upon which she sat began to vibrate and shake. Alice stretched across the cap to peer over the edge to the ground below her.

A head, clad in a stocking cap, ascended from the earth. It swung slowly, and she saw fuzzy hair, a curly beard, a bulbous nose and a pick.

So she hit him with her hookah.

Star-Crossed Lovers

Courtship among the long-lived fairies was a leisurely affair. The high elves in their island realm adhered to the old ways with children betrothed before birth. The brownies due to the great distance between families also retained the tradition.

But their parents were not cruel, knowing that the young might not approve their choice, for an eternity provided a long time to repent. The fey also maintained the custom of bundling where the affianced might spend a night with the proposed partner. The participants were placed in a common bed and swaddled, so they could converse but not touch.

The bride-to-be Arrea was first prepared for the night while the male partner, men being expected to be experienced in the affairs of love, disrobed in front of her as the proud parents watched.

Elwin stripped off his socks. Arrea gasped aghast at what she saw.

"Your feet," she said. "What's wrong with your feet?"

Elwin studied his feet. "Oh, I quite forgot. I had toelio as a child."

He stood and let his robes fold around his ankles.

"And your knees?" she asked.

"I had kneesles."

Arrea bit her tongue.

Elwin removed his pants.

The proposed bride began to struggle against her bonds.

"Oh, no. Oh, no. No, no, no."

Her parents ran up, trying to restrain her, but she found the strength to tear through the cloth that held her close. She wrapped the sheets around her tight.

"Toelio, I can stand. Kneesles too. Normal childhood ailments, but small cox. I draw the line at small cox. The wedding is off."

No, No, You Can't Make Me

Dorothy clung to the trunk of a large apple tree with a white-knuckle clutch.

"No, no, you can't make," she pleaded.

The young woman dug her nails deep into the bark. "Never! I won't do it."

The apple tree balled its branches into fists and began beating Dorothy around the neck and shoulders.

"Ouch. Ow, uh, uh. Ow, uh, uh, uh. I command you stop!" she shouted.

The Cowardly Lion and the Tin Man attempted to pry open her grip, finger by finger.

"Tin Man, Lion, I helped you," Dorothy said. "Tin Man, you got a heart because of me. Use it now and take pity on me. Cowardly Lion, you have bravery now, but, surely, you must recall what it felt like to be afraid."

The Tin Man was the first to unwrap her hand from the trunk and ducked to avoid being hit by a thrashing limb. Sensing his distraction, Dorothy turned on him, grabbing his metallic wrist so hard that it crumbled under her grip.

She spun on Scarecrow and begged. "I was your friend, once, and you were mine."

Scarecrow tapped his forehead. "I'm thinking you aren't too happy about this."

Dorothy spat at him. "Right genius. You think so? Finally figured that out, have you? Still got straw for brains, I see."

Scarecrow winced.

It was just the diversion Lion needed to rip her remaining hand from the trunk, and the metal man and the furry predator towed her closer to the hated destination.

Dorothy seized the first post she saw and tore it from the ground. She began to swing it around her head. The Lion bobbed, but she managed to flatten the left side of Tin Man's head and decapitated Scarecrow with her follow through.

Toto barked and barked excitedly. He leapt up to grab the post and hang onto it, flying in a semi-circle.

"*Et tu, Brute?* Let go, damn you." She waggled the pole up and down in the air. Toto flopped around. "Stupid dog."

Dorothy released her hold on the post and on Tin Man. He tumbled sideways. Toto landed near the well. She made a grasp at another, sturdier column, more a pillar than a post.

The skirmish began anew.

"I don't want to. I won't. I won't. I won't. You can't make me," Dorothy insisted, sticking her chin out for emphasis.

Scarecrow's body crawled around on all fours, patting the ground, while his head continued the conversation. "I don't understand. What's so awful?"

Out of the corner of his mouth he hissed to his groping body. "Here. Over here. To your left."

The body spun.

"No, not that left. Your *other* left." His gaze returned to Dorothy. "I resent your picking on me because I'm fragile."

Lion yanked Tin Man to his feet and the two started the arduous process of unwrapping Dorothy's arms from the pillar again. Toto nipped at Dorothy's heels. She kicked at him.

Head and corpse got sorted. "You've done enough damage. The Wizard wants to return to the land of his birth. It is the land of your birth too. You will accompany him – as he requests – and have the childhood you missed."

Tin Man grumbled, "Look at me. I'm going to need the tinsmith again and you know how clumsy he is."

Dorothy went limp. They tumbled tit over tail. She scrabbled back to the column, but they caught her before she could reach it and dragged her relentlessly toward the craft. When her feints did not slow them, she fought – gyrating first up and down and then back and forth.

She spied the central column in the colonnade located in Emerald City's Grand Plaza. Her arms were pinned, so she wound her legs around the mammoth structure.

Tin Man and Lion pulled, and she screamed.

A pink bubble appeared on the horizon, weaving into a landing. Glinda the Good lurched from the bubble.

Dorothy gaped. "You! You! I thought I got rid of you."

"Oh, yes," said Scarecrow. "Did we forget to tell you? We found the good fairy. She took a bit of cleaning up, but she's back."

Glinda waved her spangled wand over Dorothy's head.

The young woman eyed it, knowing the star points to be lethal.

"Help us understand," Glinda crooned.

Dorothy sputtered. "You are supposed to be good, but you never liked me. I know you didn't. You never helped me. I did it all by myself..."

"I say," said Cowardly Lion.

"You did? I distinctly remember we helped." Tin Man rubbed his dented chin.

Scarecrow interrupted. "Lost a few pieces and parts meself, I did."

Dorothy ignored their protests. "Now you send me back. I would have expected this from your sisters, the witches of west and east, but not you."

Glinda waved her wand and the girl's body tensed while her eyes continued to track the star-tipped stick.

"Well, you can't. Uh, uh, I won't let you. You can't make me," Dorothy said. "You can't make me do what I don't want to do."

The strength in her legs failed and Tin Man and Lion pulled her inexorably toward the hot air balloon where Oz beamed omnipotently.

"This is a public relations nightmare," Scarecrow growled at Tin Man. "It will take weeks to live this one down."

Glinda lowered her wand, blocking the last few steps.

She smiled at Dorothy. "I thought this was what you wanted. You always said: 'There's no place like home', didn't you?"

"I was being sarcastic. Have you ever been there? Well, have you?"

Glinda shook her head.

"It's grey. It's in black-and-white, for heaven's sake."

Glinda's mouth formed a small 'o.'

Oz entered the basket and held the door open for Dorothy to enter, but Lion and Tin Man had other ideas. They dumped her unceremoniously over the side.

Oz slammed the door shut while Tin Man chopped at the rope with his axe, and Lion bit through the opposite anchor line.

Oz fed the fire and the balloon swept majestically into the sky.

"No-o-o-o-o-o!"

Dorothy clambered into an upright position and watched Emerald City recede from view.

Scarecrow, Tin Man and Lion clapped each other on the back in a congratulatory gesture.

High above their heads, a voice reverberated. "No, no, Dorothy, no. Don't... don't do it."

A dot appeared in the heavens, a dot that grew in size and speed until it landed at their feet.

SPLAT!

Glinda the Good sniffed. "I guess she meant what she said."

Hags: So Mote It Be

The old woman clumped across the floor of the abandoned house, waiting for the contractors. A cane leaned against the wall. The crone wore the heavy orthopedic shoes of the aged and held a Zimmer frame in her hands. She pushed it before her and then waddled after it to catch up.

The floor creaked underneath her weight.

She sniffed and wondered why anyone in his right mind would attempt to fix the house and who, but the most corrupt, would contract to do the job. Better to tear down the structure and start from the beginning.

"What a dump," she muttered.

The roof – she gazed above her head – was collapsing. The woman squinted, peering through the disintegrating walls where termites chewed happily upon the studs. The supports were little more than dust.

The old woman kicked at the plaster and it dissolved into powder.

Even the sub floor was soft and spongy. She jumped with surprising agility and strength. The house shook, and a piece of ceiling fell to the floor.

The backdoor slammed open, dislodging another chunk of ceiling. "Babbs! What are you doing? The whole house trembled, and they're here now. We don't want to scare them away."

Babbs reassured her. "I know, dear, but I remember what you said: 'a forgone conclusion.' Don't worry. I'll get them."

She cocked her head to listen to the hum of the motor. "You have to get out of here or you'll ruin everything. Now, shoo, Maury. Outside. Hide."

Maury hopped through the door and vanished from view. A few minutes later a crow emerged from the misshapen shadows of the dying trees to study the ground intently, first with one glowing golden eye and then the other. The bird scratched, searching for grubs or any other critter that might make a good snack.

Babbs ignored the crow and examined the two contractors as they swaggered to the door. The brothers were tall, burly men, one heavy-set and the other muscular but lean. Like Jack Sprat and his wife.

The pudgy one knocked, and the door swung open of its own accord.

Both men stared apprehensively at the floor and stayed on the stoop. Their eyes took in the old woman. Josh spoke out of the corner of his mouth in forced stage whisper. "Hag."

Babbs stiffened and her fingers tightened on the walker.

The brothers leapt over the threshold, separating as they did so, with one moving to the right and the other to the left, for better distribution of weight on the weak floor. The three figures formed a lop-sided triangle around the pile of rubble.

"You must be the contractors," Babbs said.

Jason advanced cautiously and proffered the business card.

Babbs glanced down. "Oh, Johson and Johson."

He rubbed his nose. "Sorry, that's a typo."

The old woman shrugged. "I guess you don't have to know how to spell a builder, eh? That's most certainly not why we're hiring you, is it?" She studied one face and then the other. "You must be Jason," she said, "and you, Josh."

Jason bowed. "At your service."

"We were expecting someone, ah, a bit younger," said Josh.

"Oh, that's right. You spoke with my sister Maury. She's much younger than I am. Different mothers, don't you know."

Jason scanned the house. He gave her a greasy grin. "Quite a house you have here."

"I'll say," parroted Josh.

She ignored their comments. "I'm sorry. Maury couldn't make it. I'm here to get your bid."

Babbs began to shuffle around the room. The brothers winced at each step, watching the floorboards as they sagged under her weight. "Personally, I think she's crazy to buy this place," she said.

"Flipper?"

"No, just stupid. Maury is hoping to live here. I say burn it down to the ground, but she's a sentimentalist. She wants to save the place, says it has good bones. My creaking old bones are in better shape than the ones in this house, but you just can't talk her out of something once her mind is set. Price is no object, she says."

Both brothers beamed broadly.

"Well, we're the guys to do it," said Jason.

"I bet you are."

Josh thrust forward. "We can remodel or rebuild. Either way we will be happy to oblige. The customer is always right."

"Glad to hear you say that," Babbs said.

Then the men sauntered around the room, tape measure in hand, testing each board before they placed their weight on it.

They made slow progress around the room. Periodically, Jason jotted a figure down in his notebook.

"Now we need to check the rest of the house," he said.

"Go ahead. If you ask me, it's a complete gut job," Babbs assured them.

"Don't worry about it. Let us be the judge. We're the experts, after all," crooned Jason.

"I'm sure you are. Feel free. Break a leg."

Jason winced.

Instead of moving from room to room, the two men made a bee-line for the back door, descended to ground level and started to laugh.

Babbs lifted her walker and glided over to the broken window. She stationed herself next to the cane, took out a compact and pretended to fix her hair. She watched their reflections in the mirror and listened intently.

"What a joke!" Josh said. "The old woman is right. Better to blow this place up than fix it."

Jason held is fingers next to his lips. "Shush. It's not the old woman we need to please. It's her sister." He paused to consider the crumbling building. "I'd say this place is a gold mine. All we'd have to do is patch the hole in the roof, so it looks good, slap up some dry rock and paint it."

"But," Josh protested. He pulled at a piece of siding and it fell apart in his hand. "This place has termites. Here you can see the tunnels. The studs, joists and sub floor all need to be the replaced."

"We'll figure that into the quote, termite treatment, stud replacement, joists, roof, sheetrock, paint. The lot."

Josh looked doubtful. "This building would collapse as soon as someone tried to rent it."

"Didn't say we'd actually do it, did I? What do these old dears know about construction? Let's go back inside and give her our bid." Jason wrote a number on his pad and showed it to his brother.

Josh's eyes widened, and he nodded. "I like it."

Babbs was still fussing with her hair, her cane now resting on the walker, when the boys entered. They approached her from both sides. Jason handed her the piece of paper. "That's our bid, although if we find anything else wrong it could go up."

"It's an absolute steal," Babbs sneered.

Josh stalked around the woman and stood next to his brother.

"What about the plumbing and electrical? Does this price cover it?"

"No," Jason said. "I'll call and get bids from the plumbers and electricians and adjust the estimate accordingly. My best guess would be between ten- to fifteen-thousand dollars."

He gazed at her, waiting for a response.

She remained silent.

"We are good Christians," Jason said. "You can trust us. We won't surprise you with hidden fees. Everything up front. Once I talk to a plumber and an electrician, we can meet with your sister. For now, the estimate covers termite inspection, roof, dry wall, studs, new cabinets in the kitchen and bath, and other cosmetics like painting."

"Hmmm," Babbs said. "I'm pretty sure my sister will want to speak with you."

The brothers exchanged glances.

She seized her cane, raised it high and gave each of the contractors a round-house wallop before they had time to react.

Jason and Josh dropped to their knees. She hit them again, and they folded against each other.

"Maury!"

Her sister appeared and handed Babbs a roll of duct tape. Soon the bothers were trussed up like pigs, with arms and legs taped together from wrist to elbow and ankle to knee.

They straightened to survey their work. "All they need is an apple stuffed in their mouths," said Babbs.

Maury ducked her head in assent. She extracted a couple of filthy rags from their pockets, stuffed one in each mouth and wrapped duct tape around their heads. "It's tempting to cover their noses."

Maury passed the tape to Babbs.

The older sister examined it. "This is such marvelous stuff. So handy. So strong."

"No time to ponder modern conveniences. They could wake up soon," said Maury.

As if on cue, Jason groaned and Josh stirred.

Maury kicked Jason in the head with her hob-nailed boots while Babbs slammed Josh again with her cane.

"Did you get the keys?"

Maury patted their pockets until one jingled. She grimaced as she dug around in the pocket. She showed the keys to her sister. "Men, such nasty things. Heaven only knows what else they have in their pockets."

Babbs prodded Jason's crotch. The women twittered.

"Let's move them. You take the truck and I'll take the car," said Babbs. "Quite obliging of them to bring their tools. They'll come in handy."

"I asked them to bring their tools," Maury said.

"Nice touch."

"I thought so."

*

The truck pulled into the driveway first, followed by Babbs's grey sedan. She stopped just inside the solid wooden gate and closed it. The surrounding hedges gave the sisters complete privacy.

"*Bang, bang, bang, bang!*"

"Noisy aren't they?" Maury said as she climbed down from the cab and met her sister who was carrying walker and cane up the drive.

"*Murmph, murmph, murmph.*"

"Shut up!" Babbs shouted.

The boys fell silent when they recognized her voice.

"I'll give you Josh. He's the smaller of the two. You are eldest after all," said Maury.

"Right, you're always shoving that in my face."

Maury dropped the tailgate.

Babbs grabbed Josh's feet and stopped. "How did you know their names? Where were you?"

Maury plucked a black feather from her sleeve. "Oh, you know. I was hanging around."

148

Babbs watched the feather ride the currents down to the ground. "Don't get caught, dear."

"Oh, come on, how long have we been doing this?" Maury grasped Jason's ankles.

"Well, this time I won't argue," Babbs said.

The sisters tugged at their charges until their feet dangled from the bed of the pickup. The men struggled against their captors.

"I've got my cane," Babbs warned. She stretched her arm out, made a clasping motion, and the stick shot into her hand.

The brothers went limp.

The sisters gave a final yank to pull them from the truck. The boys fell, their heads hitting the concrete with a crack.

"Such a satisfying sound," said Maury.

"We'd better be careful. We might addle their wits," commented Babbs.

"What wits?"

The sisters giggled and dragged their charges the fifteen feet to the cellar door, opened it and continued down to the basement.

Their heads struck each step.

Smack, bounce. *Smack,* bounce. *Smack,* bounce. *Smack,* bounce. *Smack,* bounce.

They dumped the contractors on the basement floor.

"I'm tired," said Babbs. "I'd like a cup of tea."

"I'd prefer a cup of coffee."

"Well, I'm not going to make it for you," grumbled Babbs.

"I know. I know. You're old and tired. I'll go get your walker and your cane. Wouldn't want you to strain yourself."

"Better watch it, or I'll set your hair on fire."

"I remember. You did that to me when we were kids." Maury paused. "I must compliment you, though. You make the perfect feeble, little-old lady."

"I thought so."

*

Maury and Babbs came thumping up the stairs from the basement to the kitchen to be greeted by a string of invectives.

Calley glared at the snow and static emanating from the crystal. "Why you—" She lifted her arm to fling the offending article away from her.

149

"Ah!" Babbs scolded their sisters, as she would when the cats misbehaved.

The warning came too late. The ball left Calley's fingers, but Maury snatched it from the air with a deft movement. She stared at the picture that had suddenly righted itself.

"They've got me on hold!" Calley said, incensed.

A recording of eldritch shrieks, rattling chains and heart-rending moans played in an astonished *vibrato* after Calley's violent shaking.

There was a click as the recording switched tracks. The screeches and howls were replaced by a lilting ditty of New Age positivity and enthusiasm, designed for the modern Wiccan. Calley stuck her finger down her throat at the fanciful duet of lute and flute and gagged.

"Do you know many of crystals you have smashed in the last ten years? You are costing us a fortune," Babbs said.

"Well, they shouldn't put me on hold then," Calley sulked. "A nice, respectable woman like me."

Babbs suppressed a smile. "It *is* annoying, dear. Who were you calling? Can't it wait?"

"The Dracaena Emporium," said Calley. "We are almost out of dragon's blood, tooth, tongue and claw, and I sit on hold while these cretins fill orders for chamomile tea."

Crackle, hisssss!

The video showing fields of frolicking fawns and frouncy flowers changed, and a young woman made up to look like a witch – complete with hook nose, warts, green skin, wig made of straw and conical cap – appeared in the clear quartz.

The apparition threw her head back, cackled and intoned: "Your call is very important to us. There are one-hundred-and-five callers ahead of you. We are working very hard filling your needs. Please, don't zap us."

With more maniacal laughter, the face vanished, and the image of the idyllic scene returned.

Calley was up and out of her chair, fingers clawing at the air, in an instant. "Gimme that thing, I'm gonna kill it."

Maury wrapped her arms around Calley's waist to hold her back.

"One-hundred-and-fifth caller?" said Babbs. "This can wait, then. We have other business."

She set the crystal on its stand and the dancing deer winked out.

Calley relaxed and Maury released her.

Calley peered curiously at Babbs. "Oh, goody, is it something fun?"

"We thought so."

The women sat around the kitchen table.

Babbs, the eldest and leader, tapped her mug on the table. "I call the fifteen-thousand-six-hundred and fifty-sixth meeting of the Crones Club to order."

Brigdh protested. "Do you have to do that? Number the meetings. We know we're old. You don't have to rub it in."

Calley eyed her sister. "Brey, since when have you gotten so sensitive about your age? It's called the Crones Club for a reason."

"I'm not sensitive. I just don't see why we have to count them," she mumbled into her mug."

Babbs interrupted. "Let's get to business. What did you find in the court records?"

"These guys have been sued any number of times for shoddy workmanship. No criminal charges though."

"Macha, what did you discover searching through police reports?"

"One complaint was filed for assault." She distributed the reports. "Unfortunately, the woman did what most women do in the same situation. She waited too long to report it and she bathed to rid herself of their foul stench. No physical exam was conducted. The police took the report. When they confronted the two brothers, each corroborated the other. Two witnesses against one. No further investigation was conducted. It's all here. I'll give you time to read it."

Macha contemplated her notes. "Oh, yes, and I see here the police knew them. Hunting and fishing buddies. One cop was a family member. I doubt the officers would have believed the victim or done anything even if she had filmed the incident."

The sisters glared at the table.

"Typical," said Maury.

"I also found the documentation about the old woman," said Macha. "No mention of the contractors, though. The crime has been passed off as a home invasion. Perpetrator unknown. Since she died of her injuries and had no living relatives, they closed the case. Why waste police time when no one cares?"

She handed copies of the second police report to each one of her sisters.

Calley's eyes widened as she skimmed the report. "They did that! To an eighty-eight-year-old woman? Sons of bitches."

Babbs comforted her. "That's why we're here."

She turned to her left. "Mora, you were the one who discovered the woman in the hospital and overheard when hospital staff catalogued her injuries to the police. Did you get a chance to," Babbs waggled her fingers, "do your magic?"

"Not while she was still alive. I wasn't allowed to visit her in intensive care since I wasn't a family member. However, as a friend of the family I did get a chance to be alone with her for a viewing in the hospital after she died."

Mora reached to either side and clasped the hands of the nearest sister. All joined in the circle. Mora sent the images of her attackers and gave them a glimpse of what the victim experienced.

When she dropped their hands, silence descended on the group.

Macha snorted. "She was poor. She was widowed. She had no assets besides a ramshackle house badly in need of repair, and she called these bar-stewards in. Now she'll go to a pauper's grave, and her home will go the state because she had no will and no heirs."

"There's more," Mora said. "You may not have noticed this, considering the rest of the atrocities, but I believe it is pertinent."

Again the women linked hands. After a moment, Mora let go of their hands, breaking the link.

Calley blinked. "She trusted them because they were self-proclaimed Christians." She closed her eyes and rubbed them.

"They said that to us too." Babbs pointed to herself and Maury. "So, let them be judged under Christian laws."

"Oo, oo, oo." Macha raised her hand and waved it around. "I've got something about that. May I direct your attention to page six of the police report?"

"Sit still. No need to wiggle about like that," Babbs said. "We'll listen."

Macha pouted. "The police reports for the young woman mention that also."

The women read.

"This young girl trusted them because they professed to be Christians?" Calley scowled.

"Did we do any damage control?"

"Too late for this young lady. She lost her home. It was repossessed. She committed suicide, but I would ask Mora to send her sweet dreams," Macha said.

"Done," said Mora, "as soon as I get a chance. I did wipe the memories from the old woman's mind, so she can meet her maker no longer haunted by her last minutes on earth."

"Thank you, Mora, and if you could take care of this other matter." Babbs grimaced. "Tonight we have other work to do."

Maury glowered at her empty mug.

Brey stood and stamped over to the counter. "More brandy?"

"Yes, please," said Babbs.

"Yes, fill it to the brim." Maury proffered her mug.

One after another, they extended their cups for a top up.

"Maury and I can confirm that these are the same men we met this afternoon," said Babbs. "They boasted about being good Christians, therefore honorable. You all know that old house is falling down. It needs to be razed. The contractors commented on each potential job. They assured us that they'd get it treated for termites, replace the roof, the sub floor, the joists, the sheet rock, new cabinets and paint, and they'd subcontract the wiring and the plumbing, if needed. Their price was outrageous, even before they tacked on their guess-timates for plumbing and electrical; but Johson and Johson had no intention of doing anything more than cover the hole in the roof, patch the walls and paint. We both heard them."

Maury agreed. "Yep, they decided to put lipstick on this pig."

"Johson and Johson?" Brey asked.

Babbs tossed the business card to the center of the table. "That's what they call themselves on this. Evidently the brothers don't know how to spell their own name."

Maury chuckled, a deep, throaty growl. "That's comforting. Johson and Johson, So-called Handyman Services.

Brey choked on her libation. "So-called Handyman?"

All six checked the business name. So-co Handyman.

"I didn't come up with that." Maury shrugged. "I heard it on their voice mail. Don't ask me why it says that, but it seems the message is the only honest thing about these brothers. It's appropriate, don't you think? I recorded the telephone conversation. Would you like to listen to it?"

Babbs nodded. "It pertains."

Before she started the recorder, Maury clarified. "I used the name of the young woman as a reference."

"How," piped up Macha, "did know you her name? You hadn't read the police reports yet."

Babbs blew loudly between her lips. "This is Morrigan, after all."

Maury placed the digital recorder on the table. The male voice identified itself as belonging to Jason. Maury introduced herself and mentioned the woman. The conversation grew muffled. It was clear that the speaker was shouting to someone in the background.

"Hey, Josh, she recommended us."

A distant voice responded: "You are kidding."

"Evidently she liked our work." He gave an evil chuckle.

"Oh, I'm sorry," said Jason, "We do like to get referrals from satisfied customers. Do you mind if I put your call on speaker? I think my brother would like to listen to this."

"No problem," Maury purred.

"We did a bang-up job for her. I can say that for a fact." Again a vile laugh echoed through the telephone line. "For certain clients we like to go the extra mile. That is the main thrust of our operation, customer satisfaction. Perhaps we can do the same for you."

A second voice interrupted the conversion. "Are you as, um, nice as she is?"

"I would like to think so," said Maury.

The women twittered. "That's a good one," Mora said.

Maury shot her a dirty look. Her voice resounded from the recorder. "Oh, yes, I heard all about your thrust."

"Pardon?" Josh squeaked.

Maury forged ahead. "I'd like to get an estimate."

"Oh, don't worry about that," Jason said. "My brother and myself are good God-fearing Christians. We don't charge for an estimate. You can rely on us. We'll do a good job for you, I promise."

Maury snapped the digital player off. "He showed absolutely no remorse. As nice as the young lady, indeed."

Macha sniggered.

Babbs chortled. "Sure, you are as pretty as a twenty-year-old."

Maury snorted. "I believe you could say I'm well preserved."

"Well pickled you mean," commented Babbs

Maury gave an impish grin. "That too. Where's that brandy?"

Brey passed the jug.

Babbs sobered. "The judgement?"

"Guilty," the women chorused.

"Since they are Christians, we should judge these young men in terms they will understand. Charges?"

"Adulterer, fornicator," said Maury.

"Thief," said Macha.

"Liar," Mora snarled.

"Fraud," Brey said.

"Murderer," Babbs whispered.

"It's unanimous then," Maury said.

Babbs stood to pronounce the judgment: "So mote it be."

Brey frowned. "At times like this, I know why we switched from children."

"Hell." Maury wiped her sticky, wet lips on her sleeve. "You can't pry kids away from their video games long enough to walk next to a river."

"Texting may provide new opportunities," Macha countered. "Kids can now take their games outside. They never watch where they're going. Pretty soon they'll stroll into the rivers all by themselves. We won't even be needed."

"We aren't. That's why we changed our line of work," said Mora.

Maury noted: "I told you ages ago. I told you what was coming. I predicted that crime would be institutionalized, condoned, even celebrated. The only recourse a victim has is to file a civil suit. Usually, the cost represents money they don't have after they have spent it all for shoddy repairs."

The women grunted.

Maury continued: "I told you then we would risk our own lives if we stayed in the old country and upheld the old ways. The disappearance of children is noticed nowadays. The little monsters are protected. In days of yore, many parents were relieved to be rid of extraneous kids."

Calley concurred. "The switch from child to adult was necessary. You might say it was even providential and most gratifying."

"What I don't understand is why do we have to do this?" Brey indicated the piles of papers and the digital recorder.

"I understand your frustration, Brey," Babbs said. "And don't think I don't know what you do when you discover a bad man on the streets. You squeeze the life out of them. It's usually diagnosed as natural causes, a heart attack or a stroke. I trust your judgment. I even applaud your efforts. I don't mind if you give their brains a bit of a stir either."

Babbs swung on Calley. "And you push them into the street under the wheels of a car, or you freeze them."

Calley thrust her chin out. "I don't touch them."

"I know you don't," said Babbs. "But frostbite? In July?"

"It is my special gift," Calley exclaimed.

"And hitting them with a bolt of lightning on a sunny day, Brey. Really? Frozen fingers, frozen toes are okay in the wintertime, but not when it's ninety degrees outside, or lightning when there isn't a cloud in the sky. This tends to be noticed. The least you could do is wait for rain."

"But I might lose them," Brey glared at her sibling. "And you," she stabbed her finger at Babbs, "already said that I couldn't follow them."

Babbs sighed and spoke to the group. "Don't forget, there are closed circuit cameras everywhere."

She stood and laid her hands flat on the table. "All I'm saying is use some discretion. If there are too many of these mysterious incidents and your face appears on CCTV every time, where would we be? Calley, no more frostbite in the summertime; find something else. Brey, you have other talents, use them, or give 'em a nudge under the wheels of a car like Calley does, but before you do anything make sure you are not under surveillance. We are not like vampires. Our faces show up. Only Mora has the ability to remain sight unseen so necessary to her craft."

Babbs tapped the pile of papers on the table "This is different. The only way we can fit the punishment to the crime is by grabbing them from the street, so we can work someplace isolated and safe. If we snatched every wicked man from the streets will-nilly, their disappearance would be noted."

Maury interrupted: "Don't forget what happened to our cousins Jenny Green and Peg Powler. Lynched, both of them, by the mob. I told you we must be careful in this mechanized, digitalized world to continue our work."

Babbs considered for a moment. "Think of all the good we have done. Nobody bothers us. You remember the wife beater which the police refused to investigate despite the number of reports she filed. We had the paperwork. It let us fit the punishment to the crime. We made sure he would never strike or kick anyone ever again. Now *that* was justice."

Macha's eyes lit up. "His limbs sure looked funny when we released him."

Babbs went on: "Safety, our safety, is the reason why we wear the masks and use voice scramblers, so we won't be recognized or reported should they get away."

"Besides the masks scare the crap out'a them," added Maury.

Babbs glared at her sister and continued: "Even if the batterer was able to identify us as women, do you think he'd report it to his buddies? A big, strong, young cop overpowered by a bunch of senior citizens? Of course not, and if he did, he'd be laughed off the force."

"The grannies from hell." Mora snickered.

Maury elbowed her and giggled.

"Well, we have our verdict. What about punishment? I know."

Calley held a single finger in the air. "Let's slit their throats, hang 'em upside down like hogs and drain 'em,"

Babbs vetoed the suggestion. "Too easy. We want them to remember this experience as long as they live."

"Shouldn't be long, then," muttered Macha.

"Agreed," Babbs said.

"Why don't we rip out their nails, so they can't scratch their asses?" Calley mimed with a pair of pliers.

"Nails grow back and that wouldn't cover the full gamut of their crimes."

Unwilling to give up an idea, Calley countered. "Pull their nails out, slit their throats and then hang them upside. We could bathe in their blood and keep ourselves looking beautiful."

"Put them on the rack," Macha proposed.

"They're already on the rack, dear."

"Burn them with hot irons," Maury recommended.

"I like it," said Babbs. "Do they have one of those soldering machines in their tool kits?"

The sisters shrugged.

"Has anyone seen the Judas Cradle?" asked Mora.

"We're going to use their tools," Babbs said. "It seems fitting, and they got the push broom and the rake, so they... ah, er... get the point."

"How about the metal coffin? We can hang 'em in a cage outside and the crows –" the sisters traded significant glances "– can pick 'em apart."

Babbs considered for a moment. "And have them shouting all the time? The neighbors would complain, and the cops would come and arrest us. No, I say let us rely on an older code upon which Christian doctrine is based for punishment. Let us borrow from our old friend Hammurabi."

Brey went misty-eyed. "He was nice, wasn't he?"

"Not really," Maury snarled. "He just organized tyranny."

"Yummy." Brey mouthed the word.

Maury rolled her eyes toward the ceiling. "You always were a bit man-crazy."

"Am not."

"Are too."

"Girls, girls, don't bicker," said Babbs.

"So now what?" Calley inquired. "Babbs, Maury, do you need to meet Johson and Johson So-called Handyman again to entice them here?"

"Well, I'm sure we could get them here as long as there was money involved, but it's not necessary. We've a Morrigan." Babbs beamed her approval at her sister. "She knew the outcome."

Maury explained her role in the capture. "I rode shot gun and drove the company truck back here where it would not be seen."

"The young men seemed a bit disappointed when they saw me, though. Called me a hag." The women burst out laughing. Babbs waited for a moment, wiped her eyes and said: "Their disappointment was soon assuaged after they met Matilda."

Babbs rapped the floor with the heavy steel cane.

"Good old Matilda," said Maury.

"Clever girl," said Calley.

"We brought the bodies into the house and got them downstairs. Trussed 'em up as pretty as you please and stretched them out. If you don't mind, girls, there are tool boxes still in the bed of the pick-up. We'll need them. I think I saw a couple of saws, a drill, a sander, a push-broom and rake." Babbs gazed at her sisters over the rim of her glasses.

"An eye for an eye."

The four women tromped out the back door.

As soon as they exited the building, Brey began to complain. "Why do *we* have to do this? I say they brought the truck. They should unload it."

"They did, or we'd have to carry the men too," said Mora.

"Yes, but she's always bossing us around. 'Do this. Do that.'" Brey twisted her features to a passing fair imitation of Babbs's. "No lightning bolts when it's sunny and no frostbite in the summer. Who does she think she is?"

"I heard that." Babbs's voice drifted down from the kitchen window.

"She's the goddesssss of war," Macha hissed in her sister's ear.

The crones began to unload the truck. One grabbed the push-broom and the rake. They looked around for the tool boxes and found them chained and padlocked to the sides of the truck.

"No lightning without rain. Screw that," Brey snarled.

"You could always stir of up storm," Mora suggested gently.

"Too complicated, too tiring."

Lightning tore through the heavens and zapped the chains. They melted.

The sisters ran forward and yanked the boxes away from the molten metal.

"Where's the damn power tools?" said Calley.

"I guess in that big box near the cab," Macha said.

"I suppose it's locked too," Brey said. The sky parted a second time.

Calley stepped forward and provided a frosty breeze to cool the lid.

"Let it go, girls," said Macha, "let it go."

The women returned to the kitchen, tool boxes and tools dancing before them.

"Lifting heavy men, indeed," Brey sneered. "These are heavy too."

Babbs observed, "We didn't cheat like you are. Where's the fun in that?"

"Their heads made such a lovely crunching sound when they slammed on the concrete and banged against step after step, after step, after step," Maury said.

Rancor forgotten, the women roared with laughter.

"Please," gasped Mora, "don't do that. I ain't as young as I used to be."

She lowered the toolbox to the ground.

Each one of the sisters released their hold on their load, which went crashing to the floor.

Babbs winced. "So who wants to see what Maury and I baked up earlier?"

"Yes, please." Macha clapped her hands.

"We're such good cooks," crowed Maury.

Babbs smiled, revealing teeth as sharp as knives.

"I thought so."

*

The women donned the black cloaks that hung over the backs of their chairs and headed for the basement.

The sisters hefted the tool boxes and hurled them down the stairs.

Crash! Crash! Crash!

"That ought to wake them up," said Macha.

Calley was about to do the same with the power tools when Babbs stopped her. "No, some are gas-powered... They might explode. All it would take is one spark, metal hitting metal. This is no night for a fire show, and the electrical tools could break too."

Calley floated the power tools down the stairs.

Just inside the cellar door, they grabbed their masks from their hooks. They were plain linen like the executioners' masks of long ago. The women pulled them over their heads and adjusted the cloth so the voice scramblers were positioned over their mouths. Then they covered their heads with the black hoods.

Babbs thudded down the stairs, banging the cane on each tread.

The contractors' screams were muffled by the gags. The skin around the tape was bloody where they had tried to tear away their bonds.

"Mora, dear, can you help keep them quiet? They are giving me a headache," said Calley.

Mora dropped down on all fours, crept over to Jason and jumped on his chest. She stroked his head and crooned a lullaby. Her voice was raucous, like the warning cry of the crow.

She continued caressing the battered brow and Jason stilled. She sent him visions of what his future may be. His eyelids fluttered. She stroked his cheek until he fell into a sleep filled with dreams of terror.

Mora leapt from Jason's chest to his brother's. Josh's eyes popped open and he struggled. She stared into them and sang her song. She petted him. His head thrashed from side to side. She rode him like a bronco. Eventually he succumbed to her caresses. She linked the two minds to one so they could share the same dream.

Mora climbed down, wiping her hands on her skirt. "I think that will keep them for a while."

"Okay, Jason first. He's the worst. He's the eldest, and I suspect he's the ringleader. Then Josh."

The women tore the tape from arms, wrists, legs and ankles, exchanging them for shackles. The brothers moaned in unison; their eyes fluttered. Mora reinforced her spell.

The sisters pulled the heavy chains taut, first with brute force, then when strength failed, they used a crowbar as a lever. They anchored the chain closest to the wrists to a loop in the floor and then repeated the procedure on his legs.

Jason began to stir and Mora, still sitting on the floor between them, placed a hand on his forehead and reinforced her dire lullaby.

"Should we leave them alone for a bit?" Brey said.

"Mora?"

"Oh, they are having lovely dreams. They should stay under for a while."

"What did you send them?" asked Calley

"The verdict," Mora said.

"Lovely."

"Who wants a bicky?" Brey opened a tin and offered it to her sisters.

161

The women lifted their masks to take one delicate bite at a time while they contemplated their captives.

"Let's give them a few more minutes to consider their crimes," Babbs said.

"And imagine their punishments," added Mora.

Calley chuffed and hopped down from the freezer. "I'm getting bored."

"We really must treat their wounds. They look nasty where we relieved them of a layer of skin," suggested Brey.

"Of course, we mustn't be negligent," said Babbs. "Who brought the rubbing alcohol?"

"I did," said Macha. "And a little brandy in case things get rough."

"Thank you," said Maury. "We may need refreshment."

"Never amiss," agreed Babbs.

"I thought so."

*

"Ahem, ahem," *tap, tap, tap.* "Testing, testing, one, two. Is this damn thing working? Isn't it supposed to change your voice?" Babbs complained.

"Yes, dear, it does. You sound positively diabolical," said Calley.

"Don't trust these newfangled devices. I sound just like myself inside my head."

"I should hope so," Maury commented dryly.

"Don't you sass me," Babbs snapped. "Okay, ladies, surgical spirit at the ready?"

The women raised their bottles.

"Go ahead. Treat those wounds!"

The sisters saturated their rags and wrung them out over the contractors' faces and their arms.

Two pairs of eyes popped open. Two brains – or maybe, one-and-a-half – immediately regretted the decision as the liquid ran into their eyes. Two heads thrashed around. Two of the sisters knelt near the assigned brother to hold their faces steady.

The tape over their mouths grew taut as the men tried to curse.

The women applied themselves vigorously to their saturated cloths. Each tiny scratch, each wound and any area rubbed raw by chain or tape received the utmost attention, with spirit liberally applied. Then they poured a little extra over the injuries, just in case they missed a spot.

The ladies dropped the heads. The contractors whipped back and forth.

"Well, looky there, they are ruining all our hard work," Macha said.

"That's all right, we can always reapply," said Brey.

Both men froze.

"I prefer the ninety-nine percent solution. Far more effective," said Babbs.

"I thought so."

*

"Ahem, ahem..." *tap, tap, tap...* "Testing, testing, one, two."

"Quit being such an old fuddy duddy. You already did that."

"They are awake now. I want to make sure they can hear." Babbs pointed at the contractors.

"If we can hear you, they can hear you." Maury leered at the contractors and waggled the bottle of rubbing alcohol over their heads. "They can hear you all right. Right, boys?"

They tried to sit up.

"Don't do yourselves an injury that we will have to clean," Babbs crooned.

They stopped.

"Um, okay, it is the decree of our committee that you have violated the laws of God and man. As Christians you were tried. Since one law is often established on a previous one, your punishments are based on Hammurabi's code, an eye for an eye, a tooth for a tooth." Babbs examined the contractors' faces. "And as Christians, you are no doubt familiar with the Bible."

Neither man moved.

"I told you. They can't hear me," Babbs hissed.

"Oh, they can hear you," said Macha. "Look at their expressions, they are scared shitless."

Babbs glowered, not recalling that no one could see her face. "Are you familiar with the ten commandments?"

Their eyes were fixed on Babbs.

Behind her, Maury held the surgical spirit aloft.

"Girls, get closer. You blink once for yes, twice for no."

Blink.

Blink.

Babbs forged ahead. "The first commandment as outlined in Exodus states. Thou shalt have no other god before me. Secondly, it prohibits the worship of graven images. You have forsaken your God and placed your love of money above all things, and the faces found on money before the image of your Lord. Sisters exact the punishment."

The hooded figures advanced, scissors snipping, and went to work on their blue jeans.

Snip, snip, snip. Rip, rrrrrrrip!

Johson and Johson tried to fight back.

"Watch it," said Mora. "You wouldn't want to lose anything you truly love, would you?"

She observed two sets of Adams' apples bob up and down.

Snip, snip. RIP. Rip, rrrrrrrip!

The women retreated. Jason and Josh relaxed when they realized they had only lost their pockets."

"No doubt you are thinking that you can have your wives fix your trousers. Perish the thought," Mora warned. "I imagine these women work hard enough as it is."

"You have also defied the tenet 'Thou shalt not steal.' This rule is not limited to theft of another's property. It includes taking advantage of the ignorance or hardship of another. Work poorly done. Excessive claims of expenses. Its precepts require that contracts and promises be strictly observed. Girls..."

Four women shuffled forward to stand beside the four concrete blocks placed besides the men.

"For the crime of incompetent workmanship..."

The dark figures stooped to pick up their blocks and straightened. Babbs made a quick slashing sign in the air. The women dropped their burdens upon the men's arms.

There was the sound of crunching bones. One block missed its mark, bounced and landed on Jason's abdomen.

"Oops," said Calley

"No problem. Try again and, this time, don't raise it up so high. If you have any doubts, use it like a hammer," said Babbs.

"With pleasure." The hag applied herself diligently to her task.

Crunch, crunch, crunch.

"I think that should do it. You don't want to sprain something, dear. Now everyone check the arms. If any bones remain intact, get cracking."

The women manhandled the men, twisting their arms this way and that, and then used hammers and heavy wrenches to complete the job.

"For the crime of fraudulent contracts," Babbs started and then paused. "Who has the tourniquets?"

A woman advanced bearing ropes and sticks.

Unable to move their arms, all the contractors could do was watch helplessly as ropes were tied around their wrists and tightened until their fingers turned blue.

A hand twitched at Babbs's robes. "There's only two tin snips," said Macha.

"We can share," Babbs replied.

Macha handed a pair of snips to each group, one for Jason, another for Josh.

Two sets of eyes focused on their hands.

"*A sinistra,*" Babbs shouted

Snip, pinky; *snip,* ring finger; *snip,* middle finger; *snip,* index finger. *SNIIIPPPP,* thumb.

The brothers passed out.

"Ferchrissakes. Men are such wimps nowadays. Remember back in the time of the Titans. Now those were men!" said Brey.

Mora and Macha obligingly began slapping the brothers while Brey and Maury removed the wedding bands from their ring fingers, bit them and added them to the pile with the other rings they had collected through the years. The fingers were discarded on the drain.

Babbs strode forward and splashed alcohol on their hands and faces. "Wakey. Wakey. We wouldn't want you to miss any of the fun."

She retreated and gave her command. "*A droit,*"

The tin snips were passed over the bodies from left to right.

"They haven't roused yet. Shall we wait?"

"No, let's get this done. They'll just faint again."

Snip, pinky; *snip,* ring finger; *snip,* middle finger; *snip,* index finger. *SNIIIPPPP,* thumb.

"Now they'll have to use their stumps to wipe their asses," said Maury.

The women giggled and tightened the tourniquets.

"Who's for a break? This is thirsty work," Macha said.

"Ooooh, that sounds nice."

The women rose with a crackling of old bones. They pulled down their hoods and divested themselves of the executioner's masks and turned their backs on their prisoners.

Each seized an eight-ounce tumbler and stretched out their hands.

Brey filled her sisters' first and then her own. She pouted. "We're all out of brandy."

"I told you we should have gotten a keg for down here," groused Maury.

"Always complaining," Babbs said. "Just for that, you can be the next to refill the carafe."

"Jeez, let me at least get a couple of sips first."

Babbs ducked her head in assent.

The women toasted the men, threw their heads back and gulped at the brew. They emptied their tumblers in a few seconds and slammed them down on the counter.

Maury wiped her lips on her cloak. "Okay, I'll get some more." She bowed with a flourish. "Ladies, I'll be back."

The women began to paw through the tools that were scattered across the floor.

"They have plenty of razor knives. A total of six. There's one for each of us. Wouldn't want you to miss all the fun, Babbs," reported Macha.

Maury returned carrying two milk jugs full of brandy. "We shouldn't have to be climbing up and down a bunch of stairs at our age."

"Hah."

"I found a jig saw, reciprocating saw and a circular saw," Mora said.

"We have a chain saw," said Calley.

"We have crucible tongs. Now that's Biblical," Brey added.

"Clamps. Quite a few." Babbs piled her prizes between the brothers' legs.

"Vise-grips," Brey said.

"Adjustable spanners." Macha held up several.

"Standard pliers and needle-nose pliers," Brey said.

"Alligator clips!" Babbs shouted triumphantly.

"Alligator clips? What good are alligator clips? They're too small to be any good," protested Brey.

"Have you forgotten just how slippery tongues can be?"

"Ah, true. Remember the year when," she glanced over her shoulder to make sure the brothers had not awakened, "Macha lost her hand? Until it grew back, of course."

"Ah, I don't use them that much. My gift," she tapped her forehead with her index finger, "is all in the mind."

Periodically, one or the other of the sisters went to replenish their drinks.

Babbs peered myopically at the contents. "Good grief, Maury, didn't you even think to rinse the milk jugs? Were you born in a cave?"

"I was, and so were you," Maury retorted.

Babbs made a wry face. "Okay, we all were, but proprieties. Brandy should never be contaminated by milk."

Maury belched. "I thought the chunks would give it a bit of body."

As the evening progressed, their gait became a bit more unsteady.

"We need some nourishment," chimed Macha. "Where are those gingerbread men I brought down?"

The box was passed around. The crones nibbled genteelly at the biscuits, biting off the heads first. They swilled their brandy with gusto.

"Empty." Maury up-ended the jug and tossed it to Babbs.

Mora followed suit. "Empty."

Babbs stomped up the stairs. "Hope you don't mind if I rinse the jugs. Bits of clotted milk in the brandy, my word!"

Maury made a raspberry.

"Sister, you have no couth." Babbs shambled up the stairs carrying the empty jugs. A few minutes later she came bouncing down the stairs on her bottom. "That's fun. You ought to try it."

Maury prodded the nearest sister. "And she talks about proprieties."

"Better than falling down and breaking me crown." Babbs stuck her tongue out at Maury.

"That was Jack."

"Well, Jill came tumbling after, although I can well imagine that she did it with more grace than Jack did."

167

Babbs made a wobbly curtsey toward Maury. "I stand corrected."

Maury preened.

Eventually the brandy was gone and the jugs empty.

"What the hell *are* they doing?" Calley demanded.

"Playing 'possum?" suggested Brey. The crones began to cackle.

When the guffaws descended to gasps, those with some breath ran to the top of the stairs and bounced down the steps.

"She's right; that is fun."

Babbs nodded.

"I thought so."

*

The women woke to the sound of their own snoring.

Babbs raised her head gingerly and then punched the person next to her. "I think I see eyes."

"Of course, you do. We all have eyes. Even our friends, Johson and Johson So-called Handymen, have eyes."

"I mean the gleam of open eyes." Babbs leaned forward and squinted. "And, aw, cheeks glistening with tears. Isn't that sweet? They're crying."

She yanked the executioner's mask over her blue-rinse hair.

Scratching under their robes, sputtering and coughing, the others prepared themselves.

Babbs took up her position as leader. "Everyone pick the tools you need."

There were a few moments of confusion and bickering until the crones got themselves sorted.

Babbs completed the verdict. "For violating the commandment: Thou shalt not bear false witness, which includes in its definition promises made with no intent to fulfill them."

The women ripped the tape from the men's mouths. Their lips began to bleed.

"… also slander. One is guilty of calumny who harms the reputation of others and gives occasion for false judgments by remarks contrary to the truth. These sins violate both the commandment against false witness, as well as Christ's command to love one's neighbor as oneself."

Calley and Macha extracted the rags from their mouths, and the brothers began to shriek in earnest.

"A lying tongue is an abomination and shall be torn from you, for is it not said: 'If thine eye offends thee, pluck it out.'" Babbs held her hand up as she concentrated her attention on the brothers. "You are also convicted of taking the Lord's name in vain, for you falsely asserted your Christianity to convince the unwary of your honesty. Thus, we shall cleave your tongue from your throat."

Brey chased the slippery tongue around inside the mouth of her intended victim with the crucible tongs.

He clamped down.

"Maury, will you do the honors?"

Brey grabbed Jason's jaws and forced them apart.

Maury's cloak deflated, and she appeared in the form of a crow. She clamped down on the tongue with her beak and tugged at it until it was fully extended. Babbs swooped in with the alligator clamps and attached them.

"Saw or snips?" Mora asked.

"Whichever is fastest. I'd say snips."

The tongue was severed from its root and thrown upon the drain.

Maury hopped over to Josh and waited until the women could pry his jaws apart.

Maury transformed to her human form and stood stark naked, spitting and wiping her tongue with her hands. "Awk! Awk! Pah-tu, pah-tu, pah-tui. That was disgusting."

"I know, dear," said Babbs. "Thank you, though. It does help."

Maury genuflected to the group. The women gave her a smattering of applause.

"Can I have the eyes?" she asked eagerly.

"Of course, you can. You've earned them, but you have to wait."

The men began to cough and choke. The women loosened the chains and sat them upright. By this time there was no fight left in them. While two sisters steadied the brothers, two others clasped their heads so they could watch.

"For the crime of adultery when you chose to rape your clients, we will remove the temptation," she shouted: "Zippers!"

The men tried to roll their hips back and forth to evade the snapping hands.

"Gets 'em where they live, doesn't it?" muttered Maury.

"We could always use scissors or a rusty knife if you prefer," Calley bellowed.

Josh and Jason continued to thrash about.

Riipppppp!

The men lay exposed from naval to ankle.

"Because we are not cruel and would not want you to suffer from an infection, we shall shave you first. Box cutters and razor knives at ready," she barked. "Oh, and if you move too much we shall sit on you."

The rocking escalated.

"Sisters, sit on them."

The two chosen for the task, clambered onto their legs and plunked down. They began to scrape the hair off the contractors' testes.

"Now that gives a whole new meaning to the phrase whacking off," crowed Maury.

Babbs sprinkled the surgical area, with spits and the contractors emitted a bubbling screech. "Stuff the gags back into their mouths. It will, uh, help soak up the blood. Yes, that's right. Soak up the blood."

Calley winked at the convicted before shoving the greasy rags back into their mouths.

Brey attacked the men with crucible tongs. Macha attached the vice grips and ratcheted it down. Maury armed herself with needle-nose pliers.

"Babbs?" Mora said. "Uh, Babbs."

"What?" she snapped. "I was just getting ready to join the fun."

"They're dead," Mora said.

"Dead? What do you mean, dead?" Babbs said.

"Dead. No breathing, no pulse, no heart beat." Mora placed her hand on their foreheads. "No brain activity. Nothing."

She dropped the heads with a solid thwack.

"Are you sure?"

"Trust me, dead is dead, and I know dead," Mora said.

"Are we done then?" said Brey. "I'm hungry."

"We didn't even get to do the good bit," grumbled Macha.

"Not finished yet. Remember what they did to the old woman." Babbs held up the rake and the push-broom snapped her fingers. "We have these implements, unless you would prefer to use brooms on both of them, as they did the victim."

The response was immediate.

"Not mine."

"Not mine."

"Not mine."

"Not mine."

"Not mine."

"Well, I definitely don't want to use mine," said Babbs.

"The point is moot, don't you think, Babbs?" Mora said.

"A symbolic gesture, then?" Babbs clenched the push-broom in her fist and shook it.

"Give it up, Babbs." Maury clapped her sister on the back. "We did the best we could. I think they got the point."

Macha stood between the two men and kicked each of them in the ribs. "I'm disappointed. These men dish it out but can't take it."

"Oh, well." Babbs scowled. "I'm ready for another brandy. What do you think?"

"Overall, I think that was a good night's work," said Maury.

Babbs grinned.

"I thought so."

Puss in Boots

Once in a land far, far away, a miller lay dying. Few would miss him. He was not a nice man. Like many of his trade, he got rich from the losses of others. He was known for keeping his hand on the scale when it suited him and skimming more than his fair share of grain, but who could quibble? He was the only miller in town.

The man had three sons and he knew that time drew nigh for him to settle his affairs. He had three possessions to distribute – the mill, a donkey and a cat. The donkey came with a cart and a flourishing trade transporting grain. The mill was also a home. The cat, well, the cat was a cat – pernickety and demanding – but he was a good mouser.

Each son was given the opportunity to choose his bequest. The eldest as first born came first. He asked for the mill. The second son requested his father's ass. The youngest would receive the cat.

The cat was not particularly happy about this arrangement. The youngest was an idiot, and the cat did not like him. The boy had been wicked as a child, always trying to hug him, and if the cat evaded his grasp, he would catch the poor animal by the tail.

To be truthful, the cat wasn't overly fond of humanity as a whole.

The old man the cat tolerated because he was a purveyor of food and owner of the mill with its many fine, fat rats, but the miller was also the one who had dubbed the cat Puss. It did nothing for his street cred to have someone running around town calling, "Puss, Puss. Here pussy, pussy, pussy!"

The cat took over the old man's boots when he got sick. The boots were more like slippers, soft and lined. The miller had not worked in the mill for years. The eldest and the middle sons ran it and transported the grain. Their wives supplied the menial labor.

Once his affairs were settled, the old miller slipped quietly away. Each son came into his own. The eldest brothers did not mourn. The youngest, Ivan, who was simple, had never shouldered responsibility in his life. He had none now. He was carefree, and he grieved. He grabbed the cat, wept, blowing his nose in the animal's fur and got swatted for his trouble.

The town's people pitied the hapless youngest son. Some devised a scheme to help him.

*

"Father?"

"Yes, Mother," he said.

"You work too many long hours with the stables and the blacksmith's shop. You are not a young man. You need help. We have no children. Mayhap you could hire the miller's son."

"He is a simpleton," the smith objected.

"He has a strong back, and he has a cat who can keep the mice out of the feed."

"We have a cat."

"She has kittens and is preoccupied."

"Then she must work harder to provide for her brood," he said.

The wife gave him a love tap on the back of the head with the frying pan.

"Oi, woman!"

"It is the right thing to do. Ivan is an orphan and his brothers will not care for him."

"Good God, woman, he has seen twenty-three summers."

She waggled the frying pan at him. "An orphan still."

"Okay," he acquiesced to her skill with a frying pan. Then he stood to find himself some place safer to sit. Perhaps inside the forge.

Rubbing the back of his head, he mumbled, "Mark my words. No good will come of it."

The goodwife went to find the youth. Ivan was thrilled.

"I am going to be apprenticed to the blacksmith," he announced to his brothers. "I am going to learn a trade."

They rolled their eyes toward the ceiling.

The eldest nodded. "If you have been hired to help the blacksmith, take the cat."

Puss, huddled on top of the old man's slippers, opened a baleful eye and glared at them.

An expression of terror flitted across Ivan's features.

173

"And take those stinking boots with you," said the second.

Puss opened both eyes and stared at Ivan, as if daring him to try.

Ivan swallowed hard, stretched out a hand, and the cat seized his arm with all four feet, all eighteen claws, and all thirty teeth.

The brothers continued arguing.

"I tell you, I sent him out to stud, as soon as I knew the old man was dying," the second said. "He's a plucky little fellow. Two jennies are with foal. We get one for his services, and all he had to do was..." The second son nudged the air and winked twice. "We will have one to grind the grain, and a second for transport.

The eldest gazed at the youngest struggling through the yard. "How does he do that?"

"Huh? Who?"

"Ivan."

"Do what?"

"Hold onto the cat like that without screaming."

The middle son glanced over his shoulder at Ivan, cat dangling from his arm and chomping on it. "Oh, that. You know he's always trying to make friends with the animal, silly boy. He must've gotten used to it by now."

Ivan was not as stupid as people thought. He knew that Puss would not be content with his arm for long. He slapped his father's slippers on his head. Puss took the bait, and Ivan walked through the village with as much dignity as he could muster wearing his father's slippers on his head with a cat sitting astride it, hugging his head and taking an occasional swipe at his face.

By the time he reached the stables, Ivan was bleeding.

The blacksmith's wife bustled around the kitchen, collecting water and bandages to treat the wounds. The husband just shook his head and returned to the forge.

Ivan was sick for a week with cat-scratch fever, and the blacksmith breathed a sigh of relief. If he was lucky, the boy would die.

Puss was immensely satisfied. The wife was generous with the scraps and there was a multitude of rats to chase, along with a pretty little lady kitty who obviously needed his services...

*

Ivan began cleaning the stables, sporting new scars across cheeks and nose. He shoveled shit. It was a job he did relatively well, having taken care of the donkey's stall for years. Soon enough, he thought, he would work his way up to smith's apprentice and learn the magic of metal.

Ivan was always a bit lackadaisical, never paying attention to what he was doing. He spilled dung on a client's boot and, even worse, left some where a customer could slip in it.

The blacksmith ground his teeth, and his wife clucked over the young man.

Puss pursued his passions, eating, sleeping and leaping on the blacksmith's cat. Courtship, Puss-style, involved a lot of running, jumping, chasing and pouncing.

One day ten pounds of furry fury dropped from the rafter onto Ivan's head. It was not Puss, which might be expected. It was the blacksmith's cat driven to desperation by Puss's unwanted attention. Ivan attempted to peel her off his head and got swiped in the eyes, and Ivan realized the mother cat was not fighting for the fun of it, as Puss did, she was fighting for her life.

He bent over. She clung to his scalp when Puss, not about to be outdone, crashed down from above. Ivan bolted upright. Puss rode his master's back while the mother cat clung to his head.

He flailed, trying to reach Puss, who now hung from his spine and the female did a foxtrot on his scalp.

Ivan raced into the street, arms waving wildly. A donkey reared and kicked at him. The young man did a complete about face and ran blindly into the stables and through the doors into the smithy. He bumped into the rod heating on the forge and knocked it to ground.

Red hot coals splattered across the floor. The iron landed on a pile of oil-soaked rags. They burst into flame. The blacksmith cat and Puss chose to absent themselves from Ivan's person and from the smithy.

Blood streaming into his eyes, Ivan headed for the stables. He ripped off his shirt and covered the horses' eyes with it, leading them one at a time to safety.

So, that day, Ivan became a hero. He also became unemployed.

*

The blacksmith's lady convinced her sister to give the poor boy a chance.

Face still ravaged by scratches and smudged with soot, Ivan emerged from the barn where the horses were now being stabled. He washed his face in the trough, stood and contemplated a growing mound of earth rising up in an adjacent field. It turned and made a bee-line for the cottage.

The farmer and his son conferred in the corner. The farmers' wife handed Ivan the heel from a loaf of bread to break his fast.

"Look at him," said the son. "He's not even paying attention; he's just staring into space."

Ivan shook himself and pointed at the track of raised soil. "You've got moles. Really big moles."

The farmer climbed down the ladder. "Where's that cat of yours? He can kill moles. He should earn his keep."

"Puss?"

Ivan wandered off searching for his cat. "Here, Puss. Pussy? Here, pussy. Here, pussy, pussy, pussy."

The vindictive Puss sat on the roof grooming himself, still miffed at losing his home, with its warm forge, many fat rats, and a fine lady in need of courtship. Although the feline had been somewhat appeased after he discovered the farm was home to a colony of cats. He halted his ablutions when he heard his name. And he did as any cat would, he ignored it.

Unable to fetch the cat, Ivan stopped and waited until the farmer and his son concluded their conversation.

"Let him do the lugging. If you don't want him on the roof, don't let him up there. Just have him haul the bundles up the ladder and leave them on the edge. It would save you a lot of work and a lot of time.

The farmer's son grunted and yelled at Ivan. "Don't just stand there. Bring up the thatch."

The son mounted the ladder while the farmer returned to the barn to get a pitchfork.

Ivan gathered several bundles of reeds, more than he should carry; but he would please them if he could. At that moment a wagon came barreling around the bend full tilt, for the king had decreed "the coaches would run on time," and this one was late. A week late.

Puss licked himself, as cats do, and watched indifferently as the mound advanced relentlessly toward the farmyard. The cat was tired. He'd spent most of the night fighting with the other male cats that populated the farm until he achieved a position of ascendance.

*

Rumpelstiltskin tunneled through the countryside. Hearing a ruckus, he veered and decided to surface. He should be nowhere near the road. The noise came from further away. His scalp had just become visible aboveground when – "*Ooph!*" – a horse stepped on his head.

The dwarf tumbled back into the hole, hands clawing for purchase...

*

When his arms were fully loaded, Ivan shrugged, turned and began to climb the ladder.

"Don't come up here." The farmer's son patted the roof beside him. "We don't need an accident. Just place it on the edge."

Puss sat upright at full attention. Eyes trained on the path of disturbed earth as it hit the base of the ladder, Ivan began to fall, still clinging to the ladder. It rebounded off a nearby oak and back toward the house.

Ivan struggled. Having realized he was overloaded, the youth attempted to drop a bundle or two at the base of the ladder. They bounced. The ladder wobbled. Ivan threw himself forward but overbalanced.

Ivan let go of the ladder to drop to the ground too late. Momentum propelled him forward with such force that he landed on the roof and through it to the home below. He landed on the trestle table and broke it.

Up on the roof, Puss watched with moderate interest. His ears pricked when the mound of earth spoke: "What the –"

The tunnel changed direction and headed back to the pasture.

The farmer galloped into the cottage, pitchfork in hand, shrieking. The wife battered at Ivan with a fish she had bought at market that day.

"Get out!" the farmer roared, pushing him toward the door.

Head hung low, Ivan slunk away.

177

The farmer stormed up the ladder and grabbed the cat and tossed the spitting beast onto Ivan's head. "And stay out!"

Ivan was stunned. He was homeless, hurt, and now he had the cat with no boots to protect his head. The wish he had never spoken was granted as the farmer's wife threw the boots after the two of them, dejected youth and snarling cat. She hit him squarely between the shoulder blades. He fell.

Puss vacated his person.

Ivan righted himself and stumbled through the field, heading for the crossroads.

*

The people of the village, unaware of the drama unfolding at the farm, were still recoiling from the loss of the smithy and the stables. People emerged from the carriage beside the charred remains of the building. The horses stood, lathered and shaking.

Meanwhile the villagers were pre-occupied by the sight of a colorful cloak, the kind worn by the princely class, floating lazily over the smithy. A basket held in place by sturdy rope dangled at the base of the cloak. The weight drew it inexorably toward earth.

A passenger shaded her eyes from the sun and stared at the object. Her lips moved as she read it. "It says O, Z. Oz. How odd," she said.

The young woman was clearly one of the wealthy, the pampered daughter of a merchant perchance, for she was traveling first class, and she got a pillow with her ticket. She clutched at it now.

One of the observers shouted, "It's going to come down in the farmer's field."

The crowd took off, running, each thinking it might be nice to have such colorful cloth with which to make a frock, a serviceable piece of rope or sturdy basket. Each was determined to get to the pasture first before anyone else, or the farmer, could stake a claim.

*

Ivan swooned, briefly. It was all too much to bear. He had lost three homes in as many days. He pulled himself upright – his head spinning. The claw marks now stretched across his back, Puss having used it for a spring board. The cuts throbbed with each beat of his heart. The sun was in his eyes. He could no longer remember where he was going or why.

He heard the sound of thundering feet. He climbed up to his knees, swayed and sat down hard, biting on his tongue. Blood ran from his mouth.

Darkness blotted out the sun.

Ivan saw an enormous bladder, such as lucky children might have if they had toys and played games, deflating. It grew large, covering his entire field of vision.

Ivan threw himself flat upon the ground and tried to protect his bleeding head. The basket hit him, tipped, and he was surrounded by burning coals.

Screams of a mad wizard filled the air, and heat, too much heat. The sensation lasted for less than an instant. Then he felt and heard no more. The field around him burned, becoming the first crop circle in the village.

The wizard rushed off to become embroiled in yet another tale not of his choosing.

And Puss, you may ask. What became of him?

The cat was enticed by treats and the young woman's pillow. He left the village for the city where he terrorized a whole better class of felines. To the end of his days, he remained protected by his mistress, for whom he could do no wrong.

*

Crash! Rumpelstiltskin changed course again. Small village or not, this place was dangerous. He was excavating a path before him with a vengeance when he met an obstacle or, more appropriately, it ran into him.

The dwarf poked his head above ground to confront a dozy-looking rabbit chomping on a carrot.

"Who are you?" Rumpelstiltskin demanded.

The rabbit dug around in his fur, extracted a map and studied it.

"Who are you?"

The rabbit ignored his question. "Eh, doc? You wouldn't happen to know if this is Albuquerque?"

Seven in One Blow

Sometime in the reign of Charles II, a man hesitated outside the Theatre Royale on Drury Lane to adjust his accoutrement. He fluffed his ruff and his hands came away covered with the gravy from a previous meal. He extracted his kerchief and daubed at the grease, spreading it across his chest.

A fly buzzed around his head and he flicked at it.

Satisfied that nothing was found wanting, or particularly repugnant, he entered. His gaze fell upon a red-haired woman playing cards in a side room. He nodded curtly.

"Madam."

"Sir," she replied. "Are you here to join the game?"

"No, I will get some refreshment," he said.

She examined the stain on his breast and the crumbs lodged in his beard, sniffed and directed him to the gentlemen's quarters. He moved around the table and she watched him go. She did not like him. He was a puffed up little fop who put on airs far above his station just because he knew the king. He was no gentleman. His hair was greasy, his nails ingrained with dirt, hands stained with ink, and his breath smelled foul.

The woman turned her attention back to the cards in her hands. She had a lot riding on this game.

The man relaxed immeasurably once he entered the room where no woman dared cross the threshold. Women had their place, but generally he was not comforted by their presence. They were fickle, treating him dismissively as they sought another, bigger prize. He much preferred the company of men.

He ordered a drink and sipped it, contemplating the evening's entertainment. The play, *A Midsummer's Night Dream*, was ribald, and it was said that the king's bawd led the troupe.

He sighed. Times change. Women were relatively new to the theatre. Acting was considered an unseemly occupation for the softer sex. Most female parts were played by men. Women usually gained access to the theatre for their, he coughed delicately into his hand, other talents

The man studied his ink-stained fingers. Sometimes he did not know which excited him most, women in various stages of undress or men primped and strapped into female attire. Often it was hard to tell the difference between the women and the pretty boys.

A crier walked through the gentlemen's room to announce that the performance was about to begin. He rearranged himself, tucking his erection down the legs of his breeches and ensured his overskirt covered all.

He navigated the dark narrow halls to the pits and bumped into a woman, wiping her mouth, straightening her hair and shoving the shiny silver coins into her bodice.

In the lobby, the red-haired woman sighed. "That's me then. I guess I need to get to work."

She stood, tightened her corset, tugged the neckline lower to show her cleavage and her bosom to full effect.

She headed not to the stage, but to the pits where the general audience sat.

The man motioned to her. She wrinkled her nose at the thought of servicing the filthy fop. Then she pasted a smile on her face. Powder flaked onto her chest. She carried a jar of salve she had specially made for just such occasions. It had both sedative and stimulant properties.

She dug around inside his overskirt, located his penis and pulled it from its confinement. She had learned early on that many men liked to show off their wares; finding exposure as exciting as the act.

The member vibrated in her hand. He was ready. She rubbed the salve on his penis and began to tease it with lips and tongue. The man next to him poked her shoulder. She grimaced, but she had two hands she could service more than one.

She moved down the line until she counted seven heads. Still erect and still vibrating. Then she bent over and blew gently on one man after another. They ejaculated in unison and sagged against each other.

Then she straightened. She patted her breasts and heard a reassuring jingle of coins. This was enough, she decided. Let someone else come out and earn her meal.

She returned to the card game. The other women stood as she entered.

"How was it?"

"They are eager for your ministrations. Mine, you will

recognize. Seven of them. They are slumped together sleeping it off." She plunked down on her chair.

The women began to twitter. "You mean?"

"Yes, I slayed them. Seven in one blow."

In Search of the Holy Quail

Prince Rumbolt stood outside the portcullis, rubbing his rump. He could see his mother through the iron bars, wringing her hands and weeping, and his father gesticulating.

Rumbolt could have done without the kick in the ass, even if his *cuisse* had deflected most of the blow. He supposed it could have been worse. His father could have been wearing his spurs instead of his slippers.

"Go away, you ne'er-do-well," the king bellowed. "We have a wedding to plan for your brother and no time for the likes of you. Go on a quest. Find your own princess if one will have you." He hobbled back to the castle.

Rumbolt noted the old man's limp with satisfaction. He heard the clip-clop of hooves. He swung to spy a stable boy leading his destrier, Spot. The stallion got the name when it fled rather than face a larger opponent during his brother's first joust. The wounded horse was bequeathed to Rumbolt, as the youngest and least worthy of the sons.

His mother smiled, waved her kerchief in farewell, wiped her eyes, blew her nose and turned away.

The prince considered tarrying outside the gate. Perhaps his father would relent. The sun rose to median, and Rumbolt conceded that if his father were to reconsider his decision, it would not be this day.

Prince Rumbolt sighed and signed to the lad who still waited patiently next to the horse. The stable boy dropped to all fours. The prince stepped onto the youth's back and swung an armor-clad leg over the mount.

Rumbolt rode for the better part of the day, stopping often to rest and watch the butterflies. He fumed that his father thought so ill of him to force him into exile. True, he did not enjoy the joust, the drills and training that formed the greater part of his education. He reasoned rightly enough that it was the soldiers' job to defend the royal family and not his task to sacrifice himself for them. It was a matter of logistic. There were more of them than there were princes, no matter how numerous the clan.

When night fell, the youth saw the glow of a fire on the horizon. Prince Rumbolt did nothing to hide his presence or muffle the hoof falls. He could not imagine any hazard on his father's lands. The horse shambled into the clearing where a troop of knights roasted a coney over the fire. Rumbolt studied the dented, rusty armor. Obviously not among his father's best.

The men jumped to their feet, swords drawn.

Rumbolt raised his hand in the air in a placatory gesture. "Well met," he said. "Why does such a band of, ah," he hesitated, "fine gentlemen sup so far from home?"

The closest bowed. "We are on a quest. Our quest is a lofty one. Our lord sent us to seek the Holy Quail, for the banquet to honor his son's marriage."

Prince Rumbolt nodded. The quail was rumored to be quite tasty, but this was not the reason why the bird was prized. It was for their feathers of gold.

No one knew really what the quail looked like, but that never stopped the knights errant. They did as they were told, never questioning that the birds were something neither seen nor identified.

"My father sent me too to assist in this quest. Mayhap to lead."

The captain eyed him incredulous that the seventh dishonored son, known to them as a fop and a popinjay, to replace the leader. Mayhap the king had chosen to foist this ill-favored son upon them to keep him from underfoot during the preparation, for the queen still had a soft spot for this youngest of her brood.

The night passed quickly, and the troop mounted early on the morrow, but not before they had raided the prince's script for food. The noise of their preparations woke him.

"Well, young prince, are you ready to seek the famed quail? Perhaps to pluck a feather or two to make your fortune?"

Rumbolt stuck his nose up in the air. "Any feathers found would rightly belong to the king."

"Spoken like the true son of royalty." The leader clapped the youth on the shoulder, sought the eyes of his second in command and mouthed the words: "...ditch him."

The band of men clattered around the countryside on overworked equines, scaring peasants, for if their quest went bad or the season got a little bit slow, there was always rapine and pillaging to pass the time.

*

The group trotted past two birds perched high in a tree. Their blinding wings of gold blended with the brilliance of the sun.

The quail were familiar with their reputation. Scrumptious, bad attitude, an aversion to being served on plate and flightless due to the weight of their feathers.

One bird ruffled his wings and shook himself. Silly creatures, humans. What bird would evolve burdened with gold? They were carbon-based life forms after all.

"As long as they keep their eyes trained on the ground, we are safe," the second said.

"Lunch?"

"Why not?"

The birds soared into the heavens.

*

After an unsuccessful hunt, with only a hart to show for their efforts, the troop settled for the night. They could have got more meat for the king's table, but Rumbolt always seemed to stumble into the thick of things – whooping, hollering and frightening the quarry away as soon as an animal was spotted.

The leader assigned the lowest in rank to serve the prince's pleasure. As he picked his teeth, the largest knight seized Rumbolt from behind. They tied him up and left him naked under the tree.

However, Spot was far smarter than his master, leaving at the first sign of disturbance. The following morning, the horse returned armor, weaponry and other supplies clanging on his back. He nibbled at the ropes until his master was free.

As he donned his under garments, Rumbolt rued that his mother had not seen fit to supply him with a pack horse to carry his armor. Reluctantly he struggled into chest and back plates without the aid of dresser or squire.

*

Princess Sam'n'ella of the house of the Lib where no female waited for a knight to aid them, gird herself for a quest of her own. A great wyrme ravaged the people, the land and the crops while her father cowered within the castle ramparts.

She spent the greater part of the day seeking signs of smoke above smoldering fields. The heat of the sun drove her into the forest. Sam'n'ella dismounted. She removed her boots, unstrapped her cuirass and slithered from the hauberk and began to wade in the lily pond. Frogs hopped to get out of her way, landing in the water with a splash.

Once she was sufficiently cooled, she attended to her horse, bathing it with the chill water. She rested to inspect two golden birds from half-closed lids as they speared fish and frogs and swallowed them whole.

Sam'n'ella had heard the myths about the Holy Quail but paid them little heed. Indeed, these birds sported feathers as downy as any that clothed the back of a duck.

She dozed.

*

The prince twisted in the saddle uncomfortably, realizing belatedly that he had his chest plate and his back plate on back to front. He swatted at the flies that buzzed around his head, thinking it might be best if he returned to the castle to beg forgiveness for whatever crime he may have committed – be it indolence or sloth. Only as he entered the forest did he realized he had no idea where he was or in what direction the castle might lie.

*

The sun was hidden by the tangle of foliage overhead when she awoke. The horse nuzzled her. Sam'n'ella stretched and yawned. Then she sat bolt upright, for she heard the faint clop of hooves. Her head swiveled on her neck as she tried to decipher whence the sound came.

She was not completely awake when a dragon lumbered into the clearing after a human thigh bone.

The princess scrambled to her feet as the dragon swung, fixed her with a bejeweled stare and wagged its tail.

Sam'n'ella reacted on instinct when she ran it through, and the poor creature collapsed.

An area above the pond began to shimmer. A shape coalesced. Her mouth dropped open, noting the conical cap and the staff.

A wizard!

He pointed at her. Lightning blazed from his fingertips. "You killed my pet, Fluffy...."

Her skin started to feel two sizes too tight, wet and slimy. She shrank and then she fell, plop, into the water with the frogs.

*

Prince Rumbolt had stopped to admire the fair maiden sleeping in the forest. He urged Spot forward, wondering if this damsel needed saving. He froze when the dragon came barreling through the underbrush.

Spot took all decisions of heroics out of his hands when he spun and raced from the forest back onto the plains.

*

Sam'n'ella's mouth snapped shut as soon as she entered the water. Swimming was not a valued skill in land-locked Lib, and she had in the past seen the victims of drowning, with their blue-green skin and protruding eyes.

Her throat inflated, and it appeared she could breathe quite well.

The princess kicked and broke the surface of the water. She flailed to propel herself to the edge of the pool, but her arms seemed to be useless, so she kicked instead.

When she reached the grassy shore, Sam'n'ella scrabbled to find purchase and drag herself from the pond. She gaped in horror at her hands. Her fingers had become fused, connected by a slimy web not unlike the feet of a duck.

She sunk down to the shallow bottom, bunched up her legs and thrust up, leaping onto the soft ground.

Princess Sam'n'ella shuffled, overbalanced and stumbled sideways. From this defenseless position, she viewed her reflection.

She must have drowned. Her eyes formed two bulbous circles and her skin was the color of algae. She righted herself

187

and gasped, or tried, but what came out sounded more like a deep basso belch.

Sam'n'ella clapped her hand over her mouth, embarrassed, and succeeded to tumble face first onto the ledge next to the water. From this perspective, she could examine the image reflected back at her. She scanned the pond. The pieces began to drop into place.

The wizard, the staff, the lightning bolt. She was a frog surrounded by frogs.

One swam forward and climbed from the pool. "I saw it; I saw it all. Damn wizard. The land of Kee Wee is overpopulated with humans that the mage has transformed into frogs."

The frog inflated his throat in importance. "I'm such a one. I used to be the wizard's servant. My name is 'Hey you!' At least that's what he used to call me. Then one day I burned the mutton. You'd think he'd learn to make something else besides frogs. You skewered his pet, so why not turn you into a dragon to replace the one he'd lost?"

"I don't know how I'd feel about that. What with people trying to kill you and all," she said.

The frog winked at her. "How do you feel about being a frog?"

"Not very good," she said.

"See."

"I'm a princess," she protested.

"Maybe you'll find yourself a handsome prince who can return you to human form with a kiss."

"The women of Lib don't do that sort of thing. Never on the first date." Sam'n'ella frowned, but it was hard to tell considering the size and shape of her mouth.

"Suit yourself, but for now you have to register with Minister Priccus as one of the once-human contingent of frogs. Over-population, you see, and not enough flies to go around."

A fly buzzed around her head, and Sam'n'ella had to stifle the impulse to snap it up. "Looks like there are plenty of flies if you ask me."

Hey You! hopped forward, unleashed his marvelous tongue and gobbled down the insect without hesitation. "Taxes 'n' all."

"How do you find his chap Priccus?"

"His Eminence," Hey You! amended.

Sam'n'ella opened her mouth to speak, and Hey You! hurried on, "I know, I know, you're a princess, but here you are just another frog."

"If Priccus is eminent, is he royal?"

"No, that honor goes to Prince Pompous."

"Pompous?"

"Well, he is a bull frog, always puffing out his chest, making decrees and announcing proclamations. His soldiers and huntsmen are bullfrogs too, for it takes a bullfrog to fell a mouse."

"What is he called?"

"Your Magnificence, and don't stare at his eye."

"Pardon?"

"One eye droops. An old hunting accident that happened when he ran into a thorn. He's very sensitive about it. You came just in time for the jubilee. Once a year they hold a ball for all the animals in the kingdom to celebrate his coronation. You'll like his wife, the frog fairy."

"A frog with magical powers?" she yelped.

"No, a fairy who ran afoul of the wizard. She's a bit over-fond of the swamp water." Hey You! noticed Sam'n'ella's bemused expression. "The national drink. Packs quite a punch. Having lost her magic, and her looks, the frog fairy has learned to like her tipple."

"Where do they live?"

"As you might expect they dwell in a castle. Not a castle by your definition or mine. The houses resemble piles of rocks or logs. The more important the personage – or in this case, frog-age – the bigger the residence."

He indicated the direction with a wave of his webbed hand. "Beach-front property, of course. Just follow the shoreline."

Sam'n'ella followed the designated course. Hey you! dived into the water, surfaced and waved. "I'll see you at the gala on the full moon. I'm really looking forward to the band, Peachus and Herpes."

She halted. "What?"

But Hey You! was gone.

The path along the shore was easy enough, although with the long rushes, she found herself in the water several times, but swimming held no terror for her now.

189

Soon Sam'n'ella recognized the dwellings with the frogs huddled away from the sun. Piles of leaf litter, sticks and stones. She saw small frogs, big frogs, and frogs of multitudinous colors crouched beside their homes awaiting the long shadows of night. She found she didn't mind this hopping lark; it was quite an efficient form of locomotion.

By the fourth time she fell into the water, the princess emerged to a long, pebbled beach. She spied the castle, a mound made of huge granite boulders shot through with ruby and quartz.

Sam'n'ella froze.

A huge frog, almost man-high, stood at attention next to the entrance. The skin on his back formed knobs like a shield worn by a knight. The hard crust on the head, caps over each eye and circular patches to guard the ears gave the impression of a helmet.

Feeling her rank, she attempted to do the same. Stand erect. The movement turned into a leap and she bounced to a boulder above the guard's head.

"Now, wait a second, ma'am, you can't do that. You have to introduce yourself and state your business."

Sam'n'ella hopped down to a respectable position, faced him, and tried to stand again with a more controlled movement. As soon as she achieved any height, she toppled face forward.

The guard abandoned his post, solicitous. "Are you all right, little lady?"

He flopped down to a more normal stance, with legs bent and arms supporting upper torso. "I didn't mean to scare you. Just doin' my job." He offered her a hand.

"It takes some getting used to, doesn't it?" he said.

"What?" she said.

"Being morphed." The bullfrog waggled its fingers. "Not that I know how it feels, mind you, but I sees enough of it. All disoriented, not knowing what bits to put where."

When the guard was sure she had all her body parts in order, he released her. "Don't worry. It's not like I'm going to eat you."

"Eat me?" she gulped.

"Just rumors."

She gulped again and forged ahead. "I am a princess of Lib."

"Oh, a princess, are we? You'll still be looking for Minister Priccus. Capital fellow, or so I'm told. Go to the first lily pad and..." The guard waved arms this way and that.

Sam memorized his instructions.

*

The castle was a fanciful structure despite its initial foreboding appearance. The interior was punctuated by ponds lit with sunbeams shining through fissures and apertures that ran through the stone to the sky above. Sam'n'ella took the final turn and entered the Minister's Hall.

Again, the princess attempted to attain full height by clinging to the wall. Again, she made a complete cock-up of it.

She sat on her haunches. "I am Sam'n'ella of Lib. Princess of the realm."

"Princess?" Priccus waved his hand dismissively. "We already have one of them."

He began climbing on her back. "But you are a pretty little thing, aren't you?"

She shook him off. "I say."

"For a princess, perhaps, I can do you a favor if you will do something for me."

Minister Priccus placed his lips next to her head and whispered in her ear. The royal face clouded.

It would appear Minister Priccus thought he was a very handsome frog, a very handsome frog indeed, but he was not a frog. He was a great horny toad.

And he wasn't a nice toad at all.

"Why I never!" And she bounded off the walls and out the door.

And she ran or hopped.

And she hopped past the ponds with their rainbows of light, counting the turns – *droit, sinistre, droit, sinistre* – out the entrance and past the guard.

The princess bounded down the pebble beach and squatted in the water. This was a horrible place. She didn't want to be a frog with creepy old toads clambering on her back in exchange for a few flies. Come to think of it, she didn't want to eat flies at all. She shivered.

She was a princess of the realm.

"O, woe. O, woe is me," she bemoaned her fate.

*

Prince Rumbolt spent the day circling the forest. Every direction looked pretty much the same. Wide vistas and long expanses of plain with distantly seen mountains.

Prince Rumbolt too bemoaned his fate, or more importantly he bemoaned his horse. Some destriers separated from their stables could find their way unerringly toward home. The only instinct Spot had was for self-preservation.

Had Rumbolt been older when his father offered him the war horse, he might have noticed the placement of the young stallion's wound, on his rear end. Only later did he realize the injury was received while the horse was fleeing battle. If he had known then, he would have thought the better of the gift and waited for another horse.

The prince steered Spot deeper into the woods where he might take his rest.

"Oh, woe. Oh, woe. Oh, woe is me."

The prince's spirits rose.

A damsel in distress.

Perhaps he could save her from the clutches of whatever demon assailed her. The prince couldn't imagine it would be anything too horrifying in such an idyllic setting.

"Rescue the maid. Go home a conquering hero, with bride in tow." He ticked the items off on his fingers like chores on a list.

"I hope she's suitable," he muttered.

The prince dug his spurs into Spot's side. The horse cantered, dodging and darting between trees and limbs.

Rumbolt added another complaint to his inventory about Spot, after he'd been swept off the horse's back several times by low-hanging limbs.

Poor spatial relations.

Circumspect, Rumbolt dismounted and walked ahead. The sound of distress drew nigh.

The forest parted onto a beach of sparkling pebbles. A frog crouched in the center. "Oh, woe. Oh, woe. Oh, woe is me," it croaked.

He dropped the reins and advanced slowly.

The prince knelt. "Is it you who wails so?" he asked.

"Who else? Do you see anyone else around here?" Sam'n'ella retorted.

"We-e-ellll, no. Are you a frog prince or something?"

This was too much.

"Wah! You don't even know what gender I am! Wah! I am a princess. An enchanted princess," she sniveled. "A wizard put a spell on me."

The wheels in Rupert's brain began to whirr. He dropped down to his knees. "An enchanted princess? If I kiss you..."

Sam'n'ella spat at him. "What is it with you men?"

"No, I'm serious. If you and I were to kiss, would you return to your true form?" The prince leered at her.

"I don't know. Maybe."

"You're human, right? You're not the princess of slugs, are you?"

"No, I am" – she glanced down at the green skin – "or I once was as human as you are."

"Do you want to be a frog?"

"No!"

"Well then, how about a little kiss?" He puckered.

The princess flinched. "You wouldn't be my first choice."

"Nor you mine." He sat back on his haunches. "I kiss you. Wham, bam, boom. You're a princess, and you will be my bride. That's the deal. Take it or leave it."

"Wait a second. No one said that marriage was part of the proposal."

"You got a better offer. What have you got to lose? Flies for breakfast, lunch and dinner?"

She pulled a face.

He lifted her to face level. Their lips touched. A tingle rocketed between them, and they dropped.

Rumbolt stared at his green arms and feet and screamed.

"I'm a frog. I'm a bleeding frog. Look at what you made me do!"

"Me! You! You were the one who was so hot to trot, you pervert."

Rumbolt thought for a moment and settled down. "This may not be so bad. You're a frog princess and I'm a frog prince. We can still make little frog babies, can't we?"

Then she told him how it was done in the land of Kee Wee.

"You mean we can't; we don't..."

"Uh, uh."

Then they both chorused. "Help! Oh, help."

Somewhere in another part of fairy land, Glinda sat on Dorothy's former throne in a dress she had designed herself. With her powers enhanced by those of the late wizard, the good fairy was no longer destined to wear pink. She wanted something that didn't clash with the ruby slippers she inherited after Dorothy's fall from grace.

Glinda pounded on her ears as the distant pleas echoed through time and space. "*Help! Oh, help.*"

"Shut up! Shut up! Shut up! Shut up!"

*

The Holy Quail sat on either side of the nest. Their nestlings woke, raucous and famished.

The female sat on her young to muffle the sound. Her mate dropped down from the limb and stabbed Prince Rumbolt in the head, swallowing him whole.

Sam'n'ella threw herself into the water.

The bird returned to the nest, burped and tapped his chest. "'Scuse me," he said, "It must have been something I ate."

'Til Death Us Do Part

Rumpelstiltskin toiled away deep inside the bowels of the earth, avoiding human habitation. He knew he had to find *the* castle – *the right castle*. He frowned. They all looked alike to him. Then Rumpelstiltskin had a thought that caused the pick to falter mid-swing. He glanced at the rock overhead.

Of course, he had a rather skewed perspective on this castle thing.

He knew castles had turrets, fenestration, embrasures, portcullis and all that kind of stuff – the more the merrier and the wealthier the patron. Rumpelstiltskin presumed that the number of each and the configuration could differentiate one from another. But only if viewed from above ground. Digging up from down below, he was lucky if he didn't emerge in the bailey where some jackass would step on his head.

Or worse, arrive in the oubliette. Rumpelstiltskin had fallen afoul of more than one prisoner who viewed him as lunch.

To avoid these pitfalls, he listened, especially for the tread of feet. He liked to think of himself as a connoisseur of feet. Heavy traffic with the clip, clop of hooves meant road or bailey. The clatter of metal shod feet indicated the presence of knights, the armory or the war room. The soft swish of slippered feet suggested the women's realm – either the lord's lady chambers or the servants. All areas best avoided.

The dwarf also learned that there were qualities, shades of silence. He kept a deaf ear to the seductive sound of the spinning wheel. Every cottage held a spinning wheel and a loom. He could not let himself get distracted. He also tried not to be fooled by faint traffic, which might mean a lesser used portion of the castle. Like the stockroom.

Those sounds could just as easily be flocks in the far fields, with one ewe ready to cut loose as soon as his head materialized. Or it could be human habitation of the lowliest kind from the dingiest minor lord's manor to the peasant's humble hovel.

Every time Rumpelstiltskin popped his head above the surface to get his bearings straight peasants pounced on him. They rubbed him in the most embarrassing and inappropriate

195

places for good luck. Others shook him and demanded his pot of gold.

Pot of gold? What gold? If Rumpelstiltskin had a pot of gold or even a bowl he wouldn't be here grubbing around on this fruitless mission.

Damn silly idea to set a dwarf, an underground animal as much as any mole, upon a quest to climb the highest turret in the tallest tower in just the right castle.

And for what?

A spinning wheel and a wanna-be princess.

*

The woman stood at the top of the stairs, box clutched to her breast. She adjusted her body sideways, so she could see her feet.

Why did she do it? Storing winter clothes and summer clothes. She had more than she could ever need during the season. In fact, she tended to wear the same two or three pieces over and over again.

Each spring and fall she'd schlep boxes up and down the stairs. One of these days this tradition would kill her.

Tricia had a lot of clothes. Hand-me-downs, for the most part. For her weight stayed static while her friends got fat. They gave their items to her, not without a certain amount of rancor.

This did not mean Tricia was left untouched by the ravages of time. Everything she had sunk a bit here and flattened there. Muscles sagged, and the bags under her eyes stretched while the skin along her jowls formed a drape over her neck.

Thump.

She cast a nervous glance over her shoulder. The attic was comparatively civilized as attics go. It had a full wooden floor. The perfect area for storage. Anything stowed therein left smelling of warm, spicy apples.

Winter meant just a cursory search to find the boxes. It would be too cold to dawdle. She did not intend to search through everything. Each article of clothing was attached to a memory or time. Some pleasant. Most not. It was like a chronology of her life and not particularly a happy one. Usually, Tricia would fold the item up again and place it back into the box.

She concentrated on the stairs before her. They were sturdy and broad. Even laden as she was, Tricia could stick her elbows out wide and still not brush against the walls. The stairs had a handrail, a senior citizen's dream.

Except when your hands are full, she thought.

Tricia placed her foot flat on the tread, tapped it with her toe and felt around for a while. Satisfied, she distributed her weight on it. A twist, a wriggle and she could see the next step. She repeated the process one step at a time.

She was balancing on one foot, searching for the next stair, when she felt two hands on her shoulders. A picture fell from the wall. The glass shattered, spreading shards from one step to another.

She pinwheeled. The force of the initial shove caused her to bounce off the wall and propel her forward. She ricocheted, spun and tumbled head first down the stairs.

She vaguely remembered hitting the next step with her face. Her neck wrenched back with a crunching noise and slivers of glass became embedded in her cheeks and forehead.

Her first instinct was to close her eyes, but what if glass as fine as grains of sand floated on her sclera? She could grind them into her eyes if she blinked.

Tricia fought the reflex. Eyes wide, she was treated to a jumble of images, *tread, riser, ceiling, picture-laden wall* and not necessarily in the same order twice. *Riser, picture-laden wall, ceiling and tread.*

It sped up. *Ceilingtreadriserandwall.*

When her gaze locked upon the framed photos, she was haunted by the faces of her forebears going back several generations. Some leered benignly. Others – those in front of the family farm, dressed in their stuffy Sunday best and told to hold the posture too long – glowered malevolently for all posterity.

Tricia had hung the pictures on the attic stairs as an act of defiance. *Okay, I'll hang your pictures, they came to me as all things do, but I won't let you into my heart or into my home.*

Her ancestors were getting their revenge for the misuse of their images. Tricia was sure she hit every frame, back to the great-greats and great-great-greats. Some pictures fell before her and others came in hot pursuit, carried in a shower of glass.

Her mind flashed back when she was an age to do cartwheels. The sky, with a nice padding of cumulus clouds, between your feet. Grass growing beneath your hands. A flat plain of green meeting with the tangle of tree roots. A trunk seen upright, sideways, then upside down. Human visages were seen likewise, as feet, torsos, head and hair that rotated in space and time.

For a moment it seemed Tricia saw her great aunt's feet and wrinkled hose, leading to enormous breasts and scowling face.

Her chin smacked the handrail. She rebounded to make a graceless pirouette, followed by a muddled arabesque, before landing face down on the floor.

As darkness took her, Tricia found herself wishing wildly that she had been able to perform a tangled version of the dying swan before she passed out.

*

The surcease from pain brought about by unconsciousness was short-lived. Tricia opened a single eye. She focused, or at least she tried to focus, on what appeared to be a knot of wood. Tricia groaned and blinked, terrified lest she tear her retina on a shard of glass.

She paused to assess the damage. Agony rocketed up her leg to her spine.

At least, she could feel it. *That was a good thing.*

Or was it?

Must be. If her back or her neck was broken, she would have been numb from the point of fracture down.

The growing stain underneath her face must be blood. From cuts or something direr, like a hole in her scalp.

Tricia wondered if she would be able to lift her head, or if she should. The wrong move could sever her spinal cord. It was most tempting to test the theory if it meant the burning of ankle, leg, thigh and back would stop.

She shuffled through the ideas.

Call for help?

Call who? Call where? Call how? Her phone was down another flight of stairs.

Who would listen? Her home was separated from the others on the street by a hundred feet or more.

Who would care?
She had no answer for that one.
Would anyone notice her missing?
Unlikely.
Tricia knew she would have to move eventually.
Test the leg first. That would test the spine.
If she had lost use of either or both leg, it meant a break.
Tricia wondered if she could drag herself to the phone. She extended her arms tentatively.
They worked!
And they hurt.
Instead she decided to lie at the base of the stairs and rest her eyes just for a little while longer.

*

A line of long-dead relations clustered around her.

"Back up, give her room to breathe?" The self-appointed matron was also the oldest family member of the lot, a great-great-great-grandmother of unknown name. She sported the respectable widow's reeds. Her bonnet was a fanciful creation of black ribbons which stood a full foot tall. It slanted rakishly over her eyes and added to her already considerable height. The woman looked every part the matriarch. A hook nose divided an imperious expression into halves.

"Breathe why?" protested great-grandfather Milton. "She's dying."

"How about so we won't scare the crap out of her," said the plain-spoken Uncle Bob.

"Language!" the matriarch sniffed.

"Well, I mean." Bob pointed at the crumpled body. "How would you feel of you woke up to this?" He waved at their feet and legs. "To find us peering down at you?" He gestured to the matriarch. "To you, ferchrissakes. Have you seen your reflection lately?"

The great-great-great-grandmother of unknown name changed the topic. "Who wants to greet her?"

"Oh, I do, I do, I do." Sissy jumped up and down, hand waving in the air.

Tricia's mother coughed delicately in her hand. "If I remember correctly you two never got along."

A bubbled moan issued from the floor in front of them.

"Vanish," shouted great-aunt Mary.

The feet, skirts, legs, uniforms and faces faded.

*

Tricia woke to the murmur of voices. Some she recognized, like the much-beloved favorite, if somewhat inebriate, Uncle Bob. Some she hadn't a clue who the speaker may or may not be. One held the cadence of authority and sonorous language of days gone by.

Greats? Or great-greats?

Tricia viewed her familial relation and her ancestors with mixed emotions. As a child, she had been the daughter who wasn't there, much like the man who lived upon the stair. The one who was an afterthought, the unwanted and unbidden youngest. Her parents decreed her fate – to sacrifice herself and care for them in their dotage.

She rebelled and ran away to evade their plans. They never forgave her. Calls came, if they came at all, to admonish her for deserting them. When she succeeded in life beyond their expectations, they hated her even more.

Tricia was also the receptacle upon whom all the ancestral ailments had descended. In her youth, she was the one sent from here to there to take care of the sick or fix a problem. Then one-by-one the familial diseases surfaced, and still she survived.

Her family never visited her. She was told that they would not waste their vacation on her. When she moved, it took two years before they noticed she was missing,

Her childless state, a result of a hereditary disorder, provided them with a built-in excuse for condemnation – not a proper woman or daughter – and it was never acknowledged as part of a disease that ran through the family line so that the most prolific had single-child households.

If a member of the family had trouble, they called her. When a relative died, Tricia was left to sweep the home of junk and unwanted possessions, even if she never received a dime.

Until Tricia got far enough away. It took an ocean and a continent before the family stopped calling upon her to scour the messes under the family rug, and when they last died, she ended up with those things no one else wanted.

Now Tricia found herself staring up the steps to the attic among shards of glass and torn ancient photographs. Of course, she would pick an old Victorian home with high ceilings to house it all.

She harkened back to her childhood, and those small triumphs she had made on her own. Never applauded; never approved.

Tricia learned to do a cartwheel, a hand stand, a flip, specifically because her father did not approve her tomboy ways, and she became an inveterate climber of trees where no one could reach her. Tricia's sister taught her how to ride a bicycle because their parents couldn't be bothered. It was no act of love and affection. Instead it afforded Sissy an opportunity to push her younger sibling over and point out her shortcomings to their parents.

Test the leg. This time Tricia put the thought into action, trying to draw the unbent leg up to propel her forward toward the stairs and the phone.

It didn't move. Not a good sign.

Unlike many of her age, Tricia had no necklace alarm, or panic-button, to alert others to her predicament. She never seemed to have the funds.

If she wouldn't take care of her parents, they made sure no one would take care of her. Her sister got the houses and the education, and Tricia got relief from their perpetual demands.

Meanwhile an upbringing that taught little trust was not conducive to sociability. Her motto of life, her tee-shirt, had been "please, don't... kick me." The 'please don't' faded with time, but the 'kick me' remained clear.

She became a hermit.

*

"She really doesn't like us," her father noted.

"Can you blame her?" Uncle Dietrich snapped. "Elaina and I offered her a home. We wanted to adopt her; we could see how she was treated. But she was too young, too devoted to you. She gave you loyalty and love and what did you give her?"

"Shut up," William growled. "What do you know about parenting? You never had kids."

"Neither did she," said Dietrich, "And she paid for that too."

The matriarch rapped the silver-tipped cane on the floor. "If this is the way you treated each other, no wonder she retreated from the world."

Her mother, wearing a beard and the big floppy shoes of a hobo clown, bent over to examine the wreckage of her daughter's body. The thigh had snapped halfway between hip and knee. A ragged piece of bone protruded through the skin. The leg from the knee down was twisted and her foot pointed in the wrong direction. The woman turned away from the destruction. The exposed eye peered at the stair.

A single tear traced a path down her mother's cheek, smearing the grease paint.

A cousin sorted through the boxes of clothes. "Will you look at this junk? This is what she risked her life to get." He lifted up torn and shredded long-johns, frayed sweaters and patched sweat suits. "No one wears this stuff anymore. Now it's all exercise gear and leggings. I wouldn't be caught dead in these."

"You don't have to be caught dead, dear. You are dead," said Aunt Florence.

*

Somewhere above her throbbing head, people argued over her attire. Tricia smiled inwardly. She learned long ago, wearing her sister's hand-me-downs, that people avoided those who appeared poor. On her sister, the outfit looked fresh, new and clean. When she received the garment, it was worn and two sizes too large.

She had emulated that illusion, adopting the garb of the poor ever since, for humanity could be expected to turn its back on anything and anyone who struck that secret core of discomfort, poverty, the chord of atavistic fear.

There but for the grace of God go I.

The conversation drifted in and out of her consciousness, and suddenly she realized that others were discussing her fate. Instinct and hate caused Tricia to thrust herself from the floor.

Her head spun. She swayed back and forth. Then her gaze fixed upon her broken corpse.

She fainted.

"Get back!" said Milton.

"I didn't know the dead could faint," commented one little boy who Tricia recognized from a photo of a couple with nine adopted children.

Her great-grandmother Rosa indicated the thin thread that still connected body to soul. "She's not dead yet."

"But, but –"

"Hush."

The thing that Tricia was now, and not what once had been, sat up.

She scanned the clan crowded around her. "Not only, no, but hell no!"

Tricia's head swung smoothly – without the usual aches or pain – on her translucent neck to study her corpse. "I most certainly don't look well."

The faces from the photographs receded and Tricia was left alone with the memory of pain.

Somewhere beyond her visual range, voices continued to squabble.

A light appeared.

A grand white light.

The blasted light formed a halo around her sister, Sissy, and Tricia noticed that she wore the angel costume that she used as a stripper.

Tricia began to curse. She had planned to come back and haunt her sister, but it seemed Sissy had got there first. Sissy was *always* first.

Her sister's presence in her home was an insult.

"Oh, no. Uh-uh! You just back off. If Sissy is the welcoming committee to eternity, I don't need it. I don't want it."

The full gamut of relatives reappeared and advanced. They spoke about Tricia in the third person as if she wasn't there or didn't exist.

"We can show her the way."

"What way? Where?" Tricia snapped. "If I remember correctly our families' history is not exactly exemplary, and I don't want to follow you into the afterlife. Didn't we have a distant relation who was a serial killer?"

"But we can help you."

"Which one of you gave me a shove? Come on, I felt it. Was that what you call help?"

Tricia studied face after face. They were impossible to decipher since they were frozen with the expression in the photograph that was retained for all eternity.

"Who pushed me?" Tricia demanded.

"We want to help you. Guide you."

"Over a cliff, no doubt," Tricia muttered.

"Why," she shouted above the din, "would you help me?"

"Because we must. We cannot forsake you in this life as we did in the last."

*

There was mighty crash, splinters flew. A gnarled and grizzled head appeared in the stairwell. Rumpelstiltskin scrutinized the dead gathered around the body of the newly dead.

Boy, had he taken the wrong turn. This was like a scene from *Arsenic and Old Lace*. He gaped at the figure beyond the corpse. His eyes widened.

Rumpelstiltskin released the hand hold on the step and let himself fall...

*

A gleaming blade cleaved the gleaming cord that tied Tricia's spirit to flesh, and a bony hand grasped her and yanked her from her family's prattling midst.

She seized the scythe from its skeletal grasp and swung it in a wide arc, severing head from spine back through the generations. Her relatives vanished with a poof.

"So now what?" she challenged.

He rested his fingers on his iliac crest and gave her an appraising look, if two empty sockets could appear appraising.

"How did you know?" said the Reaper. "You did know, didn't you?"

She shrugged.

"You are a clever girl. As ghosts, they were neither living nor dead. You have slashed their spirits from their personalities. They exist no more either in this world or the next."

"Seemed logical. I could but hope," Tricia said.

The Grim Reaper cupped his mandible in a bony hand and scratched his skull with the scythe. "You wouldn't be interest in a part-time job, would you?"

The Magic Bumbershoot

Diddle clung to the heavy cables that lined the tunnel waiting for the next train. No few of his kind had been electrocuted when they touched the wrong wire, but he was adept. Diddle could leap upon the dragon's back and ride the tube until the next station, when he would enter the train.

He wiggled back and forth. His bladder was full, and he hoped the train would be punctual.

Times change. The olden days faded to a sepia-toned memory as a new bumptious reality supersedes. The creatures of fairy had to adjust. The high elves fled to their islands beyond the sea, leaving their cousins, the wee ones, pixies, the brownies, the gnomes to fend as they must.

The pixies, the brownies, linked to the lands, families and farms, remained where they had lived from time immemorial, but their work went unremarked. There was neither spot of cream nor bowl of milk left outside the door to thank them for their efforts, and if one appeared, the creatures of fairy had to fight with the family cat to claim their share. Most were forced to content themselves with feed from the stables and grains from the family's stores. The brave might sneak into the barn to clamp their lips around the teat of a cow, but many died in the attempt.

The wee ones never really noticed the transition unless they flew afoul of a spider's web, a flyswatter or found themselves stuck to flypaper. Otherwise, they lived their lives unchanged, with their caps of fox-glove, riding a dragonfly-back, supping on sweet pollen and drinking intoxicating dew.

No one, it seemed, could see the fairies except the homeless and those deemed insane. If they insisted on the presence of the Fay, they were soon institutionalized.

So, the former denizens of fairy were on their own. Diddle was just one of many.

The more freedom-loving gnomes of the ever-dwindling forests were not tied to a plot of land or an ungrateful family. With starvation looming, they took themselves some place where they could find sustenance.

They arrived in the cities, riding on the underside of carriages, and divided the territory between them, some to live aboveground and some to populate underworld.

The modern-day gnome is not the roly-poly, pink-cheeked creature of the past. It bore a half-starved pinched expression, its face painted in shades of dusky, dirty grey.

The gnomes, though, were witty. They found bounty in the city in the form of litter, half-consumed beef burgers abandoned in a polystyrene container, chips and occasionally fish; but they also had competition from the pigeons and rats. Sometimes, they had to battle over their repast with animals far larger than themselves. Many perished; those who survived were made of sinew and bone.

Diddle was dressed in socks purloined from people's laundry, with holes adroitly cut for heads and arms. The toe reserved as a cap; he smelled faintly of dog shit.

Of course, they were bound by their nature to serve. They could no longer attend the dryads who chose oblivion rather than face the world that cut down their resident trees for lumber. The dryads slumbered, and their trees died, shorn at the base.

The wind began to pick up. The tunnel reverberated with an unnatural roar. The cables, the tracks, even the walls began to vibrate, signaling the approach of a train.

Diddle was nearly swept off his feet. He clenched down hard on the overhead cable. As one of the first arrivals, his clan staked out a claim in the hub of London. Not all lines stopped at the station, but most ran through it.

Diddle worked the night shift after rush hour had ended. With his specialized skill, he could jump onto almost any line and ride it to the end, allowing him to harvest the food that others missed.

The best collectors got the best route. He was the best of the best. The younger, those with lesser skills, picked through the refuse inside King's Cross and Euston while Diddle gathered what others failed to notice running as they did from the crush of feet. He often doubled their take. Essentially, he was the clean-up crew, although he didn't clean up. Instead he artfully rearranged the refuse that he did not want in such a way to trip the unwary commuter.

His bladder was screaming at him. Diddle noted by the sound of the train that it was slowing down, but not stopping. It was the one he wanted.

Diddle crossed his legs momentarily and then as the engine drew abreast of him, Diddle swung from his perch and dropped on all fours to the roof of an adjacent carriage.

He swayed with the rhythm of the train, bending his knees to absorb the changes in momentum as the train slowed for Tower station. The tunnel roof far ahead the line began to glow with a lovely silver light.

Diddle blinked and rubbed his eyes with his fists. The illumination was blinding, and it could not be, could not exist. The tunnel was lit at regular intervals along the sides. There were no overhead lamps.

By this time, the train had drawn directly underneath the glare and Diddle could hear the sound of city traffic, horns, snarling motors and human voices.

A hole leading to the surface?

A whine or a whir covered the noise of the busy city. Diddle moved his fists from his eyes to his ears. The light was replaced by darkness as a globe that resembled an inverted goblet on a saucer descended through the hole, landing directly in front of him.

It was occupied by the strangest creature Diddle had ever seen, and in his time, he had known many bizarre beasts – the gryphon, the sphinx and the minotaur, or at least his cousin. This *thing* resembled an ant. It wore a helmet topped by what appeared to be a push broom. A portion of the globe opened while the saucer lowered a ramp upon which the creature marched, humming a little tune. It was trailed by the smallest – and the only green – hound Diddle had seen.

The ant-thingy wore a skirt, red long johns and trainers. The dog was similarly attired. The creature stood slightly taller than the gnome and Diddle wracked his brains, trying to recall who or what this might be.

"Hello, earthling," it said amiably enough as he leveled a tube at the bewildered gnome. "I have been sent by the Martian High Council to arrest the rabbit. Where is the rabbit?"

"Rabbit? What rabbit? You'll find no rabbit down here. Rats maybe, but no rabbits. They wouldn't last long." He pointed at the tube. "What is that?"

"It is my space modulator. You and your kind will be disintegrated if you hide the rabbit from me."

"Look around you. Does this look like a healthy environment for a rabbit?" said Diddle.

"Rabbits live underground," it noted.

"This isn't just underground; it's *The Underground, The London Underground*. A rabbit wouldn't last two minutes. It would be flattened or fried the first time it hopped around," Diddle snapped. He had missed several stops already and didn't have time for this nonsense.

"You have been warned, earthling."

He pulled another tube from his bizarre under garment. The side was marked with scratchings 'PU36'. The creature threw the tube toward the front of the train. The dog loped happily after it.

Diddle indicated the roof above his head. "If you want a rabbit, look up there. Look somewhere where you can find grass and such like. That's what rabbits eat. Why don't you try a park?"

The creature's eyes narrowed. "This one eats orange sticks."

"Carrots? Then try a market."

The dog bounded back with the tube in his mouth.

Disgusted, the creature climbed back into the globe. The dog followed, tail wagging. The globe hovered for a minute above the train. The base of the saucer dropped open and another tube, larger than the others, appeared and pointed to the ceiling overhead. The area began to glow and melt. The craft sped upward, but before it was completely clear of the tunnel, Diddle heard...

Kaboom!

The explosion was followed by a strangled: "Dammit, K-9, how many times do I have to tell you? I don't want the PU36 back."

There was muffled barking, a yipe, and the train grumbled to a halt, coasting to a stop within feet of the station.

An announcement rattled through the speakers. "We are experiencing a short delay due to..." The voice became muffled.

"What?" it said. "No one is going to believe that..."

A whispered conversation and the voice grew louder, more confident. "We are experiencing a short delay due to, ah, passenger action."

The gnome scrambled down to the tracks, muttering: "Idiot."

He walked to the darkened depot and waited. The emergency lights flared, and the train limped into the station.

This time he climbed the ladder on the side of the carriage up to the roof and crawled through vents. Six stops to the end of the line.

Diddle avoided peak periods, lest he be trodden underfoot, and he avoided the sunlit hours altogether. He preferred the end of the day when rider numbers declined, and the carriages had accumulated the greatest amount of rubbish. Some days when the harvest was great Diddle would ride to the end of the line and back again, depending on the route, where he could share his takings with others less fortunate.

He felt sorry for the other gnomes who had to brave the feet of commuters in central London, but a gnome's instinct as helpers remained intact. Scratch a gnome and find a brownie or a pixie, tied by loyalties, but with the spirit of the forest dead, gnomes turned their gazes to humanity. If the gnomes observed several humans aghast at an event, they duplicated the action. More often if it caused excitement and a loud exclamation, then it must be desirable indeed.

Gnomes took oft-used human words as names, resulting in any number of Diddles and Fiddles, Shits and Fucks, Arse or the more-formal Arsehole, Bastard and its variant Bar Steward. The youngsters leaned away from the old classics for newfangled names like Emoji, Smart, Txt, App, iPiddles, the iPoos and the most popular, Yahoo.

Diddle slithered into a vent and crawled toward the light. Years of study led gnomes to believe that man held a particular fascination with dog feces, for they swore loud and long when they stepped in it. Forsooth, this applied to anything sticky, slimy or gooey. So, when they found such items no longer deemed useful to their kind – like gum after the flavor is gone – the gnomes would rearrange it, as opportunity presented itself, in a perfect position for the human foot.

The inner-city and dayshift workers faced greater dangers than their evening cohorts. The primary hazard during nightshift was being pinned under a falling drunk. Diddle peered through the light-striped entry into the carriage and when the train ground to a halt at the next station, he slipped through it. One man snored, curled up on his seat. Diddle climbed along the cross bar, still warm from the former grasp of many human hands. He slid down the pole and scurried under the seat.

He could no longer contain himself. He lifted the sock and cut loose. He sighed as he urinated on the floor in an ever-growing pond, for clever gnomes noted that the passengers became particularly animated if they saw a fellow human urinating on the walls of the station. This, they decided, must be a pleasure to them. Thus, the gnomes did their best to oblige their human hosts. Those with aim were nominated to pee on the walls, often standing in stacks of three or four to attain greater height. Others squatted in a circle to create puddles large enough to cause injury and animate the human population. Diddle contributed his share. He drank copious amounts of water.

Diddle felt underappreciated by his target when humanity referred to his acts – the yanking of the emergency alarm or the scrambling of the announcements – as gremlins.

He was no damn gremlin. They were mythical, a human invention.

Diddle darted between a couple's feet to grab the crumbs of donuts and pastries, and then discarded scraps for something more substantial when he noticed a woman watching him. He froze. This was not supposed to happen, for the Fay had the talent of camouflage.

No one should see him. Diddle stared back at her; she pursed her lips and sniffed as he scampered underneath the seat and peered around the post.

A creature of magic?

Diddle shook his head; she looked like any other mortal, and he decided long ago that enchantment was all but dead in the human race. Occasionally he saw a glimmer of it. The believers in magic usually clattered and clanked, covered with layers of metal talismans and sparkly crystals, and they ate organically. Something that was not prized by the gnome – only a famine of chips, crisps and half-eaten sausages, could induce any self-respecting gnome to eat alfalfa sprouts.

He paused to examine the umbrella next to the old woman. It radiated with the faint sheen of magic. Something about both the female and her brolly seemed familiar, but he could not see her features, for she was facing away, no longer observing him.

Diddle squatted behind the legs of the seat. He'd wait until she left before he resumed his quest.

He dallied; he dithered, and he rearranged his accumulated treasures. One stop. Two stops.

The end of the line.

The train disgorged its passengers. The old woman exited without a backward glance.

Someone, or something, coughed. Diddle spun, slipping on a puddle of grease he'd smeared in the aisle of the train.

The bumbershoot flapped its ribs with a clatter and squawked. "Ah, er, ahem, the umbrella. You forgot the umbrella." The bumbershoot spoke softly without much conviction as if it did not wish to be heard.

"You talk!" said Diddle.

"Of course, I talk," the umbrella snapped. "I got a beak, don't I? What are you? A rodent?"

The gnome straightened to his full six-inch height. "My *name* is Diddle."

"Of course, it is," said the umbrella.

Diddle continued, "And that poor old woman forgot her umbrella."

The gnome strode down the aisle.

"Poor old woman!" the umbrella screeched. "She's a bitch. Worse than that, she's a witch. A spoonful of sugar, me ass. Arsenic more like."

The gnome climbed to the seat where he could face the umbrella handle, bent over until his head rested next to the parrot face and he could gaze into the glittering eyes.

The bumbershoot eyed the gnome warily. "You're going to return me, aren't you?"

"It is in the magical code."

"What magical code? I've never heard of no magical code."

"It is the code we gnomes maintain to do service to humankind."

"Pissing on the floor? That's a service?"

"Seems to be. Humans do it themselves; therefore, it must be esteemed."

"More like a necessity," the parrot handle countered. "Besides, she's not human. She's been around forever. She's magic. She's immortal."

"Then it's more important to help her."

"Since when? Gnomes, brownies, fairies, trolls, witches and such-like have fought among themselves for years."

"Mere squabbles over precedence." Diddle straightened. He could not maintain the upside-down stance too long. His spine popped.

The umbrella changed tactics. "I am a thing of magic. I talk. You must help me."

Diddle rubbed his chin. "I don't recall anything in the code about a magic bumbershoot."

The beak bit the gnome.

Diddle bellowed and jumped back. He slid down to the floor, so he could grab what appeared to be the safe end of the device.

The bumbershoot pleaded. "Please, please, don't. Just take me to some nice lost and found where I can rest. I hate Poppins; if you knew her, you would hate her too. She's always suffocating me, wrapping her fingers round my beak so I can't speak or breathe."

"I don't blame her," Diddle interrupted.

"Making me fly in all kinds of weather. Every time the wind changes she's off somewhere new and I must carry her. She's put on more than a couple of stone through the years, what with that spoonful of sugar, chocolates and her nips at the cooking sherry. Please. Please. Just leave me behind."

The gnome, with a series of adjustments and a few wrestling moves, managed to get the umbrella balanced on his head.

"If you could just adjust the straps that hold me bound, I'll be flying off."

Determined, Diddle ignored the brolly. He toddled to the door and jumped off the train. "Oi! Is this yours?"

Mary Poppins swung to view the bumbershoot floating parallel to the floor until it hovered abreast of her.

Diddle shoved the squawking umbrella from his head. "I believe this is yours."

She screamed, "Rat. Rat."

"I told you," the bumbershoot whispered, "wicked, she is."

The old woman grabbed the umbrella and began to hit the pavement. *Thwack.*

The blow barely missed Diddle and the wind created by the umbrella as it struck the ground sent the gnome reeling.

The umbrella passed out due to the strength of the wallop on the concrete station floor.

Diddle wrapped his arms round the parrot handle and dragged it away to slide between the boards in a newspaper stand and to safety.

Poppins thundered after them. She began to rip the boards out, one at a time. An alarm sounded. She ignored it.

Diddle loosened the straps. Then he scrounged around until he found what he needed. He upended a plastic bottle and poured the water on the carved features of the parrot handle.

The bird sputtered, heard the sound of tearing wood, felt the freedom of his limbs and acted appropriately. Diddle leapt on the umbrella before it vanished.

The landscape beneath his feet appeared as a fretwork of sparkling lights.

Back in the tube station, Mary Poppins shredded the last board from the closed stand to expose... nothing. Stacks of magazines and papers. She bent to study the wall for openings and finding none, grabbed a copy of the *Daily Mail*, and stalked to the exit.

"Probably halfway up the stairs, by now," she murmured.

She hobbled up the steps and peered at the street. She glanced up at the sky and swore. Somewhere a weathervane spun, indicating a change in the wind.

"Dammit. Now I'm going to have to walk, and my corns are killing me."

Poppins thrust her arms to the heavens and removed the gift of flight from the umbrella and no few birds.

The parrot and Diddle, pigeons and seagulls, crashed to earth.

"Awk! Awk! Ook! Gargle!"

The umbrella opened its canopy and they drifted slowly to the ground. The gnome did as the creature asked, taking it to a nice lost and found somewhere, burying it deep under the other items.

Diddle spent the rest of his life where he had landed, in the suburbs, as a garden gnome, fishing eternally in a miniature pond. It wasn't a bad life, after all.

Goldilocks

Back in the magical kingdom of Toronto lived another girl named Gilda. She was a cousin of the first unlamented, lost child. Her parents called her Goldilocks, for her lovely, long blond hair. The name was also convenient because it prevented her from being confused with the wicked Gilda.

After the first Gilda's disappearance the name Goldilocks remained.

She was a compliant child, if not necessarily well-behaved. She was dutiful enough. She agreed with all that her parents said, told them what they wanted to hear and then did what she pleased.

Her parents never questioned her. They trusted her. Mother and father left her to her own devices while they stayed at home, for there were gangs of hooligans afoot in the neighborhood. They saw Goldilocks as a resourceful child who could take care of herself. The parents always knew where she was, or thought they did, and Goldilocks always returned when she was told long before dark.

It had been Goldilocks's parents who had introduced Gilda's family to the cabins around Parry Sound.

The latter's holidays provided a happy respite from the visits of the unlovely and unloved Gilda to their house during the summer months. Goldilocks and her family also spent a month near the lake, but never at the same time when Gilda might be present.

*

The bears wandered through the forest. Their muzzles were sticky with honey. Baby Bear whimpered, for he had been stung.

"Quit whining," grumbled Father Bear. His shuffling pace faltered, and he held up a massive paw. The door was ajar... again.

Mama Bear slavered; a droplet of saliva clung to her lips. "Lunch?" she asked hopefully.

"Maybe," said Father Bear. "If there have been any damages, there will be hell to pay."

He stood on two legs, raising himself to his full height to appear as ferocious as possible, then realized he would not fit through the entrance to the den. He dropped down on all fours.

He batted the door with his paw. The door creaked slowly on its hinges. The group relaxed. This visitor they knew.

Goldilocks glanced up from her mobile phone. She could not get service, no connection to call, but she still had her games app.

"It's about time," she said. "I have been waiting for you."

Mama, papa and baby bears arranged themselves around the kitchen table.

Goldilocks respectfully pulled up a stool and sat.

"How long have you been here?" Papa Bear asked.

"Not long," said Goldilocks.

Papa Bear sputtered.

Goldilocks glanced up from her game. "Oh, you mean at the resort." She pointed to the forest beyond the open door.

Her eyes glittered. "About a week. Long enough to scope out the area and visit all the cabins."

Papa Bear rubbed his paws together.

"I have a few jobs for you." Goldilocks unrolled a rough map of the lake and surrounding cabins. She tapped on one square. "This one is unoccupied, but new people are coming next week."

"Food," said the bears.

"Money," Goldilocks corrected. The bears looked disappointed.

She noted their distress and rushed on to add: "Yes, and food. You can take as much as you would like. New arrivals always bring enough to stock the larder. These people are staying a month, so they should have plenty of both – cash and goodies. We hit them fast; we hit them hard the first day they arrive. You know the drill."

The bears nodded.

"Now here," she indicated a second square. "These people will be leaving shortly. They had a long stay. They brought all sorts of goodies, phones, CDs, games and an MP2 and an MP3 players."

Papa Bear frowned.

"You know what I'm talking about," Goldilocks said. "Of course, they will have leftovers. Food they take with them. You intercept them here, on the road, after they've left the camp."

"Hey, that is almost near the highway," said Mama Bear. "You know highways make me nervous."

"Close to the highway is an advantage. They will drive on to report the incident to the local authorities. Too close to here, they might return. There's no need to alert the camp manager. Eventually word will get back, but we can postpone it as long as possible. You don't want the game warden hunting you, do you?"

"No," Mama Bear said.

Goldilocks turned to Baby Bear. "Have you been practicing your rolls?"

Baby fell off the chair, did a somersault and sprawled in a near impossible position. Then he proceeded with cries of agony.

"Very good," she said. "They'll think they hit him and stop. You two stay out of sight until they decide to check on Baby. Wait until they have gotten close. Baby, you bounce up and chase them away from their SUV while you two swoop in."

She scrolled through her pictures until she found the one she wanted and showed it to them. "These are meant for me. You can take whatever else you want."

She then tapped on a series of cabins. "We knock them off singly at different places – the river, the lake – and at different times. The last job will be our cabin. That'll be the end of the season. The authorities might wonder if our family was left untouched. This time we can risk hitting close to home and you'll be well provisioned for the winter. You can retreat to your den and we can divvy up the loot."

Goldilocks rolled up the map. "I have all their schedules, and I've cased all the cabins. How does that sound to you?"

"Anyone have a television set? Ours was broken," Papa Bear snarled.

"Everyone does. No one comes out here to be close to nature anymore. If you need one and can carry it, take it. I can't use it. My parents would ask questions. I want the iPads, the iPhones. Those things I can fit in my luggage."

"What do you do with these things?"

"Sell 'em. You don't think I can get by on my allowance."

"Pardon?"

"Never mind," she said.

"Which reminds me," said Mama Bear. "We met your cousin. What a horrid little girl she was, but delicious. Very tasty."

Goldilocks peered at Mother Bear. A smile spread across her face. "Thank you," she said. "You did our family a great service."

Filbert Meets the Trolls

Filbert flattened his spine against the boulder and exhaled slowly. Because of his special gift he had been elected by his fellow adventurers to trace the sound of voices and the tantalizing aroma of cooking meat.

Adventuring, he'd discovered, was not at all what it was cracked up to be. So far it had consisted of getting robbed of cash, food, weapons and supplies. One thought of fulsome women, glorious mead and heroic songs, but all he got was soured wine. Now he was hugging a rock trying to figure out what to do next.

Trolls. How the hell was he supposed to steal food from a bunch of blood-thirsty, ravenous trolls?

His gift, or his inheritance, was the ability to travel unseen, provided by a cloak of invisibility. It had made him an excellent thief in the city.

Filbert was the son of the notorious Alibaba. His father never got the hang of the cloak. He thought if he put it on, presto change-o, he vanished in his entirety. He'd never really grasped that the cloak imparted invisibility only to those parts that were covered. Face, hands and feet could still be seen. As tools go, it was most useful after dark. During the daylight hours, the so-called prince of thieves presented himself as a floating face above disembodied feet.

That lack of understanding had cost him dearly, first his hands and his feet and eventually his life. It left a pretty nasty stain on the cloak where his father had been run through by a member of the guard. Later the then-convicted Alibaba died on the gallows.

His father had no head for money, spending his wealth on women of questionable repute, until all he had left was this cloak.

Alibaba Junior had been traumatized by the embarrassment done to his mother and the shame of watching his father dancing around the marketplace in broad daylight chanting "you can't see me" to an amused audience

Filbert recalled the perplexed expressions of the onlookers who observed the hands, feet and face floating without benefit of torso, legs or arms. When his father threw off his mantle Alibaba usually got a round of applause and scattering of coins. Which should have been sufficient, but old habits die hard. Instead, Alibaba cut the purse of the wrong person, a petty government official who was not only petty, but vindictive. Filbert witnessed the attack; his father pressed the cloak into his son's hands. Filbert retreated into the shadows and watched his father's undoing.

Nine guards descended on the one-time prince of thieves. They stabbed him. They would have gutted him, but a commander arrived, and the guards were forced to scrape him off the ground. They executed his remains the following day.

Filbert escaped with the cloaked tucked under his arm. He ran far to escape the embarrassment of his upbringing. He crossed deserts and seas until he found a land of green and fog. He changed his name. He borrowed a name from a traveler named Filbert and took it as his own. Thus, Filbert, born as Alibaba Junior, was left behind. He did not wish ever to be associated with the ill-fated prince of thieves in any way.

Filbert learned a great deal from his father's farce. The son squatted down so his feet would not be exposed. He pulled the hood down low to hide his features, and he wrapped it tight around his person – lest the cloak brush against a leg or stir the leaves of the forest. It was an uncomfortable posture and an even more cumbersome gait. He rarely used the cloak, and he never used it during the day. The mantle was a device meant for hiding, not for running or walking. Certainly not for evading the law, unless the bearer could find a place to crouch immobile and wait. Filbert relied on that skill when picking a pocket, filching food from a stand in the marketplace or burglarizing a home.

But Filbert carried the cape with him always. It was his father's only bequest. After years of drinking, womanizing and gambling, the cloak represented the last of the old man's treasure. It, too, had witnessed the death of the previous owner, and perhaps sparked by guilt it kept Filbert well.

The cloak was perfect, though, for a job like this where all he had to do was listen and wait, swiping any leftover mutton that he could after the creatures slept. The trolls did not set guards. Who would be foolhardy enough for attack them?

Mayhap the sun would take care of them. Filbert was familiar with the beasts or, at least, their counterparts in the lands of sand and wind. Their type was written into legend and song.

The youth pressed himself deeper into the rock. The stone warmed him. His view was unobstructed.

His ears pricked as one of the lumbering beasts spoke. He tossed a large thigh bone onto the pile. "I am sick of mutton. I need man flesh so bad I can smell it."

Filbert opened his pouch of herbs and he checked his position to make sure his toes didn't extend beyond the cloth.

One of the troll's colleagues sniffed the air. "I smell flowers."

"That sets my tummy to rumbling," said a third. "Where there are flowers there is honey."

Filbert made himself the smallest package as possible against the boulder, fitting into dimple and crag. Filbert was thin for a reason; it was a matter of professional pride.

The trolls had four carcasses roasting in the embers and two on the spit. They hung fleece and all from the stick. A flock of ten, terrified ewes gathered at the far side of a makeshift pen.

Periodically the trolls fell to fighting about who would turn the spit next. The lambs were burnt on one side and raw on the opposite side, but trolls were not known for their culinary skills or their great wit.

Filbert's mouth was watering and his stomach rumbling. He clutched the bag of herbs against his abdomen to stifle the sound.

"What was that?"

"Huh," said the second.

"I heard," the first cocked his head, "a grumbling." He pointed at the boulder.

Filbert held his breath.

"Nobody has angered the old gods, have they?" asked one.

"Calm down, it's just the crackling of the fire."

The first grunted but held his peace. The troll tore a leg from a half-cooked sheep and began munching.

The trolls had nothing to say of interest to Filbert, although they did brag about the path of destruction they had made across the countryside. Now he knew which path to avoid. Those farms and villages would be picked clean. The inhabitants who had not ended up on the trolls' menu fled and their livestock lost. The trolls had herded the animals to their camps and returned to dine on the flesh of the dead, a delicacy preferred raw.

Filbert felt ill at the thought.

After hours of bickering punctuated by pugilistic displays that resounded with the clashing of stone, Filbert became immured to their disputes. He settled to await the sun when the trolls so illuminated would turn to stone and dust. Filbert wondered if he was leaning against one of the forebears to these creatures. The stone circles adorned the high hills across this kingdom and were known as trolls' copses. The youth could think of no other logical explanation, for was it not said that the relationship between trolls and stone was established long ago?

Filbert's head began to nod, but their words penetrated.

"So what do we do?" asked the dullard.

"We wait."

"I mean when it happens. Do we whimper? Cry out? Scream?"

"Whimper? Cry out? What do you think we are? Mewling humans? Quiet now."

The conversation ceased.

*

The soft whisper of birdsong woke Filbert the following day. The sun had yet to crest the far hills, painting the horizon with a line of crimson.

A second bird raised his voice, announcing his presence and his territory. A third joined the chorus, and Filbert's blood thrilled. Soon it would be time to act. He tensed. His legs bunched ready to spring from his hiding place

The first glimmer of orange emerged on the mountain tops, with the sharp spikes of ginger that heralded the rising sun.

Within the confines of the cloak, the thief tested his joints, opening and closing his fingers, letting his head roll limp on his neck.

Snap!

He froze. The trolls held contemplative postures staring into the fire. Their appetites sated. Not one twitched a finger. No spasm of cheek indicated that they heard the crackling of his spine.

Filbert relaxed slightly.

His head swung to face the horizon. Yellow appeared floating over the hills, and the indigo night was driven back by a necklace of turquoise.

He held his breath. Deep velvet purples turned to mauve, and mauve to pink, orange to the more muted peach. Filbert knew behind him, somewhere beyond his vision, night remained in dark defiance of the day.

Filbert saw the rim of the sun jutting over the mountain range. It bore a radiant red edge and auburn center. His stomach protested loudly at the thought of food, and the youth tried to think of other things.

When the orb was one-quarter exposed, the sun sported the familiar yellow. Its rays cleaved the sky. Darkness was losing its battle. Filbert risked a glimpse back. The trolls appeared to be asleep, eyes closed, sitting upright.

The sun bathed one troll in light. The beast stood, began to scream and fell over, stone dead.

Filbert thought he heard a muffled voice inside his head say: "Idiot."

He glanced around the remaining circle as a second leapt to its feet. The creature was greeted with the full force of the sun. He halted to lean forward in a precarious attitude, facing the gap in the circle nearest the thief. Filbert was sure the creature would topple with a poke of a single finger. The young man discarded the thought.

The sun bathed the circle in light.

Time to strike.

Filbert crept cautiously forward to peer around the rock. He studied each one of the creatures and then concentrated his attention on the one left standing to check for glimmers of life, if not intelligence.

He saw naught. Still clutching the cloak tightly around him, Filbert stepped from behind the boulder that had warmed him through the night. No movement. No glint of excitement in the porcine eyes.

Filbert did a little jig around the stone. Their eyes did not follow his progress. The young man scooted along the wall of stone to the pen and freed the frightened sheep. They just stared at him. He waved his arms.

223

Nothing, no movement from either flock or trolls.

Finally, he went inside the circle. He let the cloak fall open and did a proper highland reel, capering in and out of the ring of stones. Filbert thumbed his nose at each of them.

"Nyah, nyah, nyah, nyah, nyah," he chanted.

There was the soft whoosh of air behind him, like the beat of a wing or a quiver of an arrow as it flew past his face.

Two gargantuan fingers closed around the hood of the cloak. Filbert loosed himself from the cloth and fell exposed into the light of day. His legs bent ready to scramble from the circle when another stony hand grabbed him by the leg and lifted him into the heavens. Filbert kicked and fought. A third hand clasped his other leg while two others grasped his arms.

The trolls pulled him to pieces while a fifth ripped his head from his neck.

A few minutes later the trolls licked their fingers delicately for the last drop of blood. Each satisfied with their portion, with enough body parts, legs, arms, torso and head, to provide a piquant dessert after a hearty meal.

"Not very bright. The old legend gets them every time."

The six trolls dissolved into fits of laughter. Two doubled over with the strength of their guffaws. After their mirth subsided, the trolls stretched out inside the pen of stone, for they had found the circle was the very best place to meet folk.

The End of the Tale

Rumpelstiltskin trudged up the stairs. Another set of stairs in another castle in a never ending round of castles.

This had to be it. He was pretty sure that he had run out of castles.

Castle keeps were becoming passé. No longer the fashion. Everyone went for glitz and glam. Palaces. No turrets, rarely a tower, and then there had to be two of them symmetrically placed.

He rounded a bend.

It was dreadfully silent.

Rumpelstiltskin hadn't noticed the sign on the door to the tallest turret in the tallest tower that declared that this was A Heritage Trust Estate and warned 'No Visitors Beyond this Point.'

He'd never learned to read. It was always something he was going to do, if only to read his own story and discover the end of the tale, but he never seemed to have time.

"This is it. It has to be it," the dwarf intoned, unaware he was speaking aloud. If it wasn't, he'd quit. He would happily lay down and die. Surely the grim reaper would have someone, something, for him, even if he was an immortal. A pick or a shovel should do the trick.

His joints creaked, and each step became harder than the one before.

When had he gotten old?

Rumpelstiltskin wheezed, sat on a step and waited for his breath to catch up with him. He tried to gage how many steps he had already climbed and how many he had left.

He eyed the stairs from bend to bend. How many bends had he followed? He couldn't recall.

Rumpelstiltskin patted the stone, amazed at how dusty it was. Didn't the servants clean this castle?

He glowered. He didn't think he had come very far.

This was ridiculous. This was futile. He fumed.

Then Rumpelstiltskin sighed and rose to his feet. He soldiered on, resisting the impulse to count the steps. It made the climb seem longer and more tiring if he counted them. Besides, he always got lost after ten.

The dwarf concentrated on first one foot, then the next. Right foot. Left foot. Until he got muddled and tripped over his own feet.

The air was getting thin. He must be close to the top. An eerie flicker of green lit the landing above his head.

Rumpelstiltskin went down on all fours and scrambled up the stairs. When he reached the landing, he fell flat and kissed the cold, hard stone.

When he peered at his prize, Rumpelstiltskin saw the skeletal remains of a girl in a commoner's dress, golden locks flowing over the spinning wheel. Empty sockets stared at nothing.

He stood, screaming. "No! No! NO."

He was too late; she was dead.

Rumpelstiltskin stamped his feet and jumped up and down. "NO! NO! NO!"

He ranted; he raved.

"NO! NO! NO! NO!"

The dwarf hit the floor with his pick. The stone opened up beneath his feet. The earth swallowed him whole.

-End-

Jessica Palmer was born in Chicago, Illinois. Her mother became a professional clown when she was in her teens, leaving Palmer irrevocably altered. She received her degree in nursing and worked in hospitals, starting with medical-surgical units. Eventually, she settled into psychiatric nursing where she got along famously with her patients.

Her medical background presented opportunities to write. In 1976, she was asked to develop a script for educational television, entitled *Journey to Nowhere*, about the medical aspects of addiction. Later she became a technical writer for the safety and health department at Schlumberger Well Services with an emphasis on explosives and radiation. The job took her to England where she became a British subject.

The fates decreed her combined experiences constituted a hazard to herself and others. Palmer returned to her first love, genre fiction. She wrote her first novel at the age of nine – ninety-nine typewritten pages about her then-hero Max Smart of *Get*

Smart. Altogether, she has had 28 books published in fiction and non-fiction, including university textbooks about Native American history and culture.

Palmer has received numerous awards in journalism, spanning a period from 1980 to 2014. *Dark Lullaby*, published by Pocket Books, was nominated for HWA's Bram Stoker award in 1991. Now she concentrates on satire. Parallel Universe Publications released her collection of short stories, *Other Visions of Heaven and Hell* in 2015.

To find out more about all the books
we have published
please
check our website:

http://paralleluniversepublications.blogspot.co.uk/